NICK RENNISON

VICTORIAN TALES OF THE WEIRD

NO EXIT PRESS

First published in the UK in 2025 by No Exit Press,
an imprint of Bedford Square Publishers Ltd,
London, UK

noexitpress.co.uk
@noexitpress
info@bedfordsquarepublishers.co.uk

© Nick Rennison, 2025

The right of Nick Rennison to be identified as the author of this work has been asserted in accordance with the Copyright, Designs and Patents Act 1988. All rights reserved. No part of this book may be reproduced, stored in or introduced into a retrieval system, or transmitted, in any form or by any means (electronic, mechanical, photocopying, recording or otherwise) without the written permission of the publishers.

Any person who does any unauthorised act in relation to this publication may be liable to criminal prosecution and civil claims for damages.
A CIP catalogue record for this book is available from the British Library.
This is a work of fiction. Names, characters, places, and incidents either are the product of the author's imagination or are used fictitiously, and any resemblance to actual persons, living or dead, businesses, companies, events or locales is entirely coincidental.

ISBN
978-1-83501-066-2 (Paperback)
978-1-83501-067-9 (eBook)

2 4 6 8 10 9 7 5 3 1

Typeset in Janson MT Std by Palimpsest Book Production Limited, Falkirk, Stirlingshire

Printed in Great Britain by CPI Group (UK) Ltd, Croydon CR0 4YY

The manufacturer's authorised representative in the EU for product safety is Easy Access System Europe, Mustamäe tee 50, 10621 Tallinn, Estonia
gpsr.requests@easproject.com

PRAISE FOR NICK RENNISON'S ANTHOLOGIES

'An intriguing anthology'
Mail on Sunday

'These 15 sanguinary spine-tinglers... deliver delicious chills'
Christopher Hirst, *Independent*

'A book which will delight fans of crime fiction'
Verbal Magazine

'It's good to see that Mr Rennison has also selected some rarer pieces – and rarer detectives, such as November Joe, Sebastian Zambra, Cecil Thorold and Lois Cayley'
Roger Johnson, *The District Messenger (Newsletter of the Sherlock Holmes Society of London)*

'A gloriously Gothic collection of heroes fighting against maidens with bone-white skin, glittering eyes and bloodthirsty intentions'
Lizzie Hayes, *Promoting Crime Fiction*

'Nick Rennison's *The Rivals of Dracula* shows that many Victorian and Edwardian novelists tried their hand at this staple of Gothic horror'
Andrew Taylor, *Spectator*

'*The Rivals of Dracula* is a fantastic collection of classic tales to chill the blood and tingle the spine. Grab a copy and curl up somewhere cosy for a night in'
Citizen Homme Magazine

ALSO BY NICK RENNISON

Freud and Psychoanalysis
Peter Mark Roget – The Man Who Became a Book
Robin Hood – Myth, History & Culture
A Short History of Polar Exploration
Bohemian London

The Rivals of Sherlock Holmes
The Rivals of Dracula
Supernatural Sherlocks
More Rivals of Sherlock Holmes
Sherlock's Sisters
American Sherlocks

CONTENTS

Introduction	1
Reginald Bacchus and Ranger Gull – The Dragon of St Paul's	5
Gertrude Bacon – The Gorgon's Head	31
Louisa Baldwin – The Weird of the Walfords	45
Robert Barr – The Doom of London	67
Arthur Conan Doyle – The Ring of Thoth	81
D F Hannigan – The Extraordinary Case of Mr Ebenstal	103
E and H Heron – The Story of the Grey House	117
C J Cutcliffe Hyne – The Lizard	135
Jerome K Jerome – The Dancing Partner	149
S Levett-Yeats – The Devil's Manuscript	159
Mary Louisa Molesworth – The Man with the Cough	181
Edith Nesbit – Man-Size in Marble	201
Charlotte Riddell – Sandy the Tinker	219
Phil Robinson – The Man-Eating Tree	235
T W Speight – The Green Phial	245

INTRODUCTION

This is an anthology of weird fiction published during the reign of Queen Victoria. What exactly is meant by 'weird fiction'? The American critic S T Joshi, in *The Weird Tale*, his study of writers such as Algernon Blackwood, Lord Dunsany and Arthur Machen, acknowledged how much the concept escaped easy description and ventured to assert that 'any definition of it may be impossible'. Plenty of people over the years have nonetheless attempted one. The horror writer H P Lovecraft, for example, provided his own idiosyncratic version in his 1927 essay 'Supernatural Horror in Literature'. The weird tale, he thought, must carry at the very least a 'hint' of 'that most terrible conception of the human brain – a malign and particular suspension or defeat of those fixed laws of nature which are our only safeguard against the assaults of chaos'. *Weird Tales*, the self-styled 'Unique Magazine' in which much of Lovecraft's own fiction was published, first appeared on American newsstands early in 1923.

However it is defined, weird fiction dates back, of course, much further than the 1920s. It could be argued that it has been around as long as people have been inventing stories. Ancient Greek and Roman literature contains material that could be described as 'weird'. The ironically titled *A True Story* by the satirist Lucian of Samosata, written in the second century AD, includes a voyage to the moon, an island made of cheese and a 200-mile-long whale whose belly is home to a variety of fish people. Fast-forward a millennium and more, and the romances of the Middle Ages have much that is weird and fantastical in them. *Sir Gawain and the Green Knight*, for instance, written by an anonymous English author in the fourteenth century, begins in the court of King Arthur, where Gawain decapitates a green giant, who promptly picks up his head, mounts his green horse and rides away.

In the eighteenth century, 'Gothic fiction' was enormously popular with readers. In *The Castle of Otranto* by Horace Walpole, from 1764, giants, ghosts and walking skeletons put in appearances; thirty years later, supernatural terrors regularly threaten Emily St Aubert, the heroine of Ann Radcliffe's *The Mysteries of Udolpho*, although, perhaps disappointingly, most of them turn out to have a natural explanation. The Gothic influence stretched well into the following century, the genre still popular enough to attract Jane Austen's satirical attention in *Northanger Abbey*. That most famous of all horror novels, Mary Shelley's *Frankenstein*, owes a strong debt to the eighteenth-century Gothic novel.

In America, Edgar Allan Poe, pioneer in so many genres, was hailed by Lovecraft as a founding father of 'weird fiction' and, in well-known stories like 'The Fall of the House of Usher' and 'The Pit and the Pendulum', it's easy enough to identify the later writer's reasons for doing so. Poe's countryman Nathaniel Hawthorne also flirted (and more) with the supernatural in many of his short stories. In Britain, the 1830s and 1840s saw novelists like Dickens and Emily Brontë still haunted by echoes of the Gothic.

Victoria came to the throne in 1837 and her long reign saw massive changes not only in society but in literary tastes. Most of the stories in this volume come from the last 20 years of the nineteenth century. These last decades of the old queen's reign were those in which genre fiction of all kinds came into its own. The detective story was given a new boost by Conan Doyle's invention of Sherlock Holmes. H G Wells's 'scientific romances' – *The Time Machine* (1895), *The War of the Worlds* (1898) and others – were the first masterpieces of what was not yet called science fiction. Classics of horror fiction appeared. Robert Louis Stevenson wrote *Strange Case of Dr Jekyll and Mr Hyde*, the iconic doppelgänger story, in 1886; the most famous of all vampire tales, Bram Stoker's *Dracula*, was published in 1897.

It is no surprise that these were decades in which 'weird fiction' also thrived. I have tried in this anthology to demonstrate the range and variety of stories from the late Victorian era that can be broadly categorised as such. There are no ghost stories in the selection, although all have elements of the supernatural. The ghost story, particularly the Victorian ghost story, seems to me to be a genre of its own. Many of the writers in this book, particularly women authors such as Louisa Baldwin and Charlotte Riddell, excelled at the ghost story but I have chosen other examples of their work. Some of the stories might be described as science fiction, although the term had not then been invented; others could be categorised as 'horror' stories.

Although I have included stories by very well-known writers like Sir Arthur Conan Doyle and Jerome K Jerome, I have ignored some writers (Arthur Machen, M P Shiel) whose names are regularly associated with 'weird fiction'. Their work is very frequently anthologised and I preferred to look elsewhere for examples of the genre. For that reason I have included stories by writers such as Robert Barr and Cutcliffe Hyne, whose former fame has long since faded, and by long-forgotten authors such as D F Hannigan and Reginald Bacchus whose names may not even be familiar to scholars of the period. There are works by both male and female writers. The stories are, I hope, intriguingly different. A dancing automaton runs amok at a ball; a prehistoric beast lurks in the depths of a Yorkshire cave; two statues in an ancient church come to life with fatal results; a man realises that he has married not a woman but a shape-shifting serpent. What unites them is that they all deal with experiences outside the boundaries of ordinary, everyday life. They all explore the 'weird'.

THE DRAGON OF ST PAUL'S

By Reginald Bacchus (1873–1945) and
Ranger Gull (1875–1923)

Bacchus, who was married to the actress Isa Bowman, a former child friend of Lewis Carroll, had a louche career in 1890s bohemian London, which included friendship with the notorious publisher of erotica, Leonard Smithers. He wrote several pornographic works for Smithers's Erotika Biblion Society but he also produced novels and short stories for more respectable publishers and publications. Ranger Gull was a novelist and literary journalist who was to gain his greatest fame under the pen name Guy Thorne. His 1903 novel, When It Was Dark, *told the story of the moral collapse which followed apparent disproof of Christ's resurrection. Only when this is revealed as part of a Jewish plot (the book is unashamedly anti-Semitic) is order restored. Between 1898 and his death, Gull published more than 100 novels, mostly potboilers, many of which would now be categorised as science fiction or horror. Reginald Bacchus and Ranger Gull collaborated on a number of short stories around the turn of the century, mostly published in the* Ludgate Monthly. *'The Dragon of St Paul's', which reflects the era's fascination with the prehistoric past and with the possibility there might, somewhere in the world, be survivals from it, is the most memorable of them.*

Ludgate Monthly, *April 1899*

First Episode

'It is certainly a wonderful yarn,' said Trant, 'and excellent copy. My only regret is that I didn't think of it myself in the first instance.'

'But, Tom, why shouldn't it be true? It's incredible enough for anyone to believe. I'm sure I believe it, don't you, Guy?'

Guy Descaves laughed. 'Perhaps, dear. I don't know and I don't much care, but I did a good little leaderette on it this morning. Have you done anything, Tom?'

'I did a whole buck middle an hour ago at very short notice. That's why I'm a little late. I had finished all my work for the night, and I was just washing my hands when Fleming came in with the make-up. We didn't expect him at all tonight, and the paper certainly was rather dull. He'd been dining somewhere, and I think he was a little bit cocked. Anyhow he was nasty, and kept the presses back while I did a "special" on some information he brought with him.'

While he was talking, Beatrice Descaves, his fiancée, began to lay the table for supper, and in a minute she called them to sit down. The room was very large, with cool white-papered walls, and the pictures, chiefly original black and white sketches, were all framed in *passe-partout* frames, which gave the place an air of serene but welcome simplicity. At one end of it was a great window which came almost to the floor, and in front of the window there was a low, cushioned seat. The night was very hot, and the window was wide open. It was late – nearly half-past one, and London was quite silent. Indeed the only sound that they could hear was an occasional faint burst of song and the tinkling of a piano, which seemed to come from the neighbourhood of Fountain Court.

Guy Descaves was a writer, and he lived with his sister Beatrice in the Temple. Trant, who was also a journalist on the staff of a daily paper, and who was soon going to marry Beatrice, often came to them there after his work was done. The three young people lived very much together, and were very happy in a delightful unfettered way. The Temple was quiet and close to their work, and they found it in these summer days a most peaceful place when night had come to the town.

They were very gay at supper in the big, cool room. Trant was a clever young man and very much in love, and the presence of Beatrice always inspired him to talk. It was wonderful to sit by her, and to watch her radiant face, or to listen to the music of her laugh, which rippled like water falling into water. Guy, who was more than thirty, and was sure that he was very old, liked to watch his sister and his friend together, and to call them 'you children'.

'What is the special information that the editor brought, dear?' Beatrice asked Trant, as soon as they were seated round the table.

'Well,' he answered. 'It seems that he managed to get hold of young Egerton Cotton, Professor Glazebrook's assistant, who is staying at the Metropole. Of course, various rumours have got about from the crew of the ship, but nothing will be definitely known till the inquest tomorrow. Cotton's story is really too absurd, but Fleming insisted on its going in.'

'Did he give him much for his information?' Descaves asked.

'Pretty stiff, I think. I know the *Courier* offered fifty, but he stuck out. Fleming only got it just at the last moment. It's silly nonsense, of course, but it'll send the sales up tomorrow.'

'What is the whole thing exactly?' Beatrice asked. 'All that I've heard is that Professor Glazebrook brought back some enormous bird from the Arctic, and that just off the Nore the thing escaped and killed him. I'm sure that sounds quite sufficiently extraordinary for anything; but I suppose it's all a lie.'

'Well,' said Trant. 'What Egerton Cotton says is the most extraordinary thing I have ever heard – it's simply laughable – but it will sell 300,000 extra copies. I'll tell you. I've got the whole thing fresh in my brain. You know that Professor Glazebrook was one of the biggest biologists who have ever lived, and he's been doing a great, tedious, monumental book on prehistoric animals, the mammoth and all that sort of thing that E T Reid draws in *Punch*. Some old scientific Johnny in Wales used to find all the money, and he fitted out the Professor's exploration ship, the *Henry Sandys*, to go and find these mammoths and beasts which have got frozen up in the ice. Don't you remember about two years ago when they started from Tilbury? They got the Lord Mayor down, and a whole host of celebrities, to see them go. I was there reporting, I remember it well, and Reggie Lance did an awfully funny article about it, which he called 'The Hunting of the Snark'. Well, Egerton Cotton tells Fleming – the man must be mad – that they found a whole lot of queer bears and things frozen up, but no very great find until well on into the second year, when they were turning to come back. Fleming says he's seen all the diaries and photographs and everything; they had a frightfully hard time. At last one day they came across a great block of ice, and inside it, looking as natural as you please, was a huge winged sort of dragon creature, as big as a carthorse. Fleming saw a photograph. I don't know how they faked it up, and he says it was the most horrid cruel sort of thing you ever dreamt of after lobster salad. It had big, heavy wings, and a beak like a parrot, little flabby paws all down its body like a caterpillar, and a great bare, pink, wrinkled belly. Oh, the most filthy-looking brute! They cut down the ice till it was some decent size, and they hauled the whole thing chock-a-block, like a prune in a jelly, into the hold. The ice was frightfully hard, and one of the chains of the donkey engine broke once, and the whole thing fell, but even then the block held firm. It took them three weeks to get it on board. Well, they sailed away with their beastly Snark as jolly as sandboys, and Cotton says the Professor was nearly out of his mind with joy – used to talk and mumble to himself all day. They put the thing in a huge refrigerator like the ones the Australian mutton comes over in, and Glazebrook used to turn on the electric lights and sit muffled up in furs watching his precious beast for hours.'

He stopped for a moment to light a cigarette, noticing with amusement that Guy and Beatrice were becoming tremendously interested. He made Beatrice pour him out a great tankard of beer before he would go on, and he moved to the window seat, where it was cooler, and he could sit just outside the brilliant circle of light thrown by the tall shaded lamp. The other two listened motionless, and as he unfolded the grisly story, his voice coming to them out of the darkness became infinitely more dramatic and impressive.

'Well, Cotton says that this went on for a long time. He had to do all the scientific work himself, writing up their journals and developing the photos, as the Professor was always mysteriously pottering about in the cellar place. At last, one day, Glazebrook came into the cabin at lunch or whatever they have, and said he was going to make a big experiment. He talked a lot of rot about toads and reptiles being imprisoned for thousands of years in stones and ice, and then coming to life, and he said he was going to try and melt out the dragon and tickle it into life with a swingeing current from the dynamo. Cotton laughed at him, but it wasn't any good, and they set to work to thaw the creature out with braziers. When they got close to it Cotton said that the water from the ice, as it melted, got quite brown and smelt! It wasn't till they were within almost a few hours from the Channel – you remember they put into some place in Norway for coal – and steaming for London River as hard as they could go, that they got it clear.

'While they were fixing the wires from the dynamo room, Cotton hurt his ankle and had to go to his bunk for some hours to rest. He begged Glazebrook to wait till he could help, for he had become insensibly interested in the whole uncanny thing, but it was no use. He says the fellow was like a madman, red eyes with wrinkles forming up all round them, and so excited that he was almost foaming at the mouth. He went to his cabin frightfully tired, and very soon fell asleep. One of the men woke him up by shaking him. The man was in a blue funk and told him something dreadful had happened in the hold. Cotton hobbled up to the big hatchway, which was open, and as he came near it with the mate and several of the men, he said he could hear a coughing choked-up kind of noise, and that there was a stench like ten thousand monkey houses. They looked in and saw this great beast *alive*! And squatting over Glazebrook's body picking out his inside like a bird with a dead crab.'

Beatrice jumped up with a scream. 'Oh, Tom, Tom, don't, you horrid boy! I won't hear another word. I shan't sleep a wink. Ugh! how disgusting and ridiculous. Do you mean to tell me that you've actually gone to press with all that ghastly nonsense? I'm going to bathe my face, you've made me feel quite hot and sticky. You can tell the rest to Guy, and if you haven't done by the time I come back, I won't say good night to you, there!'

She left the room, not a little disconcerted by the loathsome story which Trant, forgetting his listeners, had been telling with the true journalist's passion for sensational detail. Guy knocked the ashes slowly out of his pipe. 'Well?' he said.

'Oh, there isn't much more. He says they all ran away and watched from the companion steps, and presently the beast came flopping up on deck, with its beak all over blood, and its neck coughing and working. It got half across the hatchway and seemed dazed for about an hour. No one seemed to think of shooting it! Then Cotton says it crawled to the bulwarks coughing and grunting away, and after a few attempts actually flew up into the air. He said it flew unlike any creature he had ever seen, much higher than most birds fly, and very swiftly. The last they saw of it was a little thing like a crow hovering over the forts at Shoe'ness.'

'Well, I'm damned,' said Guy. 'I never heard a better piece of yarning in my life. Do you actually mean to tell me that Fleming dares to print all that gaudy nonsense in the paper? He must certainly have been very drunk.'

'Well, there it is, old man. I had to do what I was told, and I made a good piece of copy out of it. I am not responsible if Fleming does get his head laughed off, I don't edit his rag. Pass the beer.'

'Is the ship here?'

'Yes, it was docked about six this morning, and so far all the published news is what you had today in the *Evening Post*. It seems that something strange certainly did happen, though, of course, it wasn't that. They are going to hold an inquest, Fleming says. Something horribly beastly has happened to Glazebrook, there's no doubt of that. Something has scooped the poor beggar out. Well, I must be going, it's nearly three, and more than a little towards dawning. Tell Bee I'm off, will you?'

Beatrice came back in a minute like a fresh rose, and before he went, she drew him on to the balcony outside the window. There was a wonderful view from the balcony. Looking over the great lawns far down below, they could just see the dim purple dome of St Paul's, which seemed to be floating in mist, its upper part stark and black against the sky.

To the right was the silent river with innumerable patches of yellow light from the rows of gas lamps on Blackfriars Bridge. A sweet scent from the boxes of mignonette floated on the dusky, heavy air. He put his arm round her and kissed her sweet, tremulous lips. 'My love, my love,' she whispered, 'oh, I love you so!'

Her slender body clung to him. She was very sweet. The tall, strong young man leant over her and kissed her masses of dark, fragrant hair.

'My little girl, my little girl,' he murmured with a wonderful tenderness in his voice, 'there is nothing in the world but you, sweet little girl, dear, dear little girl, little wife.'

She looked up at him at the word and there was a great light in her eyes, a thing inexpressibly beautiful for a man to see.

'Love, good night,' he whispered, and he kissed the tiny pink ear that heard him.

After the fantastic story he had been telling them, a story which, wild and grotesque as it was, had yet sufficient *vraisemblance* to make them feel uncomfortable, the majesty of the night gave the dim buildings of the town a restful and soothing effect, and as they stood on the balcony with their love surging over them, they forgot everything but that one glorious and radiant fact.

Beatrice went with him to the head of the staircase – they lived very high up in the buildings called 'Temple Gardens' – and watched him as he descended. It was curious to look down the great well of the stone steps and to feel the hot air which rose up from the gas lamps beating on her face. She could only see Tom on each landing when he turned to look up at her – a tiny pink face perched on a little black foreshortened body.

When he got right down to the bottom he shouted up a 'good night', his voice sounding strange and unnatural as the walls threw it back to each other. In after years she always remembered the haunting sound of his voice as it came to her for the last time in this world.

Between seven and eight o'clock the next morning Guy, who was on the staff of the *Evening Post*, one of the leading lunch-time papers, left the Temple for the offices in the Strand.

It was a beautiful day, and early as it was the streets were full of people going to their work. Even now the streets were full of colour and sunshine, and every little city clerk contributed to the gayness of the scene by wearing round his straw hat the bright ribbon of some club to which he did not belong.

Guy had been working for about an hour when Gobion, his assistant – the young man who afterwards made such a success with his book *Penny Inventions* – came in with a bunch of 'flimsies', reports of events sent in by penny-a-liners who scoured London on bicycles, hoping for crime.

'There doesn't seem anything much,' he said, 'except one thing which is probably a fake. It was brought in by that man, Roberts, and he tried to borrow half a James from the commissionaire on the strength of it, which certainly looks like a fake. If it is true, though, it's good stuff. I've sent a reporter down to inquire.'

'What is it?' said Descaves, yawning.

'Reported murder of a journalist. The flimsy says he was found at four o'clock in the morning by a policeman, on the steps of St Paul's, absolutely broken up and mangled. Ah, here it is. "*The body, which presented a most extraordinary and unaccountable appearance, was at once removed to St Bride's mortuary.*" Further details later, Roberts says.'

'It sounds all right; at any rate the reporter will be back soon, and we shall know. How did Roberts spot him as a journalist?'

'Don't know, suppose he hadn't shaved.'

While the youth was speaking, the reporter entered breathless.

'Column special,' he gasped.

'Trant, a man on the *Mercury*, has been murdered, cut all to pieces. Good God! I forgot, Descaves. Oh, I am fearfully sorry!'

Guy rose quickly from his seat with a very white face, but without any sound. As he did so, by some strange coincidence the tape machine on the little pedestal behind him began to print the first words of a despatch from the Exchange Telegraph Company. The message dealt with the tragedy that had taken immediate power of speech away from him. The familiar whirr of the type wheel made him turn from mere force of habit and, stunned as his brain was, he saw the dreadful words spelling themselves on the paper with no realisation of their meaning. He stood swaying backwards and forwards, not knowing what he did, his eyes still resting on the broad sheet of white paper on which the little wheel sped ceaselessly, recording the dreadful thing in neat blue letters.

Then suddenly his eyes flashed the meaning of the gathering words to his brain, and he leant over the glass with a sick eagerness. Gobion and the reporter stood together anxiously watching him. At length the wheel slid along the bar and came to rest with a sharp click. Guy stood up again.

'Do my work today,' he said quietly. 'I must go to my sister,' and taking his hat he left the room.

When he got out into the brilliant sunshine which flooded the Strand, his senses came back to him and he determined that obviously the first thing to be done was to make sure that the body at St Bride's was really the body of his friend.

Even in moments of deep horror and sorrow the mind of a strong, self-contained man does not entirely lose its power of concentration. The telegraphic news had left very little doubt in his mind that the fact was true, but at the same time he could not conceive how such a ghastly thing could possibly have happened. According to the information he had, it seemed the poor fellow had been struck dead only a few minutes after he had left the Temple the night before, and within a few yards of his chambers. 'On the steps of St Paul's,' the wire ran, and Trant's rooms were not sixty yards away, in a little old-fashioned court behind the Deanery.

It was incredible. Owing to the great shops and warehouses all round, the neighbourhood was patrolled by a large number of policemen and watchmen. The space at the top of Ludgate Hill was, he knew, brilliantly lighted by the street lamps, and besides, about four it was almost daylight. It seemed impossible that Tom could have been done to death like this. 'It's a canard,' he said to himself, 'damned silly nonsense,' but even as he tried to trick himself into disbelief, his subconscious brain told him unerringly that the horrid thing was true.

Five minutes later he walked out of the dead house knowing the worst. The horror of the thing he had just seen, the awful inexpressible horror of it, killed every other sensation. He had recognised his friend's right hand, for on the hand was a curious old ring of beaten gold which Beatrice used to wear.

Second Episode

Mr Frank Fleming, the editor of the *Daily Mercury*, was usually an early riser. He never stopped at the office of the paper very late unless some important news was expected, or unless he had heard something in the House that he wished to write about himself. Now and then, however, when there was an all-night sitting, he would steal away from his bench below the gangway and pay a surprise visit before Trant and his colleagues had put the paper to bed. On these occasions, when he was kept away from his couch longer than was his wont, he always slept late into the morning. It was about twelve o'clock on the day of Trant's death that he rose up in bed and pressed the bell for his servant. The man brought his shaving water and the morning's copy of the *Mercury*, and retired. Fleming opened his paper and the black headline and leaded type of the article on Professor Glazebrook's death at once caught his eye. He read it with complacent satisfaction. Trant had done the thing very cleverly and the article was certainly most striking. Fleming, a shrewd man of the world and Parliamentary adventurer, had not for a moment dreamt of believing young Egerton Cotton, but he nevertheless knew his business. It had got about that there was something mysterious in the events that had occurred on board the *Henry Sandys*, and it had also got about that the one man who could throw any authentic light on these events was Cotton. It was therefore the obvious policy to buy Cotton's information, and, while disclaiming any responsibility for his statements, to steal a march on his contemporaries by being the first to publish them. As he walked into the pretty little dining-room of his flat, Mr Fleming was in an excellent temper.

He was dividing his attention between the kidneys and the *Times*, when his man came into the room and told him that Mr Morgan, the news editor, must see him immediately.

He could hear Morgan in the *entresol*, and he called out cheerily, 'Come in, Morgan; come in, you're just in time for some breakfast.'

The news editor entered in a very agitated state. When Fleming heard the undoubted fact of Trant's death he was genuinely moved, and Morgan, who had a very low opinion of his chief's human impulses, was surprised and pleased. It seemed that Morgan had neither seen the body nor been to the scene of the crime, but had simply got his news from some men in the bar of the Cheshire Cheese, in Fleet Street, who were discussing the event. Trant had been a very popular man among his brethren, and many men were mourning for him as they went about their work.

'What you must do,' said Fleming to his assistant, 'is this. Go down to the mortuary on my behalf, explain who Trant was, and gain every morsel of information you can. Go to the place where the body was found as well. Poor Tom Trant! He was a nice boy – a nice boy; he had a career before him. I shall walk down to the office. This has shaken me very much, and I think a walk will buck me up a little. If you get a fast cab and tell the man to go hell for leather, you will be back in Fleet Street by the time I arrive. I shall not walk fast.' He heaved a perfectly sincere sigh as he put on his gloves. As he left the mansions and walked past the Aquarium he remembered that a cigar was a soothing thing, and, lighting one, he enjoyed it to the full. The sunshine was so radiant that it was indeed difficult to withstand its influence. Palace Yard was a great sight, and all the gilding on the clock tower shone merrily. The pigeons, with their strange iridescent eyes, were sunning themselves on the hot stones. The editor forgot all about Trant for some minutes in the pure physical exhilaration of it all. As he advanced up Parliament Street he saw Lord Salisbury, who was wearing an overcoat, despite the heat.

Fleming turned up Whitehall Court and past the National Liberal Club to the Strand, which was very full of people. Fleming had always been a great patron of the stage. He knew, and was known to, many actors and actresses, and you would always see his name after a ten-guinea subscription on a benefit list. He liked the Strand, and he walked very slowly down the north side, nodding or speaking to some theatrical acquaintance every moment.

When he came to the bar where all the actors go, which is nearly opposite the Tivoli Music Hall, he saw Rustle Tapper, the famous comedian, standing on the steps wearing a new white hat and surveying the bright and animated scene with intense enjoyment.

The two men were friends, and for a minute or two Fleming mounted the steps and stood by the other's side. It was now about half-past one.

'Well,' said the actor, 'and how are politics, very busy just now? What is this I see in the *Pall Mall* about the murder of one of your young men? It's not true, I hope.'

'I am afraid it is only too true. He was the cleverest young fellow I have ever had on the paper. I got him straight from Balliol, and he would have been a very distinguished man. I don't know anything about it yet but just the bare facts; our news editor has gone down to find out all he can.'

They moved through the swing doors into the bar, talking as they went.

The Strand was full of all its regular frequenters, and in the peculiar fashion of this street everyone seemed to know everyone else intimately. Little groups of more or less well-known actors and journalists stood about the pavement or went noisily in and out of the bars, much impeding the progress of the ordinary passer-by. There was no sign or trace of anything out of the common to be seen. It was just the Strand on a bright summer's day, and the flower-girls were selling all their roses very fast to the pretty burlesque actresses and chorus girls who were going to and fro from the agents' offices.

About two o'clock – the evening papers said half-past two, but their information was faulty – the people in Bedford Street and the Strand heard a great noise of shouting, which, as far as they could judge, came from the direction of the Haymarket or Trafalgar Square. The noise sounded as if a crowd of people were shouting together, but whether in alarm or whether at the passing of some great person was not immediately apparent. It was obvious that something of importance was happening not very far away. After about a minute the shouting became very loud indeed, and a shrill note of alarm was plainly discernible.

In a few seconds the pavements were crowded with men, who

came running out from the bars and restaurants to see what was happening. Many of them came out without their hats. Fleming and the actor hurried out with the rest, straining and pushing to get a clear view westwards. One tall, clean-shaven man, with a black patch on his eye, his face bearing obvious traces of greasepaint, came out of the Bun Shop with his glass of brandy and water still in his hand.

It was a curious sight. Everyone was looking towards Trafalgar Square with mingled interest and uncertainty, and for the time being all the business of the street was entirely suspended. The drivers of the omnibuses evidently thought that the shouting came from fire-engines which were trying to force their way eastwards through the traffic, for they drew up by the kerbstone, momentarily expecting that the glistening helmets would swing round the corner of King William Street.

Fleming, from the raised platform at the door of Gatti's, could see right down past Charing Cross Station, and as he was nearly six feet high, he could look well over the heads of the podgy little comedians who surrounded him. Suddenly the noise grew in volume and rose several notes higher, and a black mass of people appeared running towards them.

The next incident happened so rapidly that before anyone had time for realisation it was over. A huge black shadow loped along the dusty road, and, looking up, the terror-stricken crowd saw the incredible sight of a vast winged creature, as large as a dray-horse, gliding slowly over the street. The monster, which Fleming describes as something like an enormous bat with a curved bill like a bird of prey, began to hover, as if preparing to descend, when there was the sudden report of a gun. An assistant at the hosier's shop at the corner of Southampton Street, who belonged to the Volunteers, happened to be going to do some range firing in the afternoon, and fetching his rifle from behind the counter, took a pot shot at the thing. His aim, from surprise and fear, was bad, and the bullet only chipped a piece of stone from the coping of the Tivoli. The shot, however, made the creature change its intentions, for it swerved suddenly to the right against some telegraph wires, and then, breaking through them, flew with extraordinary swiftness away over the river, making, it appeared, for the Crystal Palace upon Sydenham Hill. A constable on Hungerford foot-bridge, who saw it as it went over the water, said that its hairless belly was all cut and bleeding from the impact of the wires. The excitement in the Strand became frantic. The windows of all the shops round the Tivoli were broken by the pressure of the crowd, who had instinctively got as near as possible to the houses. The cab and omnibus horses, scenting the thing, were in that state of extreme terror which generally only an elephant has power to induce in them. The whole street was in terrible confusion. The only person who seemed calm, so a report ran in a smart evening paper, was a tall man who was standing at the door of a bar wearing a patch over one eye, and who had a glass of brandy in his hand. A reporter who had been near him, said that as soon as the monster had disappeared over the house-tops, he quietly finished his glass of brandy, and straightway went inside to have it replenished.

Special editions of the evening papers were at once issued. The *Globe*, owing to the nearness of its offices, being first in the field.

The sensational story of the *Mercury*, which had been the signal for increasing laughter all the morning, came at once into men's minds, and, incredible as it was, there could now be no doubt of the truth.

A creature which, in those dim ages when the world was young and humanity itself was slowly being evolved in obedience to an inevitable law, had winged its way over the mighty swamps and forests of the primeval world, was alive and preying among them. To those who thought, there was something sinister in such an incalculable age. The order of nature was disturbed.

The death of young Trant was immediately explained, and at dinner time the wildest rumours were going about the clubs, while in the theatres and music halls people were saying that a whole foul brood of dragons had been let loose upon the town.

The sensation was unique. Never before in all the history of the world had such a thing been heard of, and all night long the telegraphs sent conflicting rumours to the great centres of the earth. London was beside itself with excitement, and few people going about in the streets that night felt over-secure, though everyone felt that the slaughter of the beast was only a matter of hours. The very uneasiness that such a weird and unnatural appearance excited in the brains of the populace had its humorous side, and when that evening Mr Dan Leno chose to appear upon the stage as a comic St George, the laughter was Homeric. Such was the state of the public opinion about the affair on the evening of the first day, but there was a good deal of anxiety felt at Scotland Yard, and Sir Edward Bradford was for some time at work organising and directing precautionary measures. A company of sharp-shooters was sent down to the Embankment from the Regent's Park Barrack, and waited in readiness for any news. Mounted police armed with carbines were patrolling the whole country round Sydenham and, even as far as Mitcham Common, were on the alert. Two or three of them rode constantly up and down the Golf Links.

A warning wire was despatched to Mr Henry Gillman, the general manager of the Crystal Palace, for at this season of the year the grounds were always full of pleasure-seekers. About nine o'clock the chief inspector on duty at the police headquarters received the following telegram:

'Animal appeared here 8.30, and unfortunately killed child. Despite volley got away apparently unharmed. Heading for London when last seen. Have closed Palace and cleared grounds.'

It appears what actually happened was as follows:—

A Dr David Pryce, a retired professor from one of the Scotch Universities, who lived in a house on Gipsy Hill, was taking a stroll down the central transept after dinner, when he was startled to hear the noise of breaking glass high up in the roof. Some large pieces of glass fell within a few yards of him into one of the ornamental fountains. Running to one side, he looked up, and saw that some heavy body had fallen on to the roof and coming through the glass was so balanced upon an iron girder. Even as he looked, the object broke away and fell with a frightful splash into the basin among the goldfish. Simultaneously he heard the crack of rifles firing in the grounds outside.

He was the first of the people round to run to the fountain, where he found, to his unspeakable horror, the bleeding body of a child, a sweet little girl of six, still almost breathing.

The news of this second victim was in the streets about ten o'clock, and it was then that a real panic took possession of all the pleasure-seekers in Piccadilly and the Strand.

The special descriptive writers from the great daily papers, who went about the principal centres of amusement, witnessed the most extraordinary sights. Now and again there would be a false alarm that the dragon – for that is what people were beginning to call it – was in the neighbourhood, and there would be a stampede of men and women into the nearest place of shelter. The proprietor of one of the big Strand bars, afterwards boasted that the panic had been worth an extra £50 to him.

The Commissioner of Police became so seriously alarmed, both at the disorderly state of the streets, and at the possible chance of another fatality, that he thought it wiser to obtain military assistance, and about half-past eleven London was practically under arms. Two or three linesmen were stationed at central points in the main streets, and little groups of cavalry with unslung carbines patrolled from place to place.

Although the strictest watch was kept all night, nothing was seen of the monster, but in the morning a constable of the C Division, detailed for special duty, found traces at the top of Ludgate Hill which proved conclusively that the animal had been there some time during the night.

Third Episode

The widespread news that the terror had been in the very heart of London during the night created tremendous excitement among the authorities and the public at large. The City Police held a hurried consultation in Old Jewry about nine o'clock in the morning, and after hearing Sergeant Weatherley's account of his discovery, came to the conclusion that the dragon had probably made its lair on the top of St Paul's Cathedral.

A man was at once sent round to the Deanery for a pass which should allow a force of police to search the roofs, and came back in half an hour with an order written by Dean Gregory himself requesting the officials to give the police every facility for a thorough examination.

It was then that the fatal mistake was made, which added a fourth victim to the death roll.

About 9.30 a telegram was received at New Scotland Yard from a professional golfer at Mitcham, saying that some caddies on their way to the club-house had sighted the monster hovering over the Croydon road early in the morning. A wire was at once despatched to the local police station on the lower green, directing that strict inquiries should be made, and the result telegraphed at once. Meanwhile Scotland Yard communicated with Old Jewry, and the City Police made the incredible blunder of putting off the search party till the Mitcham report was thoroughly investigated.

It was not allowed to be known that the police had any suspicion that St Paul's might harbour the dragon, and the fact of Sergeant Weatherley's discovery did not transpire till the second edition of the *Star* appeared, just about the time the final scene was being enacted on the south roof.

Accordingly the omnibuses followed the usual Cannon Street route, and the City men from the suburbs crowded them as usual. In the brilliant morning sunshine – for it was a perfect summer's day – it was extremely difficult to believe that anything untoward was afoot.

The panic of the night before, the panic of the gas lamps and the uncertain mystery of night, had very largely subsided. Many a city man who the night before had come out of the Alhambra or the Empire seized with a genuine terror, now sat on the top of his City bus smoking the after-breakfast cigarette and almost joking about the whole extraordinary affair. The fresh, new air was so delightful that it had its effect on everybody, and the police and soldiers who stood at ease round the statue of Queen Anne were saluted with a constant fire of chaff from the waggish young gentlemen of the Stock Exchange as they were carried to their daily work.

'What price the Dragon!' and 'Have you got a muzzle handy!'

resounded in the precincts of the Cathedral, and the merry witticisms afforded intense enjoyment to the crowds of ragamuffins who lounged round the top of Ludgate Hill.

Then, quite suddenly, came the last act of the terrible drama.

Just as a white Putney bus was slowly coming up the steep gradient of the hill, the horses straining and slipping on the road, a black object rose from behind the clock tower on the facade of the Cathedral, and with a long, easy dive the creature that was terrorising London came down upon the vehicle. It seemed to slide rapidly down the air with its wings poised and open, and it came straight at the omnibus. The driver, with great presence of mind and not a moment too soon, pulled his horses suddenly to the right, and the giant enemy rushed past with a great disturbance of the air hardly a yard away from the conveyance.

It sailed nearly down to the railway bridge before it was able to check its flight and turn.

Then, with a slow flapping of its great leathery wings, it came back to where the omnibus was oscillating violently as the horses reared and plunged.

It was the most horrible sight in the world. Seen at close quarters the monstrous creature was indescribably loathsome, and the stench from its body was overpowering. Its great horny beak was covered with brown stains, and in its eagerness and anger it was foaming and slobbering at the mouth. Its eyes, which were half-covered with a white scurf, had something of that malignant and horrible expression that one sometimes sees in the eyes of an evil-minded old man.

In a moment the thing was right over the omnibus, and the people on the top were hidden from view by the beating of its mighty wings. Three soldiers on the pavement in front of the Cathedral knelt down, and taking deliberate aim, fired almost simultaneously.

A moment after the shots rang out, the horses, who had been squealing in an ecstasy of terror, overturned the vehicle. The dragon, which had been hit in the leather-like integument stretched between the rib-bones of its left wing, rose heavily and slowly, taking a little spring from the side of the omnibus, and giving utterance to a rapid choking sound, very like the gobbling of a turkey. Its wings beat the air with tremendous power and with the regular sound of a pumping engine, and in its bill it held some bright red object, which was screaming in uncontrollable agony. In two seconds the creature had mounted above the houses, and all down Ludgate Hill the horror-bitten crowd could see that its writhing, screaming burden was a soldier of the line.

The man, by some curious instinct, had kept tight hold of his little swagger-stick, and his whirling arms bore a grotesque resemblance to the conductor of an orchestra directing its movements with his baton. Some more shots pealed out, and the screaming stopped with the suddenness of a steam whistle turned off, while the swagger-stick fell down into the street.

Over the road, from house to house, was stretched a row of flags with a Union Jack in the centre, which had been put up earlier in the morning by an alderman who owned one of the shops, in order to signalise some important civic function. In mounting, the monster was caught by the line which supported the flags, and then with a tremendous effort it pulled the whole arrangement loose. Then, very slowly, and with the long row of gaudy flags streaming behind it, it rose high into the air and sank down behind the dome of St Paul's. As it soared, regardless of the fusillade from below, it looked exactly like a fantastic Japanese kite. The whole affair, from the time of the first swoop from St Paul's until the monster sank again to its refuge, only took two or three seconds over the minute.

The news of this fresh and terrible disaster reached the waiting party in Old Jewry almost immediately, and they started for the Cathedral without a moment's delay. They found Ludgate Hill was almost empty, as the police under the railway bridge were deflecting the traffic into other routes. On each side of the street hundreds of white faces peered from doorways and windows towards St Paul's. The overturned omnibus still lay in the middle of the road, but the horses had been taken away.

The party marched in through the west door, and the ineffable peace of the great church fell round them like a cloak and made their business seem fantastic and unreal. Mr Harding, the permanent clerk of the works, met them in the nave, and held a consultation with Lieutenant Boyle and Inspector Nicholson, who commanded the men. The clerk of the works produced a rough map of the various roofs, on any one of which the dragon might be. He suggested, and the lieutenant quite agreed, that two or three men should first be sent to try and locate the exact resting-place of the monster, and that afterwards the best shots should surround and attack it. The presence of a large number of men wandering about the extremely complicated system of approaches might well disturb the creature and send it abroad again. He himself, he added, would accompany the scouts.

Three men were chosen for the job, a sergeant of police and two soldiers. Mr Harding took them into his office, and they removed their boots for greater convenience in climbing. They were conducted first of all into the low gallery hung with old frescoes which leads to the library, and then, opening a small door in the wall, Mr Harding, beckoning the others to follow, disappeared into darkness.

They ascended some narrow winding steps deep in the thickness of the masonry, until a gleam of light showed stealing down from above, making their faces pale and haggard. Their leader stopped, and there was a jingling of keys. 'It is unlikely it'll be here,' he said in a low voice, 'and anyway it can't get at us quickly, but be careful. Sergeant, you bring one man and come with me, and the last man stay behind and hold the door open in case we have to retreat.' He turned the key in the lock and opened the narrow door.

For a moment the brilliant light of the sun blinded them, and then the two men who were yet a few steps down in the dark heard the other say, 'Come on, it's all safe.'

They came out into a large square court floored with lead. Great stone walls rose all around them, and the only outlet was the door by which they had come. It was exactly like a prison exercise yard, and towering away above their heads in front was the huge central dome. The dismal place was quite empty.

'The swine isn't here, that's certain,' said one of the soldiers.

'No, we must go round to the south side,' said the clerk of the works. 'It's very much like this, only larger. But there's a better way to get to it. Let us go back at once.'

They went down again to the library corridor, and turning by the archway debouching on the whispering gallery – they could hear the strains of the organ as they passed – went up another dark and narrow stairway. They came out on to a small ledge of stone, a kind of gutter, and there was very little room between the walls at their backs and the steep lead-covered side of the main roof which towered into the air straight in front.

'Now,' said Mr Harding, 'we have got to climb up this slant and down the other side, and if he's anywhere about we shall see him there. At the bottom of the other slope is a gutter, like this, to stand in, but no wall, as it looks straight down into a big bear pit, like the one we went to first. We shall have to go right down the other slant, because if he's lying on the near side of the pit – and it's the shady side – we shan't be able to see him at all. You'll find it easy enough to get up, and if you should slip back this wall will bring you up short, but be very careful about going down. If you once begin to slide, you'll toboggan right over the edge and on to the top of the beast, and even if he isn't there, it's a 60-foot drop.'

As they climbed slowly up the steep roof, all London came into clear and lovely view – white, red, and purple in the sun. When at length they reached the top and clung there, for a moment, high in the air, like sparrows perching on the ridge of a house, they could only just see the mouth of the drop yawning down below them.

One of the soldiers, a lithe and athletic young fellow, was down at the bottom considerably before the others, and crouching in the broad gutter, he peered cautiously over the edge. They saw his shoulders heave with excitement, and in a moment he turned his head towards them. His face was white and his eyes full of loathing. They joined him at once, and the horror of what they saw will never leave any of the four.

The Dragon was lying on its side against the wall. Its whole vast length was heaving as if in pain, while close by it lay the remains of what was once a soldier of the queen.

It was soon killed. The marksmen were hurriedly brought up from below, and after a perilous climb, owing to the weight of their rifles, lined the edge of the pit. They fired repeated volleys into the vast groaning creature. After the first volley it began to cough and choke, and vainly trying to open its maimed wings, dragged itself into the centre of the place. The mere sight of the malign thing gave a shock to the experience that was indescribable. It fulfilled no place in the order of life, and this fact induced a cold fear far more than its actual appearance. A psychologist who talked to one of the soldiers afterwards got near to some fundamental truths dealing with the natural limits of sensation, in a brilliant article published in *Cosmopolis*. In its death agonies, agonies which were awful to look at, it crawled right across the floor of the court, and it moved the line of flags, which still remained fixed to one paw, in such a way that when they got down to it they found that, by a strange and pathetic coincidence, the Union Jack was covering the body of the dead soldier.

In this way the oldest living thing in the world was destroyed, and London breathed freely again.

THE GORGON'S HEAD

By Gertrude Bacon (1874–1949)

Born in Cambridge, the daughter of a well-known astronomer, Gertrude Bacon became her father's collaborator in scientific work while still a teenager. In her twenties she accompanied him on three expeditions to witness solar eclipses in Lapland, India and North Carolina, and together they ascended in a hot-air balloon to observe the Leonid meteor shower, an adventure which saw them nearly disappear across the Atlantic before they made an emergency landing near Neath. Gertrude suffered a broken arm but this did not deter her from further exploits in the air. She became an aeronautical pioneer and was one of the first British women to fly in an aircraft. Her books on early aviation history include How Men Fly *(1911) and* All About Flying *(1915), and she was a member of the Aeronautical Society from 1905. Her account of her experiences observing the meteor shower from above the clouds is reported to have influenced Sir Arthur Conan Doyle when he came to write his 1913 weird story, 'The Horror of the Heights'. She was also a botanist of some note.*

As a young woman in the 1890s, Gertrude Bacon was a contributor to The Strand Magazine, *producing both non-fiction articles and short stories, including this one in which two sailors in the nineteenth century encounter a monster from ancient Greek mythology.*

The Strand Magazine, *December 1899*

'They that go down to the sea in ships' see strange things, but what they tell is ofttimes stranger still. A faculty for romancing is imparted by a seafaring life as readily and surely as a rolling gait and a weather-beaten countenance. A fine imagination is one of the gifts of the ocean – witness the surprising and unlimited power of expression and epithet possessed by the sailor. And a fine imagination will frequently manifest itself in other ways besides swear words.

Captain Brander is one of the most gifted men in this way in the whole merchant service. His officers say of him with pride that he possesses the largest vocabulary in the great steamship company of which he is one of the oldest and most respected skippers, and his yarns are only equalled in their utter impossibility by the genius he displays in furnishing them with minute detail and all the outward circumstance of truth.

I first learned this fact from the second engineer the evening of the sixth day of our voyage, as we leant across the bulwarks and watched the sunset. The second engineer was a bit of a liar – or, I should say, romancer – himself. The day he took me down into the engine-room he told me, as personal experiences, tales of mutinous Lascar firemen, unpopular officers who disappeared suddenly into the fiery maw of blazing furnaces, and so forth, which, whatever foundation of fact they may have possessed, certainly did not lose in the telling. As a humble aspirant in the same branch of art, he naturally was quick to recognise the genius of that past master, the captain, and his admiration for his chief was as boundless as it was sincere.

'I say, Miss Baker,' he said, apropos of nothing, 'have you had the skipper "on" yet?'

'Not that I am aware of,' I said. 'What do you mean?'

'Why, has he been spinning you any yarns yet? There isn't a man in the service can touch him for stories. I don't deny that he has seen some service, and been in some tight places, but for a real out-and-out lie, commend me to old Monkey Brand!' (It was by this sobriquet, I regret to say, suggested partly by his name, and mostly by his undoubted resemblance to a well-known advertisement, that the worthy captain was known in the unregenerate engine-room.)

'Oh, I should just love to hear him,' I cried. 'There is nothing I should like better. Do tell me how I can manage to draw him.'

'Well, he doesn't want much drawing as a rule,' said the engineer. 'He likes to give vent to his imagination. Let me see,' he continued, 'tomorrow afternoon we shall be about passing the Grecian Islands. Ask him about them, and try and get him on the subject of Gorgons.'

'Gorgons!' I said. 'What a strange topic! Why, since I've left school I have almost forgotten what they were. Weren't they mythological creatures who turned people into stone when they looked at them?'

'That's about it, I believe,' said the engineer, 'and a fellow called Perseus cut off their heads, or something of that kind. It's a lie anyhow, but you ask the skipper.'

It was the custom of Captain Brander every afternoon to make a kind of royal progress among his passengers. Going the entire circuit of the ship; passing slowly from group to group, with a joke here and a chat there, and bestowing his favours in lordly and impartial fashion – especially among the ladies. I have watched him often coming the whole length of the promenade deck, making some outrageous compliment to one girl, patting another on the shoulder, even chucking a third under the chin; a sense of supreme self-satisfaction animating his red cheeks, curling his grey hair, and suffusing his whole short, portly person. Eccentric he was; indifferent to his personal appearance – his battered old cap had seen almost as much service as he had – but a more popular man or an abler officer never walked the bridge. On this particular occasion I was at the end of the deck, and had so arranged that an inviting deck chair stood vacant beside me. Wearied by his progress by the time he reached me, he fell at once into my little trap, and sat down on the empty chair, leant back, and spread his legs. He and I were fast friends, and had been since the day when I tried to photograph him, and he had frustrated my design by unscrewing the front lens of my camera and keeping it in his pocket for the rest of the morning.

'Captain,' I said, pointing to a cloudy grey outline faintly visible against the eastern horizon, 'what land is that?'

'My dear young lady,' said he, 'I am quite sick of answering that question! If I have been asked it once I have been asked it twenty times in the last half-hour. That old Mrs Matherson in the red shawl buttonholed me on the subject to such an extent that I thought I should never get away again. Wonderful thirst for information that old party has! And she appears to think that because I'm captain I must have a complete knowledge of geography, geology, history, etymology, mythology, and navigation. Well, for the twenty-first time, then, we are passing the isles off the coast of Greece, and that one straight ahead is Zante.'

'So that is Greece, is it?' I mused aloud. 'Well, from here at least it looks old enough and romantic enough to be the home of all those ancient heroes we read about – Alexander and Hercules and – and – Gorgons and those sort of things.' I felt I had introduced the subject somewhat lamely, after all, and the captain looked me full in the face as if suspecting a plot. But if I am not very adroit in conversation, I can at least look innocent upon occasions, and he merely said, 'And what do you know about Gorgons, pray?'

'Oh, as much as most people, I expect!' I answered. 'They are only a sort of fairy tale, you know.'

'I am not so sure of that,' said Captain Brander. 'Those fairy tales, as you call them, have often truth at the bottom of them. And as to

Gorgons, why, I could tell you a little incident that happened to me once – but it's rather a long story.'

Then I urged my best persuasions – not that he needed much pressing – and pushing his old cap off his bald forehead, and speaking slowly and with that almost American accent peculiar to him, he unfolded his tale of wonder as follows:—

'It's nearly thirty years ago, Miss Baker – that's long before you were ever born or thought of – that I was fourth officer of the *Haslar*, 2,000-ton vessel of this same company I serve to this day. How times have altered, to be sure! The *Haslar* was reckoned a fine ship in those days, and if you had told me that I should presently command an 8,000-tonner, such as I do this day, with 11,000 horse power engines, and more men for the crew alone than the *Haslar* could hold when she was packed her tightest, I very probably wouldn't have believed you. However, that is neither here nor there. But thirty years ago in the spring time—now I come to think of it, it was in the month of April—we were cruising in this very neighbourhood, and one thick foggy night our skipper lost his bearings a bit, got too near the coast, and ran us ashore off the south point of Zante.

'Of course there was a great fuss, and everybody came up on deck with life-belts, and all the girls screamed, and all the young fellows swore to save them or die in the attempt; and the skipper turned as white as paper – not that he was afraid, for he was no coward – none of our officers are that – but because he knew his prospects were ruined, and he would be turned out of the company and perhaps lose his certificate, and he'd got a wife and a big family, poor chap! Of course that consideration didn't affect me, for I was in my bunk and asleep at the time, but it was certainly unfortunate for him.

'Well, it was very soon discovered that the ship wasn't going down in a hurry, and nobody got into the boats, though they were lowered ready. And when daylight came we saw we were fast on the rocks, with half the stern under water, and the saloon and a lot of the cabins flooded. But more than that, the *Haslar* couldn't sink, and at low water you might almost walk dryshod on to the shore. There was no getting her off, however, and so all the passengers were landed and sent home as best they could across country, and a rough time they had of it, for Zante is not an over-hospitable sort of a place; while we officers had to stick to the ship till we could get help, and then till she was repaired sufficiently to work her into dock somewhere.

'It was a tedious job, for help was slow in coming; and then all her boilers had to be taken out before she would float, and we fellows got jolly sick of it, I can tell you, for we were hard worked, and Zante is a wretched hole to spend more than half an hour in. Our one amusement, when we were off duty, was to go ashore on foot or row round the island in a boat, shooting wild fowl and exploring the country. There was precious little to see and not much to shoot, and it was slow fun altogether till, one day, the second officer came back from a tramp ashore and told us he had found his way to some very remote village on the eastern coast, where there was a cave among the hills which the villagers warned him not to enter. He could not gather for what reason, because he didn't understand enough of their outlandish tongue, but as it was then growing late he was obliged to return to the ship without further investigation.

'I was always one for adventure when I was a lad, and directly the second officer told his tale I made up my mind to go and explore that cave before any of the rest had a chance. It so happened that next day was my turn for going ashore, and I went and looked up one of the assistant engineers and persuaded him to come with me.

I wanted him because he was a chum of mine, and also he was the only one of us who could talk the language a bit. He had been in those parts before, and generally acted as interpreter in our dealings with the natives. His name was Travers, a queer little dark chap, with black eyes and a hot temper, but a pleasant fellow enough if you did not rub him up the wrong way, and game for anything under the sun. He readily agreed to come with me, and we started as soon as we could get away, telling no one of our destination, for we had no wish to be forestalled.

'It was a long tramp, right across the island, to the village which Jenkins, the second officer, had indicated. But at last, after climbing a weary hill, we looked down on some clustering huts standing amid vineyards in the valley beneath, while another and much sheerer cliff rose on the opposite side, whose rugged scarp was all rent and riven as by an earthquake, and intersected by a deep ravine. Here and there among the rocks were dark shadows and black patches which might be the entrances to caverns in the crag. "This must be the place," I said, "and one of those is the forbidden cave. How are we to find out which?"

'As if in answer to my question, at this moment there came along the hill-top towards us a burly countryman with a sunburned face and tattered garments. He regarded us with astonishment, as well he might, for they get few strangers in those parts, and he made some remark to us in his queer language, which, of course, I didn't understand, but Travers did and replied to it. Finding he was understood, the countryman stopped and talked.

'"Ah!" he said, or so Travers interpreted. "So you have reached the valley of the Haunted Cavern! It is far to seek and hard to find, but it lies spread beneath you."

'"But which is the Haunted Cavern, and why is it so called?" asked Travers.

"'It lies in yonder cleft of the hills," answered the man, pointing to the opposite ravine, "and it is called the Haunted Cavern because none who venture there return alive. Nay, they return not either alive or dead. They are seen no more!"

"'Tell that to the Marines!" said Travers, only he translated it into Greek, of course, or what the Zante people think is Greek. "You don't expect me to believe such a yarn as that! Why, what is there up in that place?"

"'That is what none can tell," replied the peasant, "for none come back to say. And, indeed, it is the truth I speak. Many men have attempted to find the secret. In bygone days, I have heard, a whole party of soldiers were sent there to search for brigands supposed to be in hiding, but not one was seen again. The cavern has an evil name, and now is shunned by one and all, but every now and again there arises a youth venturesome beyond the rest; and he heeds not the warnings of the old, but hopes to break the spell and find the treasure that some say is hidden there, and he starts in high hope and courage, but never again do we behold his face!"

"'But what is the reason?" persisted Travers, the incredulous.

"'Nay, that we cannot say," reiterated the man. "A short distance can one go up the ravine that leads to the cavern. I have been there myself, and truly there is nothing that can be seen except a barren valley, scattered all over with big black stones. Nothing more, and farther than the entrance none must venture."

"'Oh, I say!" exclaimed Travers, in delight. "Did you ever hear such an old liar? This beats anything I could have believed possible in the nineteenth century. Come on, Brander! We are in luck this time!" And the impetuous fellow dashed off down the hill, I at his heels, leaving the countryman dumb with amazement behind us.

'At the foot of the hill we entered the little village. An old, white-haired man of rather superior appearance was crossing the road before us. Travers accosted him and asked him the way to the Haunted Cavern. The old man turned quite pale with astonishment and apprehension.

'"The Haunted Cavern, my son!" he said, in quavering tones. "Surely you are not going thither?"

'"Yes, we are, though," said Travers, his eyes dancing with excitement. It is wonderful what enterprise that boy – he was little more – had in him. "And if you won't tell us, we'll find the way out for ourselves!" And he pushed past the old man, who held out his skinny hands as if to detain him.

'Before we had got clear of the hamlet the news had somehow got circulated that we were about to explore the ravine, and the whole of the inhabitants turned out in the wildest excitement. Some were for staying us forcibly, till Travers began to get quite nasty, drew his revolver, and talked of firing. Many reiterated and emphasised alarming warnings and assurances that we should never return. All watched us with the most intense interest, and followed close on our footsteps until we began to near the fatal spot, when they fell off singly or in parties, till finally at the very entrance of the ravine we had left even the boldest spirits behind us.

'In truth, it was a strange spot to which we had penetrated. The narrow path had led us suddenly round the spur of the mountain, and now, look which way we might, the giant rocks towered up sheer above us, hundreds of feet high, in inaccessible grey walls. The sinking sun was now too low to shine within this well-like space, which his rays could only reach at midday, and the very air struck damp and chill. We were in an open valley, thus shut in by the cliffs, of considerable extent, but not to be reached by any path except that we had traversed. The ground was firm and smooth, but littered all over with the strangest black stones of all sorts of shapes, and in all positions, though of a fairly uniform size, and alike in material. There was something uncanny and weird about these queer black boulders, which strewed the valley the thicker the farther we advanced, till at the far end of the space, where a huge back hole yawned ominous in the cliff, they almost entirely blocked the way.

'The dark cavern looked terribly grim and forbidding in the fading light. A little stream issued from its mouth and trickled among the stones. It did not gurgle and glisten as most mountain streams, but flowed noiselessly, sluggish, and dull, and gathered in stagnant pools on its rocky bed. No birds sang in that dismal nook; no sound from without penetrated to its recesses. All was silent, dim, and chill as the tomb itself.

'Despite my utmost efforts, I felt the spell of the weird, wild spot stealing over me, and a cold shudder crept down my backbone. There was but room for one at a time in the ever-narrowing track, and I was at first leading. My steps became slower and slower, and finally I paused altogether and turned to look back on Travers to see if he too was feeling the oppressive sense of evil that seemed to hang heavy in the very air. But in his face was only visible an ecstasy almost of eagerness and delight. His dark eyes sparkled again, his cheeks were flushed, his breath came quick, and his whole body was quivering with excitement.

'"Go on, Brander!" he cried. "What are you stopping for, man? This is grand! This is luck, indeed! Did you ever see such a place? Come on, I want to get to that cave!"

'I felt utterly ashamed to confess my weakness, but it was that cave that I had begun to dread more and more. Whatever else I may be, Miss Baker, it is not boasting to say I am no coward. I have seen danger, aye, and courted it all my life, and until that moment I doubt if I had known what fear was. But I knew then: the blind, unreasoning fear that saps the strength of mind and limb and melts the heart and paralyses all thought save that one overpowering instinct to fly – somewhere. Yet, in face of Travers's eagerness, I could not bear to show the white feather. I turned my back therefore on the dark cavern, now just ahead of us, and endeavoured to temporise.

"'Travers," I said, "did you ever see such queer stones? How do you suppose they have got here? They are quite a different nature from these cliffs, so they could not have fallen from the sides."

"'Oh, bother the stones!" said Travers. "I can't look at them now, I want to get into the cave. Quick, before it gets dark!" And as I still hesitated, he pushed past me into a more open space beyond, almost at the cavern's mouth. I did not dare to leave him, and was scrambling after him as best I might, when I suddenly heard him cry out in a voice such as I had never heard before, and hope never to again. A shrill, high-pitched cry in which there were surprise, wonder, disgust, alarm, and awful horror all combined in one: a cry of astonishment, a shriek of agony, a shout of dismay. "Look, Brander! Look! Look!"'

'I could have sworn that when he spoke my companion was in full view, close beside me, touching me almost, though at the exact moment my eyes were looking from him; but when I turned my head in answer to his cry he was gone.

'For one second only had my gaze been averted, but in that time he had utterly vanished from sight, disappeared in a flash, gone – whither? A large black stone stood close beside me, similar to the rest in that ghostly valley; yet it struck me somehow that I had not noticed it there before. I placed my hand upon it as I peered round behind to see if Travers were there, and a shudder I could not explain ran up my arm, for the stone felt warm to the touch. I had not time then to analyse my unreasonable horror at this trivial circumstance; I was too eager to find my friend. I rushed madly among the stones, I yelled his name again and again, but the weird echoes of my cry, returned in countless reflections from cliff and cavern, alone answered me.

'In a frenzy of despair I continued my search, for certain was I that by no natural means could Travers have disappeared so utterly in so brief a space. Blind panic seized me, and I knew not what I did, till my eye suddenly fell on a shallow pool of water collected in a rocky hollow at my very feet. It was not more than a couple of inches deep, and scarce a yard across, but on its placid face were reflected the overhanging rock and opening of the cavern just behind it, and also something else that glued my eyes to it in horror and rooted my flying feet to the ground.

'Just above the cavern's mouth was a narrow ledge of rock, running horizontally, and of a few inches in width. On this natural shelf, reflected in the water, I saw, hanging downwards, a decayed fragment of goat-skin, rotten with age, but which might have been bound round something, long years before. Upon this, as if escaped from its folds, rested a Head.

'It was a human head, severed at the neck, but fresh and unfaded as if but newly dead. It bore the features of a woman – of a woman of more perfect loveliness than was ever told of in tale, or sculptured in marble, or painted on canvas. Every feature, every line, was of the truest beauty, cast in the noblest mould – the face of a goddess. But upon that perfect countenance was the mark of eternal pain, of deathless agony and suffering past words. The forehead was lined and knit, the death-white lips were tightly pressed in speechless torment; in the wide eyes seemed yet to lurk the flame of an unquenchable fire; while around the fair brows, in place of hair, curled and coiled the stark bodies of venomous serpents, stiff in death, but their loathsome forms still erect, their evil heads yet thrust forward as if to strike.

'My heart ceased beating, and the chill of death crept over my limbs, as with eyes starting from their sockets I stared at that awful head, reflected in the pool. For hours it seemed to me I gazed fascinated, as the bird by the eye of the snake that has charmed it. I was as incapable of thought as movement, till suddenly forgotten school-room learning began to cross my brain, and I knew that I looked at the reflection of Medusa, the Gorgon, fairest and foulest of living things, the unclean creature, half-woman, half-eagle, slain by the hero Perseus, and one glimpse of whose tortured face turned the luckless beholder into stone with the horror of it.

'If I once raised my eyes from the reflection to the actual head above I knew that I too should freeze in a moment into another black block, even as poor Travers, and every other who had entered the accursed valley had done before. And as this thought occurred to me, the longing to lift my eyes and look upon the real object became so overpowering that, in sheer self-preservation, I inclined my face closer and closer to the water till I seemed almost to touch it, when my senses fled and I knew no more.

'When I woke at last it was far on in the night, and a bright moon, riding high, shone full down upon the valley, revealing the ragged rocks and scattered stones with a cold brilliance that almost equalled the day. I was lying chilled and stiff beside the pool, and I started up in amazement, unable to recall to my mind, for a moment, where I was or what I was doing there. I had my back to the cavern, fortunately, and as I gazed over the ghostly and deserted scene the events of the day suddenly returned to my mind in a single flash of terror.

'To escape from this ghastly place was now my only thought, and in order to do this I resolved to look no more at the pool at my feet in case the terrible fascination should again take possession of me. What it cost me to adhere to this resolution I cannot tell you, but with the courage of despair I pressed blindly forward to the mouth of the ravine, only pausing a second to lay my hand upon the now ice-cold stone that once was Travers.

'Poor Travers! Gay, light-hearted fellow! Ever in the forefront of mischief, of danger, of adventure. How eager he had been to solve the secret of the haunted valley, which now must be his tomb for ever. How full of health and spirits he had scrambled a few hours before among those very boulders, one of which now, standing stiffly erect among its forest of brethren, was at once the monument and sole relic of a fearless lad, a cheery friend, and a gallant seaman. Dear old Travers! Brave, foolish boy! My heart was heavy, indeed, for his awful fate, as I reverently touched the stone and murmured to the night breeze, stealing around the rocks, "Good-bye, old fellow; sleep sound!"

'It seemed to me, in my loneliness and terror, that my fearsome journey would never be ended: that, lost in a labyrinth, I should tread that valley for ever. But at last, after endless ages, I reached the mouth of the ravine, and once on open ground I stretched my cramped limbs and ran, without ceasing, till I once more reached the ship.'

Here the captain paused, more from want of breath than anything else, I think.

'Go on, Captain Brander,' I cried. 'You haven't half finished yet. What did they say when you returned, and how did you explain about poor Travers?'

'Young lady,' said Captain Brander, 'don't ask any more questions. I think I have told you enough for one afternoon.' And here, an officer coming up and summoning him, he left me.

THE WEIRD OF THE WALFORDS

By Louisa Baldwin (1845–1925)

*Louisa Macdonald was one of four remarkable sisters, born into a Methodist family in the early years of Victoria's reign. Three of them married artists of varying degrees of prominence. The oldest, Alice, became the wife of Lockwood Kipling and moved with him to India, where she gave birth in 1865 to a son they named Rudyard after the lake in Staffordshire where they had first met. Agnes married Edward Poynter, later President of the Royal Academy; Georgiana became the wife of Pre-Raphaelite painter Edward Burne-Jones. Louisa herself married an industrialist and future MP, Alfred Baldwin. Their son, Stanley, became British prime minister in the 1920s and 1930s. Louisa was a talented writer, who produced novels (*A Martyr to Mammon; The Story of a Marriage*), poetry and short stories. Her shorter fiction, particularly her ghost stories, mostly collected in the volume* The Shadow on the Blind, *published in 1895, is still read and admired. 'The Weird of the Walfords', one of the tales in* The Shadow on the Blind, *is not really a ghost story. Although the word 'weird' in its title does not have the meaning one might think at first glance (it refers to an Anglo-Saxon term for 'fate'), the narrative itself definitely falls into the category of 'weird'.*

Longman's Magazine, *November 1889*

On a summer's day in the year 1860 I, Humphrey Walford, did a deed for which I should have been disinherited by my father and disowned by my ancestors. I laid sacrilegious hands on the old carved oak four-post family bedstead and destroyed it.

Alone I could not have accomplished the work of destruction. The massive posts, canopy, and panels would have resisted my single efforts; but I compelled two reluctant men to lend me their aid, and by the help of saws and hatchets we reduced the whole structure to billets of wood such as one might kindle a cheerful flame with in the parlour grate on a damp summer evening.

It was a bed with a history to me so unspeakably melancholy that I had resolved when I was my own master I would destroy the gloomy structure, and rid me of the nightmare-like feeling with which the sight of it never failed to inspire me.

The bed itself was upwards of 300 years old, carved in oak grown on our land, while the heavy dark-green hangings, faded and musty-smelling, dated only from the time of my great-grandfather Walford. I have the dimensions of the huge hearse-like thing by heart. It was ten feet long by eight feet wide, and ten feet high; and when as a small child I was brought to see my young mother die in the recesses of the vast bed, I looked up at its tall posts with something of the awe with which I should now regard the loftiest tree.

For three centuries this bed had been the cradle and grave of our family. Its heavy drapery had deadened the sound of the first cry and the last groan of the generations of Walfords who had been born or died in Walford Grange. In its solemn depths the newly wedded brides of the family lay the first few nights in their new home, till the wedding festivities were ended, and the squire and his wife began their everyday married life by occupying a less stately but more comfortable bed. I knew the history of the gloomy old piece of furniture as family tradition had preserved it for three centuries. Ten Squire Walfords had either died in that bed or had lain on it after death awaiting their burial. I was the eleventh squire dating from the epoch of the bed, and I would neither die in it nor be laid upon it after my death; and to make sure of this there was no way but now, in my youth and strength, to fall upon it with hatchet and saw and utterly destroy it.

I did not fear death more than my forefathers, but I resented being bidden by family tradition and custom to die in a given spot. I rebelled at having a definite place assigned to me to lie down in and die – a place so fraught with dismal associations as the ancient, hearse-like bed. I could not endure to think that, wander wide as I would, I must return to this bed of death at last, and here, among stifling pillows and heavy curtains, end my life precisely where it began.

Must this ghastly horror of my childhood be the goal towards which I tend? When I am sailing on mid-ocean, the ship ploughing her way through the furrows of the sea, shall I only be speeding, sooner or later, towards this dismal bed? When I climb mountains and breathe the keen air of the heights, is it but to end in the exclusion of light and air? Must every step I take, every journey I make, be but a stage on the road that ends in the stifling pillows of this bed of death? No, a thousand times no, and I brought my axe down on the footboard with a crash.

How vividly both the dead and the living who had occupied this ancient bed rose before my mind's eye! Here had lain Ralph Walford, killed in the Civil Wars, fighting for the king, and his wounded body was brought home and stretched on what had been his bridal bed to await his burial. And here died Squire Ralph's young widow, who a short time after her husband's sad homecoming gave birth to his posthumous child, and never again left this ill-omened bed till they carried her out feet foremost. Ralph Walford's brother Heneage, the next squire, thought to make the old bed festive with gold and crimson hangings, to forget that his brother's corpse had lain on it, his orphan child been born in it, and his widow died in it, and by the upholsterer's wit to convert a hearse into a bridal bower.

Brighter times came to our family with the Restoration. We had spent our blood and treasure in the king's cause, for which he did not suffer us to go unhonoured; for shortly after his joyful restoration his gracious majesty was travelling within ten miles of Walford Grange, and, the weather proving stormy, and there being no other Royalist house of consideration near, he made shift to pass a night under the roof of his faithful servant Heneage Walford.

My father often told me the history of that memorable visit, as it had been handed down from generation to generation. How gracious and witty was the king's majesty, how merry and light-hearted, as little troubled by the murder of his royal father and the heavy misfortunes of his house as by the brave lives lost and families impoverished in his cause! Squire Heneage was as loyal a man as ever drew sword for the king, yet he was heard to say that it was a cursed day for him when his gracious majesty honoured him by being his guest, for it turned his wife Mistress Johanna's head, and she was never again the woman she had been. She grumbled and bemoaned herself that the king had not knighted her husband, so that she might have ruffled it a step above the squirearchy. But one abiding comfort remained with her from the royal visit. And this was that both at coming and going the king had saluted her, and she ever after prettily described the royal manner of kissing, which she affirmed to differ from that practised by ordinary men. Mistress Johanna's serving woman, Anne Grimshaw, said that the king had saluted her too; but this her mistress would not hear of, and when she appealed to Squire Heneage he set the vexed question at rest by giving his opinion that, judging it as a matter of probability, it was more likely that a vain woman should tell a lie than that his sacred majesty should kiss Anne Grimshaw, who had a foul face of her own.

If I have somewhat enlarged on the fact of the king's visit to Walford Grange, it is not so much on account of any tokens of his royal favour that he was pleased to bestow on my ancestors, as because he lay in the best chamber, in the great oak bed with its brave new hangings. But the king was tormented by terrible dreams, and woke in the morning haggard and weary, as though he had been ridden by witches. And that I attributed to a malign influence in the hearse-like bed itself, and with that I crashed into it afresh.

I had long promised myself this fierce, destructive joy, when I in my turn should be master of Walford Grange. My father had died in this bed three years ago, and I had been travelling in the south of Europe ever since, urged partly by the restless curiosity of youth, and partly by the belief that no Squire Walford had ever crossed the seas before. Some younger sons and thriftless members of our family, in pursuit of the fortune denied them at home, had ventured into foreign lands, but the head of the house never. My father met any wishes or arguments I advanced on the subject of travel by a statement that seemed to him conclusive – namely, that a man sees enough in his own country that he can't understand, without going abroad to complete his confusion. But now on my return home I hastened to carry out my design on the hated ancestral bed.

What consternation prevailed in the house when it was understood what I was about, and when I and Gillam the carpenter and his man, having stripped the great bed of its drapery, proceeded to take to pieces the panels of the carved oak canopy! Mrs Barrett, the old housekeeper, stood wiping her honest eyes and bewailing my impiety.

'Don't 'ee do it, squire, don't 'ee do it! You may come to know the want of a good feather bed to die in yet! Such a bed as it's been for lyings in and layings out, and I'd hoped to ha' seen you laid in it, like your poor father before you.'

What Mrs Barrett's expectation of life may have been I know not, but she was sixty-five, and I twenty-four years of age.

'My good Barrett, I have determined that this bed shall utterly perish. We will not contribute one more corpse to its greedy maw. But if it be its feathers that you bewail, you are welcome to its pillows to line your nest with, but the bed itself must perish.'

'What, squire, the bed that your Great-Uncle Geoffrey was found dead in, when he'd gone upstairs overnight as well and as hearty as man ever was, and making his ungodly jokes, the Lord forgive him! The very bed as your grandfather lay in two whole years before he died, and all the house heard his groans; and where your Aunt Hester was laid with the water drip, drip, from every limb, just as they brought her in drowned from the brook!'

'Yes, my good Barrett, because of these very things the bed must perish.'

Then Gillam began, as he took off his paper cap and wiped his brow: 'If it's as the bed don't seem nateral like to sleep in after so many o' your kin has laid stiff and stark in it, won't you sell it, squire, to them as knows nothing of its ways? That there panel with the berried ivy on it is a deal too pretty a bit of carving to make firewood on.'

'No, Gillam, I shall not sell it. The man who would take money for the bed his ancestors died in, would sell their bones to make knife handles of. Besides, the bed has existed long enough; it has served my family to die in for ten generations. It's my own property, Gillam; mayn't I do what I will with my own?'

'Ay, surely, squire; there's no law to hinder a man making any fool of hisself as he pleases wi' what's his own. But I sides with the chap as made the bedstead, and I shouldn't like to think as in a matter o' two or three hundred years a bit o' my work 'ud be chopped up for firing.'

'Be under no uneasiness, Gillam; you and I do not live in an age that produces lasting work. Our glue-and-tintack carpentry is not done with a view to posterity.'

'Well, squire,' continued Gillam, returning to his first idea, 'if you won't sell the bedstead whole nor piecemeal, you might give me them panels with the carved ivy on 'em. I could find you some bits o' wood as 'ud burn brighter and better.'

'I don't mind giving you the old ivy carving, Gillam,' I said, 'but only on condition that I shall never see anything more of it, in any shape or form.'

'That's easy promised, sir, and thank you kindly. I'll make it up into something as'll surprise itself.'

Having weakly consented to his request, I saw him lay aside two or three beautiful panels, richly carved with branches of berried ivy, as salvage from the general wreck. If the gloomy horrors of the old bed had not eaten into my very heart, I could never have lent a hand at such a work of destruction. I should at least have saved the footboard with its carving in high relief of Adam and Eve under the tree, a man-headed serpent twining round the trunk, and the branches bending beneath their load of fruit. But I could not look at it without thinking of the dying eyes that had fixed their fading gaze on it, so my axe and saw made havoc of a work of art. When the floor was littered over with billets of wood, and the men were wiping their hot faces, I felt a strange lightness of heart, a comfortable sense of work postponed at length happily accomplished.

'Gillam,' I said, 'there was timber enough in that huge thing to build a man-of-war, drapery to make her sails, and rope enough for all her rigging.'

'Ay, there was a'most,' and, hastily throwing his tools into his basket, he added, sarcastically I thought, 'There'll be nothing else I can help you to pull down or to smash up, squire?'

I soon found that my destructive toil had benefited me in more ways than one. Not only had it freed me from an intolerable oppression of spirit, but it established for me in the neighbourhood a reputation for eccentricity, which I maintained afterwards at the smallest cost, and found of great service. The carrying out of my long-cherished purpose was regarded as evidence of a wild and lawless disposition, bordering on mental derangement. Night after night at the alehouse Gillam recounted to a breathless audience the story of the scene of destruction at which he had assisted professionally; and it grew in the telling till, without the slightest intention of lying, he added that the squire's rage against the old place was such that he had been obliged to menace him with the screwdriver to keep him from tearing down the mantelshelf and wainscot.

I was evidently a man whom it was not wise to thwart or contradict. My servants flew at my least word with an alacrity I had not before observed. My bidding was promptly done, my orders were not disputed, and whatever I said was agreed to with servility. While enjoying the sweets of mental health, as my neighbours voted me on such insufficient grounds on the borderland of insanity, I availed myself of the liberty it gave me to speak and act as I chose. Their hasty judgement had made me free of the wide domain of conduct. There was nothing I could do, however extravagant, but was clearly shadowed forth in the destruction of the ancestral oak bed.

I began to grow lonely in Walford Grange. My good Barrett died suddenly, and in my solitude I wanted someone to sit and talk with me in the long evenings, for even the bright wood fire flickering on the hearth could not satisfy all my desires for cheerful companionship. I should not have wished to marry if I had had a brother to live with me, to share my thoughts and occupations, and who would himself marry and preserve the name. But I was the last of the family, and I did not mean to let an ancient race die out. I began seriously to think of marrying, though whom I had not an idea, for so far I had not seen the woman I should care to marry, nor could I suppose that anyone looked with an eye of favour upon me. But when a man makes up his mind to marry, and sets out on his travels by land and sea, resolved never to return to his home till he brings a wife with him, it would be hard if he could not effect his purpose.

It happened that I met with my wife unexpectedly, and where I should have thought I was least likely to meet her – in a log house in the far west of America. Her name was Grace Calvert, and she was only eighteen years old, fair and fresh as an unfolding flower, and full of the high spirits and delight of life suited to her age and her free and simple bringing up. I fell in love with her at first sight, and we were married after a short courtship, for I had obtained the object of my travels, and my little wife was wild with curiosity and impatience to see England. She had a most romantic conception of the land of her forefathers, and delighted me by her belief that every village in England contained a church, vast and venerable as Westminster Abbey, and was engirt with hills crowned by frowning fortresses.

Grace had never seen houses built either of brick or stone, and had I not been able to show her a photograph of Walford Grange, it would have been impossible to give her any idea of an object so strange that there was nothing within the narrow limits of her experience with which to compare it. Her imagination was greatly stirred by the picture of the old house. Not a detail escaped her, from the fluted chimneys to the stone seats in the wide porch. The oriel windows, with their diamond panes, pleased my young wife more than anything, and especially she admired the broad windows of the best bed chamber, in which some two years before I had wrought my destructive will on the ancestral bed. The room was now bare and stripped of furniture, and since Mrs Barrett's death I had kept it constantly locked.

Grace was fascinated with the position of the room, with its large window over the porch, looking down the avenue of limes by which the house was approached, to the open country, and the line of low hills that bounded the horizon.

'That room must be lighter than those on the ground floor,' she said. 'See how the upper storey projects and throws a shadow over the lower rooms. We will make it our sitting-room, will we not?'

The request gave me a strange sinking of heart, and I felt that not even the society of my young wife could induce me to live in the room that had so long contained the hearse-like bed. I temporised with her in a vague manner, neither granting nor denying her request. I begged her to wait till she could see for herself how much better adapted to the comfort of daily life were the rooms on the ground floor than those on the upper storey.

In all her short life Grace had not been further than twenty miles from the spot where she was born, and I feared lest taking her away from all she loved, and from everything with which she was familiar, might prove too keen a pain.

There was a brief tempest of tears at parting with the dear ones she was never to meet again, but it was an April shower succeeded by smiles. Each outburst of weeping was of shorter duration, and the sunny intervals between them were longer, till in a few days Grace was her bright self again. The excitement of the journey was so overwhelming as to swallow up every other feeling.

We reached our home one November afternoon as the setting sun looked out through a rift in the clouds, and his level beams lighted up every casement with a red glow. As we drove up the leafless avenue, heavy drops fell from the bare boughs overhead, and Grace, clinging to my arm, said in a frightened whisper: 'O Humphrey, that light in the window is not like sunshine! It looks as if your old house was on fire!' and, raising my eyes, I caught for one moment the full effect of the illusion. But, the sun sinking into his bed of cloud, the red glow faded from the windows and left them dark and dim. 'Welcome, my darling, to your English home!' I said, and I took my little wife by the hand and led her up the wide oak staircase; and before we sat down to our evening meal I had taken her over the house from garret to basement, preceding her, candle in hand, through the darkening rooms. She expressed unbounded admiration for the house and its furniture, but the old family portraits and pictures excited her utmost enthusiasm, for Grace had never seen anything more venerable or older than her grandparents and the log house in which she was born. When her raptures had toned down sufficiently to allow her to eat a little, and we were seated at supper in the oak parlour, my little wife suddenly said: 'Humphrey, there ought to be a ghost in a house like this.'

'Why should there be?' I asked, while I smiled at her extreme gravity.

'Because so many generations of men and women cannot have been born and died in this house without leaving some trace of themselves for us who come after,' and I saw that works of fiction had penetrated into the far west, for Grace had certainly been reading romances.

'I object to talking about ghosts at supper,' I said. 'Breakfast is the best time for such conversation, and not a word should be uttered on the subject later than 12 o'clock at noon,' and I rose, and taking one of the candles with me, and holding it so as to throw the light on a dark painting over the mantelshelf, I asked: 'Do you know who that is?'

My little wife looked earnestly at the portrait, with her head inclined dubiously, and with a puzzled expression of face.

'I am not surprised that you do not know who that dark sinister-looking man is, for the backwoods of America are not hung with portraits of Charles the Second. Yes, that is King Charles; and the melancholy cast of his features must be merely an inherited expression – certainly nothing in his nature answered to it – for he passed through grief and tragedy with a light heart. He once spent a night in this very house; we have the tradition of his visit, with many quaint details, preserved to this day.'

'Oh, how wonderful to think of!' said Grace eagerly. 'And would the king sup in this very room where you and I are now?'

'Yes, in this very room, and would you like to know what he had for supper?'

'No, that is not the kind of thing that makes me curious. I want to know how the king looked, how he was dressed, and in which of those solemn-looking old bedrooms upstairs he slept. No doubt you still have the bed the king slept in?'

'No,' I replied with decision, 'that I am sure we have not.'

'Then tomorrow, Humphrey, you will show me the room the king slept in, and the bed I can imagine for myself.'

The bed she could imagine for herself! My little wife did not know what she was talking about. The next day the event occurred which might have been expected. I was walking in the garden, when Grace came to me, and, slipping her hand through my arm, drew me towards the porch.

'You see that large window,' she said, pointing towards it as she spoke, 'that is the one I admired so much in the picture of the house. I have looked out of every window but that, and I fancy the room must be locked, for I cannot open it, so I have fetched you to unlock it for me.'

I walked in silence by her side while she led me into the house and upstairs to the door of the hated room, talking with so much animation herself that she did not notice that I had not spoken a word.

'This is the room,' she said gaily, and she turned the latch of the door to and fro, saying as she did so, 'You see it is locked.'

'I know it is,' I said sullenly.

'Then fetch the key and open it,' and Grace gave the door handle a little impetuous shake.

'My dearest, don't ask me again to open that door, for I shall not do it.'

'Not do what I ask you to do? How cruel of you!' and her eyes filled with tears.

I knew that my young wife thought me brutal, but I could only say, 'Anything else in my power I will do for you, only this one thing, this one little thing, I beg you will not ask me to do.'

'If you admit that it is such a very small thing, there can be no reason why you should refuse to grant me such a trivial request,' persisted Grace, 'when I ask you simply to unlock a door in your own house, and you refuse to do it, I can only think that you do not love me, or else that there is some horrid mystery about the room that you wish to keep hidden from me,' and she wiped away a hasty tear, that proceeded rather from indignation than from grief.

'My dear Grace, do not let us be tragic about nothing. There is no secret connected with this room that I have ever heard of, and I love you so much that I cannot bear to see you troubling yourself with absurd imaginations. The fact is this. I have a feeling – call it superstition, what you will – but I have a feeling that would make it very painful to me to open this door and take you into the room. And what pleasure could there be in seeing a bare, unfurnished room, precisely like any other empty room?'

'But I should set about furnishing it at once.'

'Let us come away,' I said, gently removing her dear obstinate hand from the lock. 'I repeat I have a feeling about that room that would prevent my ever being happy in it,' and I added lightly, 'Don't let my Eve spoil our paradise by longing after the forbidden fruit.'

But Grace said quickly, 'It was not Adam who forbade Eve to eat of the fruit. If it had been, I can't see that there would have been any great harm in disobeying him.' And we said no more about the locked door, but a cloud had come between us, and the unalloyed sweetness of our first happiness was lost.

One day, a few weeks after this folly, when I was beginning to hope that my little wife had forgotten her curiosity, I saw from her constrained and uneasy manner that something had happened to disturb her.

'My dear Grace, you certainly are not happy this morning – will you not tell me what ails you?' I asked. Her voice trembled and her face flushed as she replied, 'Humphrey, I did not think you could tell me an untruth!'

'My child, what do you mean? We are playing at cross purposes. Be so good as to explain your meaning, that we may not misunderstand each other for a moment.'

'You told me that the big bedroom you keep locked was empty.'

'So it is,' I said, growing impatient at this childish scene, 'but what is the untruth I have told you?'

'Why, the room is not empty. I can prove what I say.'

'The room not empty! Nonsense! I keep the key, and no one but myself has entered it these two years.'

'How can you persist in such an untruth, Humphrey? I am not ashamed to confess that I looked through the keyhole – I wonder I did not do it before – and I saw in the middle of the room, between the door and the window, an enormous old bed. I could only see the two foot-posts, but they went up to the ceiling, and the footboard was high and richly carved, and the curtains a gloomy, dark green. So you have deceived me about the room, and I am afraid there is some secret connected with it that you dare not tell me. What ails you, Humphrey?' and my wife rose with a terrified exclamation, for I thought I was fainting, and all the life seemed to have gone out of the air.

'Grace,' I said, when I had shaken off the sense of oppression, 'let us go at once to that unlucky room, and settle this preposterous dispute. You say that the room has furniture in it, I say that it is empty. We will see which of us is right, and then we will never mention the subject again,' and I asked my wife to come with me and assure herself that the room was, as I said, absolutely bare and unfurnished. My hand shook as I turned the key, and, flinging the door open till it strained on its hinges, we entered the room together. Grace shrank back with a low cry, and covered her face with her hands.

'Where is it gone to, the great bed that I saw standing on this very spot? I cannot have been deceived. O Humphrey! why do you play me such cruel tricks? You terrify me.'

'My little wife,' I said, assuming an air of cheerfulness I was far from feeling, 'this comes of what I must call your overweening curiosity. If my dear girl had been content to let me keep this door locked, she would not have grown so curious that her little brain is almost turned, and she has taken to seeing housewifely spectral illusions of domestic furniture. Depend upon it, what you think you saw was nothing but the creature of your own imagination, that has dwelt so long on the idea of furnishing the room that you have only to peep through the keyhole, and, hey, presto! the thing is done, and beds and tables start forward at your bidding. But henceforward you can enter the room as often as you like, only we will not live in it, and I will not have it furnished.'

This appeared to satisfy Grace, and though I could not fully persuade her that the great bed she had seen when she peeped through the keyhole was an illusion begotten of curiosity and a lively imagination, yet with the door of the room unlocked she felt that she had some control over any tricks I might play her in the future.

I was deeply disturbed by what she had told me. I had not breathed a word to my wife about the destruction of the ancestral bed. Mrs Barrett was dead before we were married, and I had changed my servants since her death, and, as we saw nothing of our neighbours, Grace could not have heard from anyone of the ghastly old bed, which nevertheless she had accurately described to me.

I could never tell her the truth now. It would shake her nerves, and impress her with the idea that there was something weird about the house. I wished I had not destroyed the old bed. Better far that she should have known the gloomy reality than behold a presentment of it that was neither an embodiment of memory nor a vivid picturing of it from imagination. I tried if I could summon up a like hallucination, but in vain. Though my memory of the ancient bed was perfect, and every detail stamped on my mind, never could I call it up before my external vision, however earnestly I tried to do so.

Grace completely regained her accustomed cheerfulness, and in the spring was busy making a thousand little preparations for the expected arrival of an infant, which was to surpass any yet born into this world. I could hardly believe the gentle obstinacy of my wife, when after all I had said about the empty room she asked me one day if she might not make it into a nursery.

'Do you not remember, dear, that I said we would not furnish that room?' I said.

'Oh, of course, not furnish it; a nursery needs no furniture; but it is much the most cheerful and sunny room in the house.'

And again I had to appear inhuman and refuse my little wife a trivial request.

One morning as I sat in my room busy with my accounts Grace came to tell me that she was going to drive to the county town, some eight miles distant, for a round of shopping, such as her soul loved. I said that if she would wait till the next day I should be able to take her myself, but she tapped the barometer on the wall, that had stood for some time at 'set fair', and assured me it would rain tomorrow, and that she must avail herself of the fine weather today. So away drove my self-willed darling, nodding a gay farewell as the carriage drove away from the house.

Grace returned late in the afternoon in the best of spirits, bringing with her an enormous package, such as none but a country woman, or one, like my little wife, from the far west, would dream of bringing with her in an open carriage. It must have broken the coachman's heart to drive with it through the streets of the county town.

'What in the name of wonder have you brought home with you?' I asked.

'Ah!' she said, laughing. 'It is a trial for your curiosity now! Anything else you may ask me I will tell you, only I cannot let you know anything about this mysterious package.'

'Then have it put out of sight,' I said, 'or depend upon it I shall find some hole in the wrapper to peep through. You ought to know what a devouring passion curiosity is.'

As the unwieldy bundle was carried upstairs its cover slipped aside, and revealed a pair of black oak rockers. But I said nothing; Grace should tell me her little secret in her own way and at her own time.

We thought ourselves the happiest creatures in the world when our little son Heneage was born. The gloom that brooded over the house from the death of many generations was lessened by the joy of birth, and my young son's life was like the sprouting acorn that sends up its vigorous shoot through the earth, fed by the fallen leaves of a hundred autumns. On the third day of our happiness my wife sent for me, and told me she had a very pretty surprise for me.

'I can tell you all about the big mysterious package now. It was a beautiful old-fashioned cradle that I bought in Carlyon from a man called Gillam, who keeps an old furniture shop there. I fell in love with it at once, for I knew how well it would suit this house with its old oak. Gillam said he could swear it was old work; in fact, he said it was originally part of a fine old bedstead a poor mad gentleman in the neighbourhood actually destroyed in a fit of frenzy, but he was lucky enough to secure a portion of the wreck, and made it up into that cradle, and baby looks lovely in it. I'm afraid I gave a great deal of money for it, but one does not meet with such a beautiful thing every day,' and the nurse removed a screen from before the cradle, that its beauties might burst upon me suddenly and with the more effect.

Cold drops stood on my brow as I recognised, in the high sides and head of the cradle, the carving of ivy branches and berries I had so madly given Gillam when I destroyed the old bed.

'I thought you would have been so pleased,' said Grace, disappointed by my silence as I stood spellbound, my eyes following every line of the hated carving. 'I thought you would have been so pleased to see baby in a cradle really worthy of him.'

But I could not speak; I was oppressed by a sense of coming doom.

'It is very unkind of you,' said Grace. 'I had prepared a pretty surprise for you, and instead of being pleased, you stand and sigh and look as if you saw a ghost. Nurse, take baby out of his lovely cradle; we must get him a common wicker thing to lie in instead!'

And the nurse did as her mistress bade her, and lifted little Heneage from his cradle of death, for while we talked the child had slept his feeble life away.

I have no memory of what happened day by day during the few weeks following. It was my one consuming fear that my wife too should die. Six weeks after our child's death I carried her downstairs, and this was the only progress made towards recovery. She remained at the same stage of convalescence, made wayward by grief, with shattered nerves, and so weak in mind and body that I dared not thwart her in anything. As the dim, sunless days of autumn drew on, my little wife said to me as though we had never spoken on the subject before, 'I want the big empty room furnished for my sitting-room, Humphrey. I shall have a little sunshine there sometimes to cheer me in your dismal English winter, and it will amuse me to furnish it.'

As I looked at her white wistful face, I felt that nothing mattered to me now, and I said, 'Do exactly as you like, dear, in everything,' and she was too listless to thank me.

But the work of transforming the sombre room into a bright boudoir proceeded rapidly, for Grace said with a shudder, 'I will have no more old oak furniture.'

My little wife always went to extremes, and now, in her antipathy to old oak, she filled the room with tawdry chips of furniture, chairs made of gilded matchsticks tied together with ribbons, that must sink into feeble ruins if a cat so much as jumped on them.

I entered into all her little fancies, and feigned excessive admiration of each fresh idea she had on the subject of decoration. I did her bidding, even to placing her couch on the very spot where the hated bed had stood. Thus was my resistance broken down, and I, who three years ago had tried by sheer physical force to thwart destiny, was now unconsciously working to bring about its fulfilment. It did not tarry long.

One gloomy November afternoon, Grace lay on her couch covered with soft shawls, and the window curtains were drawn back to give as much light as possible. The glow of the setting sun illuminated the room, and lent a more living hue to the grey pallor of her face.

'How like the day when I first came to Walford Grange!' she said. 'The sun is setting with the same fiery light. Do go into the garden, Humphrey, and see if the windows are aglow with red light as they were then.' And I left her to do as she asked me.

Seen from the garden, the house looked precisely as it had done on the day of our homecoming. From garret to basement every window glowed red in the light of the setting sun, as though from fire within. Everything that my eyes rested on was as it had been a year ago. Grace and I only were changed – changed in ourselves and changed to each other. I felt impatient of the changeless aspect of nature and of inanimate things around me, and I entered the house, now dark in contrast with the twilight without, and returned to my wife's room with a heavy heart.

'The house looks as it did when you first saw it,' I said. 'Till the sun sank behind the hill, the windows were lighted up with the same strange effect of fire that you noticed a year ago,' and I threw a fresh log on the embers as I spoke, sending a bright train of sparks up the wide chimney. 'Shall I light the candles?' I asked, turning towards my wife's couch. 'The room is growing dark.'

But there was no reply. I was speaking to the dead. In vain I had baulked the old bed of its prey, for there on the very spot where it had stood, where three centuries of my ancestors had died, the wife of the last of the Walfords lay dead.

I buried my sweet Grace by our little son, and on the night of the funeral, alone in my desolate home, I conceived the idea of freeing myself for ever from the horror of darkness that had fallen on Walford Grange. I sent every servant away. I would have the house and my sorrow to myself.

When I was assured that I was alone in the house, I went rapidly from room to room in a strange exultation, speaking aloud and flinging open doors and windows till the cold night air rushed through chambers and passages, and curtains and hangings flapped in the wind.

'When I destroyed the old bed of death,' I said, 'I thought to restore joy and brightness to Walford Grange. But I should have destroyed not it alone, but the room in which it stood, and the very house of which it formed a part. Never more shall man dwell in this house glutted with death. Never more shall the voice of the bride and bridegroom be heard in its chambers, or footsteps of children be heard on its stairs. Never more shall fire subdued to harmless household use be kindled on its hearth, but fire untamed in its ferocity shall devour the accursed pile.' And I seized the burning log from the hearth and threw it on the couch where Grace had died.

Carrying a lighted brand, I sped from room to room of the doomed house, leaving in each a fiery token of my presence, and then, descending the wide staircase, where flickering shadows were cast from every open door, and the silence was broken by the crackling sound of flames, I let myself out into the darkness, closing the heavy door behind me with a crash. On through the cold damp air I ran, the moon through a rift in the clouds guiding me by her fitful light, till, drawing her shroud around her, she left me again in darkness. Not once did I turn to right or left or look behind me till I had gained the summit of the hills that bounded the valley. Then

I stood and turned to take a last look at the home of my fathers. Just then the moon, issuing forth in cold splendour from her bed of cloud, shed a solemn lustre far and wide. And I saw for the last time the house of my birth, the cradle and grave of my race, and every window from basement to garret glowed with fire, no mere reflected glare, but red from the raging fire within, and keen flames darted from the casement of the room above the porch.

I stood long to watch the fire of my own kindling, till, when a sudden burst of light and leaping splendour of flame showed me that the gabled roof had fallen in, I shouted, took off my hat, and waved a last farewell to Walford Grange.

THE DOOM OF LONDON

By Robert Barr (1850–1912)

A Scotsman who had grown up in Canada and returned to the UK to forge a literary career, Robert Barr was a productive writer whose works encompassed everything from travel sketches to historical fiction. His best-remembered creation is the French detective Eugène Valmont, a former head of the Parisian police now in exile in London, who first appeared in stories published in Windsor Magazine *and* Pearson's Magazine *in 1904–05. These were collected in a volume entitled* The Triumphs of Eugène Valmont *in 1906. Barr was also the author of one of the very earliest parodies of Sherlock Holmes. 'Detective Stories Gone Wrong: The Adventures of Sherlaw Kombs' was published in 1892 in* The Idler, *the magazine he founded with the collaboration of Jerome K Jerome. Several of Barr's collections of short stories include work that can be described as fantasy or horror. 'The Doom of London', which appeared first in his own magazine and then in the volume entitled* The Face and the Mask, *published in 1894, is a fine example of the thriving 'disaster' story subgenre in late Victorian Britain. Readers in the 1890s seemed to lap up tales of society disintegrating in some kind of unforeseen cataclysm. H G Wells's* The War of the Worlds *is the best and most archetypal example but Barr's vision of death and destruction in the imperial capital works well.*

The Idler, *November 1892*

Nick Rennison

The Self-Conceit of the 20th Century

I trust I am thankful my life has been spared until I have seen that most brilliant epoch of the world's history—the middle of the 20th century. It would be useless for any man to disparage the vast achievements of the past fifty years, and if I venture to call attention to the fact, now apparently forgotten, that the people of the 19th century succeeded in accomplishing many notable things, it must not be imagined that I intend thereby to discount in any measure the marvellous inventions of the present age. Men have always been somewhat prone to look with a certain condescension upon those who lived fifty or a hundred years before them. This seems to me the especial weakness of the present age; a feeling of national self-conceit, which, when it exists, should at least be kept as much in the background as possible. It will astonish many to know that such also was a failing of the people of the 19th century. They imagined themselves living in an age of progress, and while I am not foolish enough to attempt to prove that they did anything really worth recording, yet it must be admitted by any unprejudiced man of research that their inventions were at least stepping-stones to those of today. Although the telephone and telegraph, and all other electrical appliances, are now to be found only in our national museums, or in the private collections of those few men who take any interest in the doings of the last century, nevertheless, the study of the now obsolete science of electricity led up to the recent discovery of vibratory ether which does the work of the world so satisfactorily. The people of the 19th century were not fools, and although I am well aware that this statement will be received with scorn where it attracts any attention whatever, yet who can say that the progress of the next half-century may not be as great as that of the one now ended, and that the people of the next century may not look upon us with the same contempt which we feel toward those who lived fifty years ago?

Being an old man, I am, perhaps, a laggard who dwells in the past rather than the present; still, it seems to me that such an article as that which appeared recently in *Blackwood* from the talented pen of Prof. Mowberry, of Oxford University, is utterly unjustifiable. Under the title of 'Did the People of London Deserve their Fate?' he endeavours to show that the simultaneous blotting out of millions of human beings was a beneficial event, the good results of which we still enjoy. According to him, Londoners were so dull-witted and stupid, so incapable of improvement, so sodden in the vice of mere money-gathering, that nothing but their total extinction would have sufficed, and that, instead of being an appalling catastrophe, the doom of London was an unmixed blessing. In spite of the unanimous approval with which this article has been received by the press, I still maintain that such writing is uncalled for, and that there is something to be said for the London of the 19th century.

Why London, Warned, Was Unprepared

The indignation I felt in first reading the article alluded to still remains with me, and it has caused me to write these words, giving some account of what I must still regard, in spite of the sneers of the present age, as the most terrible disaster that ever overtook a portion of the human race. I shall not endeavour to place before those who read, any record of the achievements pertaining to the time in question. But I would like to say a few words about the alleged stupidity of the people of London in making no preparations for a disaster regarding which they had continual and ever-recurring warning of. They have been compared with the inhabitants of Pompeii making merry at the foot of a volcano. In the first place, fogs were so common in London, especially in winter, that no particular attention was paid to them. They were merely looked upon as inconvenient annoyances, interrupting traffic and prejudicial to health, but I doubt if anyone thought it possible for a fog to become one vast smothering mattress pressed down upon a whole metropolis, extinguishing life as if the city suffered from hopeless hydrophobia. I have read that victims bitten by mad dogs were formerly put out of their sufferings in that way, although I doubt much if such things were ever actually done, notwithstanding the charges of savage barbarity now made against the people of the 19th century.

Probably, the inhabitants of Pompeii were so accustomed to the eruptions of Vesuvius that they gave no thought to the possibility of their city being destroyed by a storm of ashes and an overflow of lava. Rain frequently descended upon London, and if a rainfall continued long enough it would certainly have flooded the metropolis, but no precautions were taken against a flood from the clouds. Why, then, should the people have been expected to prepare for a catastrophe from fog, such as there had never been any experience of in the world's history? The people of London were far from being the sluggish dolts present-day writers would have us believe.

The Coincidence That Came at Last

As fog has now been abolished both on sea and land, and as few of the present generation have even seen one, it may not be out of place to give a few lines on the subject of fogs in general, and the

London fogs in particular, which through local peculiarities differed from all others. A fog was simply watery vapour rising from the marshy surface of the land or from the sea, or condensed into a cloud from the saturated atmosphere. In my day, fogs were a great danger at sea, for people then travelled by means of steamships that sailed upon the surface of the ocean.

London at the end of the 19th century consumed vast quantities of a soft bituminous coal for the purpose of heating rooms and of preparing food. In the morning and during the day, clouds of black smoke were poured forth from thousands of chimneys. When a mass of white vapour arose in the night these clouds of smoke fell upon the fog, pressing it down, filtering slowly through it, and adding to its density. The sun would have absorbed the fog but for the layer of smoke that lay thick above the vapour and prevented the rays reaching it. Once this condition of things prevailed, nothing could clear London but a breeze of wind from any direction. London frequently had a seven days' fog, and sometimes a seven days' calm, but these two conditions never coincided until the last year of the last century. The coincidence, as everyone knows, meant death – death so wholesale that no war the earth has ever seen left such slaughter behind it. To understand the situation, one has only to imagine the fog as taking the place of the ashes at Pompeii, and the coal-smoke as being the lava that covered it. The result to the inhabitants in both cases was exactly the same.

The American Who Wanted to Sell

I was at the time confidential clerk to the house of Fulton, Brixton & Co., a firm in Cannon Street, dealing largely in chemicals and chemical apparatus. Fulton I never knew; he died long before my time. Sir John Brixton was my chief, knighted, I believe, for services to his party, or because he was an official in the City during some royal progress through it; I have forgotten which. My small room was next to his large one, and my chief duty was to see that no one had an interview with Sir John unless he was an important man or had important business. Sir John was a difficult man to see, and a difficult man to deal with when he was seen. He had little respect for most men's feelings, and none at all for mine. If I allowed a man to enter his room who should have been dealt with by one of the minor members of the company, Sir John made no effort to conceal his opinion of me. One day, in the autumn of the last year of the century, an American was shown into my room. Nothing would do but he must have an interview with Sir John Brixton. I told him that it was impossible, as Sir John was extremely busy, but that if he explained his business to me, I would lay it before Sir John at the first favourable opportunity. The American demurred at this, but finally accepted the inevitable. He was the inventor, he said, of a machine that would revolutionise life in London, and he wanted Fulton, Brixton & Co. to become agents for it. The machine, which he had in a small handbag with him, was of white metal, and it was so constructed that by turning an index it gave out greater or less volumes of oxygen gas. The gas, I understood, was stored in the interior in liquid form under great pressure, and would last, if I remember rightly, for six months without recharging. There was also a rubber tube with a mouthpiece attached to it, and the American said that if a man took a few whiffs a day, he would experience beneficial results. Now, I knew there was not the slightest use in showing the machine to Sir John, because we dealt in old-established British apparatus, and never in any of the new-fangled Yankee contraptions. Besides,

Sir John had a prejudice against Americans, and I felt sure this man would exasperate him, as he was a most cadaverous specimen of the race, with high nasal tones, and a most deplorable pronunciation, much given to phrases savouring of slang; and he exhibited also a certain nervous familiarity of demeanour towards people to whom he was all but a complete stranger. It was impossible for me to allow such a man to enter the presence of Sir John Brixton, and when he returned some days later I explained to him, I hope with courtesy, that the head of the house regretted very much his inability to consider his proposal regarding the machine. The ardour of the American seemed in no way dampened by this rebuff. He said I could not have explained the possibilities of the apparatus properly to Sir John; he characterised it as a great invention, and said it meant a fortune to whoever obtained the agency for it. He hinted that other noted London houses were anxious to secure it, but for some reason not stated he preferred to deal with us. He left some printed pamphlets referring to the invention, and said he would call again.

The American Sees Sir John

Many a time I have since thought of that persistent American, and wondered whether he left London before the disaster, or was one of the unidentified thousands who were buried in unmarked graves. Little did Sir John think when he expelled him with some asperity from his presence, that he was turning away an offer of life, and that the heated words he used were, in reality, a sentence of death upon himself. For my own part, I regret that I lost my temper, and told the American his business methods did not commend themselves to me. Perhaps he did not feel the sting of this; indeed, I feel certain he did not, for, unknowingly, he saved my life. Be that as it may, he showed no resentment, but immediately asked me out to drink with him, an offer I was compelled to refuse. But I am getting ahead of my story. Indeed, being unaccustomed to writing, it is difficult for me to set down events in their proper sequence. The American called upon me several times after I told him our house could not deal with him. He got into the habit of dropping in upon me unannounced, which I did not at all like, but I gave no instructions regarding his intrusions, because I had no idea of the extremes to which he was evidently prepared to go. One day, as he sat near my desk reading a paper, I was temporarily called from the room. When I returned I thought he had gone, taking his machine with him, but a moment later I was shocked to hear his high nasal tones in Sir John's room alternating with the deep notes of my chief's voice, which apparently exercised no such dread upon the American as upon those who were more accustomed to them. I at once entered the room, and was about to explain to Sir John that the American was there through no connivance of mine, when my chief asked me to be silent and, turning to his visitor, gruffly requested him to proceed with his interesting narration. The inventor needed no second invitation, but went on with his glib talk, while Sir John's frown grew deeper, and his face became redder under his fringe of white hair. When the American had finished, Sir John roughly bade him begone, and take his accursed machine with him. He said it was an insult for a person with one foot in the grave to bring a so-called health invention to a robust man who never had a day's illness. I do not know why he listened so long to the American, when he had made up his mind from the first not to deal with him, unless it was to punish me for inadvertently allowing the stranger to enter. The interview distressed me exceedingly, as I stood there helpless, knowing Sir John was becoming more and more angry with every word the foreigner uttered, but, at last, I succeeded in drawing the inventor and his work into my own room and closing the door. I sincerely hoped I would never see the American again, and my wish was gratified. He insisted on setting his machine going, and placing it on a shelf in my room. He asked me to slip it into Sir John's room some foggy day and note the effect. The man said he would call again, but he never did.

How the Smoke Held Down the Fog

It was on a Friday that the fog came down upon us. The weather was very fine up to the middle of November that autumn. The fog did not seem to have anything unusual about it. I have seen many worse fogs than that appeared to be. As day followed day, however, the atmosphere became denser and darker, caused, I suppose, by the increasing volume of coal-smoke poured out upon it. The peculiarity about those seven days was the intense stillness of the air. We were, although we did not know it, under an air-proof canopy, and were slowly but surely exhausting the life-giving oxygen around us, and replacing it by poisonous carbonic acid gas. Scientific men have since showed that a simple mathematical calculation might have told us exactly when the last atom of oxygen would have been consumed; but it is easy to be wise after the event. The body of the greatest mathematician in England was found in the Strand. He came that morning from Cambridge. During the fog there was always a marked increase in the death rate, and on this occasion the increase was no greater than usual until the sixth day. The newspapers on the morning of the seventh were full of startling statistics, but at the time of going to press the full significance of the alarming figures was not realised. The editorials of the morning papers on the seventh day contained no warning of the calamity that was so speedily to follow their appearance. I lived then at Ealing, a western suburb of London, and came every morning to Cannon Street by a certain train. I had up to the sixth day experienced no inconvenience from the fog, and this was largely due, I am convinced, to the unnoticed operations of the American machine.

On the fifth and sixth days Sir John did not come to the City, but he was in his office on the seventh. The door between his room and mine was closed. Shortly after ten o'clock I heard a cry in his room, followed by a heavy fall. I opened the door, and saw Sir John lying face downwards on the floor. Hastening towards him, I felt for the first time the deadly effect of the deoxygenised atmosphere, and before I reached him I fell first on one knee and then headlong. I realised that my senses were leaving me, and instinctively crawled back to my own room, where the oppression was at once lifted, and I stood again upon my feet, gasping. I closed the door of Sir John's room, thinking it filled with poisonous fumes, as, indeed, it was. I called loudly for help, but there was no answer. On opening the door to the main office I met again what I thought was the noxious vapour. Speedily as I closed the door, I was impressed by the intense silence of the usually busy office, and saw that some of the clerks were motionless on the floor, and others sat with their heads on their desks as if asleep. Even at this awful moment I did not realise that what I saw was common to all London and not, as I imagined, a local disaster, caused by the breaking of some carboys in our cellar. (It was filled with chemicals of every kind, of whose properties I was ignorant, dealing as I did with the accountant, and not the scientific side of our business.) I opened the only window in my room, and again shouted for help. The street was silent and dark in the ominously still fog, and what now froze me with horror was meeting the same deadly, stifling atmosphere that was in the rooms. In falling, I brought down the window, and shut out the poisonous air. Again I revived, and slowly the true state of things began to dawn upon me.

I was in an oasis of oxygen. I at once surmised that the machine on my shelf was responsible for the existence of this oasis in a vast desert of deadly gas. I took down the American's machine, fearful in moving it that I might stop its working. Taking the mouthpiece between my lips I again entered Sir John's room, this time without feeling any ill effects. My poor master was long beyond human help. There was evidently no one alive in the building except myself. Out in the street all was silent and dark. The gas was extinguished, but here and there in shops the incandescent lights were still weirdly burning, depending, as they did, on accumulators, and not on direct engine power. I turned automatically towards Cannon Street Station, knowing my way to it even if blindfolded, stumbling over bodies prone on the pavement, and in crossing the street I ran against a motionless 'bus, spectral in the fog, with dead horses lying in front, and their reins dangling from the nerveless hand of a dead driver. The ghostlike passengers, equally silent, sat bolt upright, or hung over the edge boards in attitudes horribly grotesque.

The Train With its Trail of Dead

If a man's reasoning faculties were alert at such a time (I confess mine were dormant), he would have known there could be no trains at Cannon Street Station, for if there was not enough oxygen in the air to keep a man alive, or a gas-jet alight, there would certainly not be enough to enable an engine fire to burn, even if the engineer retained sufficient energy to attend to his task. At times instinct is better than reason, and it proved so in this case. The railway from Ealing in those days came under the City in a deep tunnel. It would appear that in this underground passage the carbonic acid gas would first find a resting-place on account of its weight; but such was not the fact. I imagine that a current through the tunnel brought from the outlying districts a supply of comparatively pure air that, for some minutes after the general disaster, maintained human life. Be this as it may, the long platforms of Cannon Street Underground Station presented a fearful spectacle. A train stood at the down platform. The electric lights burned fitfully. This platform was crowded with men, who fought each other like demons, apparently for no reason, because the train was already packed as full as it could hold. Hundreds were dead under foot, and every now and then a blast of foul air came along the tunnel, whereupon hundreds more would relax their grips, and succumb. Over their bodies the survivors fought, with continually thinning ranks. It seemed to me that most of those in the standing train were dead. Sometimes a desperate body of fighters climbed over those lying in heaps and, throwing open a carriage door, hauled out passengers already in, and took their places, gasping. Those in the train offered no resistance, and lay motionless where they were flung, or rolled helplessly under the wheels of the train. I made my way along the wall as well as I could to the engine, wondering why the train did not go. The engineer lay on the floor of his cab, and the fires were out.

Custom is a curious thing. The struggling mob, fighting wildly for places in the carriages, were so accustomed to trains arriving and departing that it apparently occurred to none of them that the engineer was human and subject to the same atmospheric conditions as themselves. I placed the mouthpiece between his purple lips and, holding my own breath like a submerged man, succeeded in reviving him. He said that if I gave him the machine he would take out the train as far as the steam already in the boiler would carry it. I refused to do this, but stepped on the engine with him, saying it would keep life in both of us until we got out into better air. In a surly manner he agreed to this and started the train, but he did not play fair. Each time he refused to give up the machine until I was in a fainting condition with holding in my breath, and, finally, he felled me to the floor of the cab. I imagine that the machine rolled off the train as I fell and that he jumped after it. The remarkable thing is that neither of us needed the machine, for I remember that just after we started I noticed through the open iron door that the engine fire suddenly became aglow again, although at the time I was in too great a state of bewilderment and horror to understand what it meant. A western gale had sprung up – an hour too late. Even before we left Cannon Street those who still survived were comparatively safe, for one hundred and sixty-seven persons were rescued from that fearful heap of dead on the platforms, although many died within a day or two after, and others never recovered their reason. When I regained my senses after the blow dealt by the engineer, I found myself alone, and the train speeding across the Thames near Kew. I tried to stop the engine, but did not succeed. However, in experimenting, I managed to turn on the air brake, which in some degree checked the train, and lessened the impact when the crash came at Richmond terminus. I sprang off on the platform before the engine reached the terminal buffers, and saw passing me like a nightmare the ghastly trainload of the dead. Most of the doors were swinging open, and every compartment was jammed full, although, as I afterwards learned, at each curve of the permanent way, or extra lurch of the train, bodies had fallen out all along the line. The smash at Richmond made no difference to the passengers. Besides myself, only two persons were taken alive from the train, and one of these, his clothes torn from his back in the struggle, was sent to an asylum, where he was never able to tell who he was; neither, as far as I know, did anyone ever claim him.

THE RING OF THOTH

By Arthur Conan Doyle (1859–1930)

Conan Doyle, born in Edinburgh, came from a family of artists – his uncle worked as a cartoonist for Punch *and his father illustrated a number of books until his life was clouded by alcoholism and depression – but he trained originally as a doctor. He began to write and publish short stories in the 1880s and* Micah Clarke, *the first of his historical novels, appeared in 1889. Famously, Conan Doyle wanted to be remembered more for his historical fiction than as the creator of Sherlock Holmes. It was not to be. His greatest claim to fame will always be that he gave to the world the finest of all fictional detectives. He also showed a fascination with the weird and macabre throughout his life and many of his non-Holmes stories reflect this. Published a month before* The Sign of Four, *the second Sherlock Holmes novel, and 18 months before 'A Scandal in Bohemia', the first Holmes short story, 'The Ring of Thoth' reflects that late Victorian fascination with ancient Egypt which can also be seen in, for example, some of the fiction of Rider Haggard. (Doyle himself wrote another weird tale, 'Lot No. 249', which involves a student of Egyptology possessed of an ancient mummy that returns to life.) Most of the collections of short stories he published in the 1890s –* The Gully of Bluemansdyke, The Great Keinplatz Experiment *and others – include tales that fit broadly into the 'weird' category.*

The Cornhill Magazine January 1890

Mr John Vansittart Smith, FRS, of 147-A Gower Street, was a man whose energy of purpose and clearness of thought might have placed him in the very first rank of scientific observers. He was the victim, however, of a universal ambition which prompted him to aim at distinction in many subjects rather than pre-eminence in one.

In his early days he had shown an aptitude for zoology and for botany which caused his friends to look upon him as a second Darwin, but when a professorship was almost within his reach he had suddenly discontinued his studies and turned his whole attention to chemistry. Here his researches upon the spectra of the metals had won him his fellowship in the Royal Society; but again he played the coquette with his subject, and after a year's absence from the laboratory he joined the Oriental Society, and delivered a paper on the Hieroglyphic and Demotic inscriptions of El Kab, thus giving a crowning example both of the versatility and of the inconstancy of his talents.

The most fickle of wooers, however, is apt to be caught at last, and so it was with John Vansittart Smith. The more he burrowed his way into Egyptology the more impressed he became by the vast field which it opened to the inquirer, and by the extreme importance of a subject which promised to throw a light upon the first germs of human civilisation and the origin of the greater part of our arts and sciences. So struck was Mr Smith that he straightway married an Egyptological young lady who had written upon the sixth dynasty and, having thus secured a sound base of operations, he set himself to collect materials for a work which should unite the research of Lepsius and the ingenuity of Champollion. The preparation of this magnum opus entailed many hurried visits to the magnificent Egyptian collections of the Louvre, upon the last of which, no longer ago than the middle of last October, he became involved in a most strange and noteworthy adventure.

The trains had been slow and the Channel had been rough, so that the student arrived in Paris in a somewhat befogged and feverish condition. On reaching the Hôtel de France, in the Rue Laffitte, he had thrown himself upon a sofa for a couple of hours, but finding that he was unable to sleep, he determined, in spite of his fatigue, to make his way to the Louvre, settle the point which he had come to decide, and take the evening train back to Dieppe. Having come to this conclusion, he donned his greatcoat, for it was a raw rainy day, and made his way across the Boulevard des Italiens and down the Avenue de l'Opéra. Once in the Louvre, he was on familiar ground, and he speedily made his way to the collection of papyri which it was his intention to consult.

The warmest admirers of John Vansittart Smith could hardly claim for him that he was a handsome man. His high-beaked nose and prominent chin had something of the same acute and incisive character which distinguished his intellect. He held his head in a birdlike fashion, and birdlike, too, was the pecking motion with which, in conversation, he threw out his objections and retorts. As he stood, with the high collar of his greatcoat raised to his ears, he might have seen from the reflection in the glass case before him that his appearance was a singular one. Yet it came upon him as a sudden jar when an English voice behind him exclaimed in very audible tones, 'What a queer-looking mortal!'

The student had a large amount of petty vanity in his composition which manifested itself by an ostentatious and overdone disregard of all personal considerations. He straightened his lips and looked rigidly at the roll of papyrus, while his heart filled with bitterness against the whole race of travelling Britons.

'Yes,' said another voice, 'he really is an extraordinary fellow.'

'Do you know,' said the first speaker, 'one could almost believe that by the continual contemplation of mummies the chap has become half a mummy himself?'

'He has certainly an Egyptian cast of countenance,' said the other.

John Vansittart Smith spun round upon his heel with the intention of shaming his countrymen by a corrosive remark or two. To his surprise and relief, the two young fellows who had been conversing had their shoulders turned towards him, and were gazing at one of the Louvre attendants who was polishing some brass-work at the other side of the room.

'Carter will be waiting for us at the Palais Royal,' said one tourist to the other, glancing at his watch, and they clattered away, leaving the student to his labours.

'I wonder what these chatterers call an Egyptian cast of countenance,' thought John Vansittart Smith, and he moved his position slightly in order to catch a glimpse of the man's face. He started as his eyes fell upon it. It was indeed the very face with which his studies had made him familiar. The regular statuesque features, broad brow, well-rounded chin, and dusky complexion were the exact counterpart of the innumerable statues, mummy-cases, and pictures which adorned the walls of the apartment.

The thing was beyond all coincidence. The man must be an Egyptian. The national angularity of the shoulders and narrowness of the hips were alone sufficient to identify him.

John Vansittart Smith shuffled towards the attendant with some intention of addressing him. He was not light of touch in conversation, and found it difficult to strike the happy mean between the brusqueness of the superior and the geniality of the equal. As he came nearer, the man presented his side face to him, but kept his gaze still bent upon his work. Vansittart Smith, fixing his eyes upon the fellow's skin, was conscious of a sudden impression that there was something inhuman and preternatural about its appearance. Over the temple and cheek-bone it was as glazed and as shiny as varnished parchment. There was no suggestion of pores. One could not fancy a drop of moisture upon that arid surface. From brow to chin, however, it was cross-hatched by a million delicate wrinkles, which shot and interlaced as though Nature in some Maori mood had tried how wild and intricate a pattern she could devise.

'*Où est la collection de Memphis?*' asked the student, with the awkward air of a man who is devising a question merely for the purpose of opening a conversation.

'*C'est là,*' replied the man brusquely, nodding his head at the other side of the room.

'*Vous êtes un Égyptien, n'est-ce pas?*' asked the Englishman.

The attendant looked up and turned his strange dark eyes upon his questioner. They were vitreous, with a misty dry shininess, such as Smith had never seen in a human head before. As he gazed into them he saw some strong emotion gather in their depths, which rose and deepened until it broke into a look of something akin both to horror and to hatred.

'*Non, monsieur; je suis Français.*' The man turned abruptly and bent low over his polishing. The student gazed at him for a moment in astonishment, and then, turning to a chair in a retired corner behind one of the doors, he proceeded to make notes of his researches among the papyri. His thoughts, however, refused to return into their natural groove. They would run upon the enigmatical attendant with the sphinx-like face and the parchment skin.

'Where have I seen such eyes?' said Vansittart Smith to himself. 'There is something saurian about them, something reptilian. There's the *membrana nictitans* of the snakes,' he mused, bethinking himself of his zoological studies. 'It gives a shiny effect. But there was something more here. There was a sense of power, of wisdom – so I read them – and of weariness, utter weariness, and ineffable despair. It may be all imagination, but I never had so strong an impression. By Jove, I must have another look at them!' He rose and paced round the Egyptian rooms, but the man who had excited his curiosity had disappeared.

The student sat down again in his quiet corner, and continued to work at his notes. He had gained the information which he required from the papyri, and it only remained to write it down while it was still fresh in his memory. For a time his pencil travelled rapidly over the paper, but soon the lines became less level, the words more blurred, and finally the pencil tinkled down upon the floor, and the head of the student dropped heavily forward upon his chest.

Tired out by his journey, he slept so soundly in his lonely post behind the door that neither the clanking civil guard, nor the footsteps of sightseers, nor even the loud hoarse bell which gives the signal for closing, were sufficient to arouse him.

Twilight deepened into darkness, the bustle from the Rue de Rivoli waxed and then waned, distant Notre Dame clanged out the hour of midnight, and still the dark and lonely figure sat silently in the shadow. It was not until close upon one in the morning that, with a sudden gasp and an intaking of the breath, Vansittart Smith returned to consciousness. For a moment it flashed upon him that he had dropped asleep in his study-chair at home. The moon was shining fitfully through the unshuttered window, however, and, as his eye ran along the lines of mummies and the endless array of polished cases, he remembered clearly where he was and how he came there. The student was not a nervous man. He possessed that love of a novel situation which is peculiar to his race. Stretching out his cramped limbs, he looked at his watch, and burst into a chuckle as he observed the hour. The episode would make an admirable anecdote to be introduced into his next paper as a relief to the graver and heavier speculations. He was a little cold, but wide awake and much refreshed. It was no wonder that the guardians had overlooked him, for the door threw its heavy black shadow right across him.

The complete silence was impressive. Neither outside nor inside was there a creak or a murmur. He was alone with the dead men of a dead civilisation. What though the outer city reeked of the garish nineteenth century! In all this chamber there was scarce an article, from the shrivelled ear of wheat to the pigment-box of the painter, which had not held its own against four thousand years. Here was the flotsam and jetsam washed up by the great ocean of time from that far-off empire. From stately Thebes, from lordly Luxor, from the great temples of Heliopolis, from a hundred rifled tombs, these relics had been brought. The student glanced round at the long silent figures who flickered vaguely up through the gloom, at the busy toilers who were now so restful, and he fell into a reverent and thoughtful mood. An unwonted sense of his own youth and insignificance came over him. Leaning back in his chair, he gazed dreamily down the long vista of rooms, all silvery with the moonshine, which extend through the whole wing of the widespread building. His eyes fell upon the yellow glare of a distant lamp.

John Vansittart Smith sat up on his chair with his nerves all on edge. The light was advancing slowly towards him, pausing from time to time, and then coming jerkily onwards. The bearer moved noiselessly. In the utter silence there was no suspicion of the pat of a footfall. An idea of robbers entered the Englishman's head. He snuggled up further into the corner. The light was two rooms off. Now it was in the next chamber, and still there was no sound. With something approaching to a thrill of fear the student observed a face, floating in the air as it were, behind the flare of the lamp. The figure was wrapped in shadow, but the light fell full upon the strange eager face. There was no mistaking the metallic glistening eyes and the cadaverous skin. It was the attendant with whom he had conversed.

Vansittart Smith's first impulse was to come forward and address him. A few words of explanation would set the matter clear, and lead doubtless to his being conducted to some side door from which he might make his way to his hotel. As the man entered the chamber, however, there was something so stealthy in his movements, and so furtive in his expression, that the Englishman altered his intention. This was clearly no ordinary official walking the rounds. The fellow wore felt-soled slippers, stepped with a rising chest, and glanced quickly from left to right, while his hurried gasping breathing thrilled the flame of his lamp. Vansittart Smith crouched silently back into the corner and watched him keenly, convinced that his errand was one of secret and probably sinister import.

There was no hesitation in the other's movements. He stepped lightly and swiftly across to one of the great cases, and, drawing a key from his pocket, he unlocked it. From the upper shelf he pulled down a mummy, which he bore away with him, and laid it with much care and solicitude upon the ground. By it he placed his lamp, and then squatting down beside it in Eastern fashion he began with long quivering fingers to undo the cerecloths and bandages which girt it round. As the crackling rolls of linen peeled off one after the other, a strong aromatic odour filled the chamber, and fragments of scented wood and of spices pattered down upon the marble floor.

It was clear to John Vansittart Smith that this mummy had never been unswathed before. The operation interested him keenly. He thrilled all over with curiosity, and his birdlike head protruded further and further from behind the door. When, however, the last roll had been removed from the four-thousand-year-old head, it was all that he could do to stifle an outcry of amazement. First, a cascade of long, black, glossy tresses poured over the workman's hands and arms. A second turn of the bandage revealed a low, white forehead, with a pair of delicately arched eyebrows. A third uncovered a pair of bright, deeply fringed eyes, and a straight, well-cut nose, while a fourth and last showed a sweet, full, sensitive mouth, and a beautifully curved chin. The whole face was one of extraordinary loveliness, save for the one blemish that in the centre of the forehead there was a single irregular, coffee-coloured splotch. It was a triumph of the embalmer's art. Vansittart Smith's eyes grew larger and larger as he gazed upon it, and he chirruped in his throat with satisfaction.

Its effect upon the Egyptologist was as nothing, however, compared with that which it produced upon the strange attendant. He threw his hands up into the air, burst into a harsh clatter of words, and then, hurling himself down upon the ground beside the mummy, he threw his arms round her, and kissed her repeatedly upon the lips and brow. '*Ma petite!*' he groaned in French. '*Ma pauvre petite!*' His voice broke with emotion, and his innumerable wrinkles quivered and writhed, but the student observed in the lamplight that his shining eyes were still as dry and tearless as two beads of steel. For some minutes he lay, with a twitching face, crooning and moaning over the beautiful head. Then he broke into a sudden smile, said some words in an unknown tongue, and sprang to his feet with the vigorous air of one who has braced himself for an effort.

In the centre of the room there was a large circular case which contained, as the student had frequently remarked, a magnificent collection of early Egyptian rings and precious stones. To this the attendant strode, and, unlocking it, he threw it open. On the ledge at the side he placed his lamp, and beside it a small earthenware jar which he had drawn from his pocket. He then took a handful of rings from the case, and with a most serious and anxious face he proceeded to smear each in turn with some liquid substance from the earthen pot, holding them to the light as he did so. He was clearly disappointed with the first lot, for he threw them petulantly back into the case, and drew out some more. One of these, a massive ring with a large crystal set in it, he seized and eagerly tested with the contents of the jar. Instantly he uttered a cry of joy, and threw out his arms in a wild gesture which upset the pot and sent the liquid streaming across the floor to the very feet of the Englishman. The attendant drew a red handkerchief from his bosom, and, mopping up the mess, he followed it into the corner, where in a moment he found himself face to face with his observer.

'Excuse me,' said John Vansittart Smith, with all imaginable politeness. 'I have been unfortunate enough to fall asleep behind this door.'

'And you have been watching me?' the other asked in English, with a most venomous look on his corpse-like face.

The student was a man of veracity. 'I confess,' said he, 'that I have noticed your movements, and that they have aroused my curiosity and interest in the highest degree.'

The man drew a long flamboyant-bladed knife from his bosom. 'You have had a very narrow escape,' he said. 'Had I seen you ten minutes ago, I should have driven this through your heart. As it is, if you touch me or interfere with me in any way you are a dead man.'

'I have no wish to interfere with you,' the student answered. 'My presence here is entirely accidental. All I ask is that you will have the extreme kindness to show me out through some side door.' He spoke with great suavity, for the man was still pressing the tip of his dagger against the palm of his left hand, as though to assure himself of its sharpness, while his face preserved its malignant expression.

'If I thought—' said he. 'But no, perhaps it is as well. What is your name?'

The Englishman gave it.

'Vansittart Smith,' the other repeated. 'Are you the same Vansittart Smith who gave a paper in London upon El Kab? I saw a report of it. Your knowledge of the subject is contemptible.'

'Sir!' cried the Egyptologist.

'Yet it is superior to that of many who make even greater pretensions. The whole keystone of our old life in Egypt was not the inscriptions or monuments of which you make so much, but was our hermetic philosophy and mystic knowledge, of which you say little or nothing.'

'Our old life!' repeated the scholar, wide-eyed; and then suddenly, 'Good God, look at the mummy's face!'

The strange man turned and flashed his light upon the dead woman, uttering a long doleful cry as he did so. The action of the air had already undone all the art of the embalmer. The skin had fallen away, the eyes had sunk inwards, the discoloured lips had writhed away from the yellow teeth, and the brown mark upon the forehead alone showed that it was indeed the same face which had shown such youth and beauty a few short minutes before.

The man flapped his hands together in grief and horror. Then mastering himself by a strong effort, he turned his hard eyes once more upon the Englishman.

'It does not matter,' he said, in a shaking voice. 'It does not really matter. I came here tonight with the fixed determination to do something. It is now done. All else is as nothing. I have found my quest. The old curse is broken. I can rejoin her. What matter about her inanimate shell so long as her spirit is awaiting me at the other side of the veil!'

'These are wild words,' said Vansittart Smith. He was becoming more and more convinced that he had to do with a madman.

'Time presses, and I must go,' continued the other. 'The moment is at hand for which I have waited this weary time. But I must show you out first. Come with me.'

Taking up the lamp, he turned from the disordered chamber, and led the student swiftly through the long series of the Egyptian, Assyrian, and Persian apartments. At the end of the latter he pushed open a small door let into the wall and descended a winding stone stair. The Englishman felt the cold fresh air of the night upon his brow. There was a door opposite him which appeared to communicate with the street. To the right of this another door stood ajar, throwing a spurt of yellow light across the passage. 'Come in here!' said the attendant shortly.

Vansittart Smith hesitated. He had hoped that he had come to the end of his adventure. Yet his curiosity was strong within him. He could not leave the matter unsolved, so he followed his strange companion into the lighted chamber.

It was a small room, such as is devoted to a concierge. A wood fire sparkled in the grate. At one side stood a truckle bed, and at the other a coarse wooden chair, with a round table in the centre, which bore the remains of a meal. As the visitor's eye glanced round, he could not but remark with an ever-recurring thrill that all the small details of the room were of the most quaint design and antique workmanship. The candlesticks, the vases upon the chimney-piece, the fire-irons, the ornaments upon the walls, were all such as he had been wont to associate with the remote past. The gnarled heavy-eyed man sat himself down upon the edge of the bed, and motioned his guest into the chair.

'There may be design in this,' he said, still speaking excellent English. 'It may be decreed that I should leave some account behind as a warning to all rash mortals who would set their wits up against workings of Nature. I leave it with you. Make such use as you will of it. I speak to you now with my feet upon the threshold of the other world.

'I am, as you surmised, an Egyptian – not one of the down-trodden race of slaves who now inhabit the Delta of the Nile, but a survivor of that fiercer and harder people who tamed the Hebrew, drove the Ethiopian back into the southern deserts, and built those mighty works which have been the envy and the wonder of all after generations. It was in the reign of Tuthmosis, sixteen hundred years before the birth of Christ, that I first saw the light. You shrink away from me. Wait, and you will see that I am more to be pitied than to be feared.

'My name was Sosra. My father had been the chief priest of Osiris in the great temple of Abaris, which stood in those days upon the Bubastic branch of the Nile. I was brought up in the temple and was trained in all those mystic arts which are spoken of in your own Bible. I was an apt pupil. Before I was sixteen I had learned all which the wisest priest could teach me. From that time on I studied Nature's secrets for myself, and shared my knowledge with no man.

'Of all the questions which attracted me there were none over which I laboured so long as over those which concern themselves with the nature of life. I probed deeply into the vital principle. The aim of medicine had been to drive away disease when it appeared. It seemed to me that a method might be devised which should so fortify the body as to prevent weakness or death from ever taking hold of it. It is useless that I should recount my researches. You would scarce comprehend them if I did. They were carried out partly upon animals, partly upon slaves, and partly on myself. Suffice it that their result was to furnish me with a substance which, when injected into the blood, would endow the body with strength to resist the effects of time, of violence, or of disease. It would not indeed confer immortality, but its potency would endure for many thousands of years. I used it upon a cat, and afterwards drugged the creature with the most deadly poisons. That cat is alive in Lower Egypt at the present moment. There was nothing of mystery or magic in the matter. It was simply a chemical discovery, which may well be made again.

'Love of life runs high in the young. It seemed to me that I had broken away from all human care now that I had abolished pain and driven death to such a distance. With a light heart I poured the accursed stuff into my veins. Then I looked round for someone whom I could benefit. There was a young priest of Thoth, Parmes by name, who had won my goodwill by his earnest nature and his devotion to his studies. To him I whispered my secret, and at his request I injected him with my elixir. I should now, I reflected, never be without a companion of the same age as myself.

'After this grand discovery I relaxed my studies to some extent, but Parmes continued his with redoubled energy. Every day I could see him working with his flasks and his distiller in the Temple of Thoth, but he said little to me as to the result of his labours. For my own part, I used to walk through the city and look around me with exultation as I reflected that all this was destined to pass away, and that only I should remain. The people would bow to me as they passed me, for the fame of my knowledge had gone abroad.

'There was war at this time, and the Great King had sent down his soldiers to the eastern boundary to drive away the Hyksos. A Governor, too, was sent to Abaris, that he might hold it for the King. I had heard much of the beauty of the daughter of this Governor, but one day as I walked out with Parmes we met her, borne upon the shoulders of her slaves. I was struck with love as with lightning. My heart went out from me. I could have thrown myself beneath the feet of her bearers. This was my woman. Life without her was impossible. I swore by the head of Horus that she should be mine. I swore it to the Priest of Thoth. He turned away from me with a brow which was as black as midnight.

'There is no need to tell you of our wooing. She came to love me even as I loved her. I learned that Parmes had seen her before I did, and had shown her that he too loved her, but I could smile at his passion, for I knew that her heart was mine. The white plague had come upon the city and many were stricken, but I laid my hands upon the sick and nursed them without fear or scathe. She marvelled at my daring. Then I told her my secret, and begged her that she would let me use my art upon her.

'"Your flower shall then be unwithered, Atma," I said. "Other things may pass away, but you and I, and our great love for each other, shall outlive the tomb of King Chefru."

'But she was full of timid, maidenly objections. "Was it right?" she asked. "Was it not a thwarting of the will of the gods? If the great Osiris had wished that our years should be so long, would he not himself have brought it about?"

'With fond and loving words I overcame her doubts, and yet she hesitated. It was a great question, she said. She would think it over for this one night. In the morning I should know her resolution. Surely one night was not too much to ask. She wished to pray to Isis for help in her decision.

'With a sinking heart and a sad foreboding of evil I left her with her tirewomen. In the morning, when the early sacrifice was over, I hurried to her house. A frightened slave met me upon the steps. Her mistress was ill, she said, very ill. In a frenzy I broke my way through the attendants, and rushed through hall and corridor to my Atma's chamber. She lay upon her couch, her head high upon the pillow, with a pallid face and a glazed eye. On her forehead there blazed a single angry purple patch. I knew that hell-mark of old. It was the scar of the white plague, the sign-manual of death.

'Why should I speak of that terrible time? For months I was mad, fevered, delirious, and yet I could not die. Never did an Arab thirst after the sweet wells as I longed after death. Could poison or steel have shortened the thread of my existence, I should soon have rejoined my love in the land with the narrow portal. I tried, but it was of no avail. The accursed influence was too strong upon me. One night as I lay upon my couch, weak and weary, Parmes, the Priest of Thoth, came to my chamber. He stood in the circle of the lamplight, and he looked down upon me with eyes which were bright with a mad joy.

'"Why did you let the maiden die?" he asked. "Why did you not strengthen her as you strengthened me?"

'"I was too late," I answered. "But I had forgot. You also loved her. You are my fellow in misfortune. Is it not terrible to think of the centuries which must pass ere we look upon her again? Fools, fools, that we were to take death to be our enemy!"

'"You may say that," he cried with a wild laugh. "The words come well from your lips. For me they have no meaning."

'"What mean you?" I cried, raising myself upon my elbow. "Surely, friend, this grief has turned your brain." His face was aflame with joy, and he writhed and shook like one who hath a devil.

'"Do you know whither I go?" he asked.

'"Nay," I answered, "I cannot tell."

'"I go to her," said he. "She lies embalmed in the further tomb by the double palm-tree beyond the city wall."

"'Why do you go there?" I asked.

"'To die!" he shrieked, "To die! I am not bound by earthen fetters."

"'But the elixir is in your blood," I cried.

"'I can defy it," said he. "I have found a stronger principle which will destroy it. It is working in my veins at this moment, and in an hour I shall be a dead man. I shall join her, and you shall remain behind."

'As I looked upon him I could see that he spoke words of truth. The light in his eye told me that he was indeed beyond the power of the elixir.

"'You will teach me!" I cried.

"'Never!" he answered.

"'I implore you, by the wisdom of Thoth, by the majesty of Anubis!"

"'It is useless," he said coldly.

"'Then I will find it out," I cried.

"'You cannot," he answered. "It came to me by chance. There is one ingredient which you can never get. Save that which is in the ring of Thoth, none will ever more be made."

"'In the ring of Thoth!" I repeated. "Where then is the ring of Thoth?"

"'That also you shall never know," he answered. "You won her love. Who has won in the end? I leave you to your sordid earth life. My chains are broken. I must go!" He turned upon his heel and fled from the chamber. In the morning came the news that the Priest of Thoth was dead.

'My days after that were spent in study. I must find this subtle poison which was strong enough to undo the elixir. From early dawn to midnight I bent over the test-tube and the furnace. Above all, I collected the papyri and the chemical flasks of the Priest of Thoth.

Alas! they taught me little. Here and there some hint or stray expression would raise hope in my bosom, but no good ever came of it. Still, month after month, I struggled on. When my heart grew faint I would make my way to the tomb by the palm-trees.

'There, standing by the dead casket from which the jewel had been rifled, I would feel her sweet presence, and would whisper to her that I would rejoin her if mortal wit could solve the riddle.

'Parmes had said that his discovery was connected with the ring of Thoth. I had some remembrance of the trinket. It was a large and weighty circlet, made, not of gold, but of a rarer and heavier metal brought from the mines of Mount Harbal. Platinum, you call it. The ring had, I remembered, a hollow crystal set in it, in which some few drops of liquid might be stored. Now, the secret of Parmes could not have to do with the metal alone, for there were many rings of that metal in the Temple. Was it not more likely that he had stored his precious poison within the cavity of the crystal? I had scarce come to this conclusion before, in hunting through his papers, I came upon one which told me that it was indeed so, and that there was still some of the liquid unused.

'But how to find the ring? It was not upon him when he was stripped for the embalmer. Of that I made sure. Neither was it among his private effects. In vain I searched every room that he had entered, every box, and vase, and chattel that he had owned. I sifted the very sand of the desert in the places where he had been wont to walk; but, do what I would, I could come upon no traces of the ring of Thoth. Yet it may be that my labours would have overcome all obstacles had it not been for a new and unlooked-for misfortune.

'A great war had been waged against the Hyksos, and the Captains of the Great King had been cut off in the desert, with all their bowmen and horsemen. The shepherd tribes were upon us like the locusts in a dry year. From the wilderness of Shur to the great bitter lake there was blood by day and fire by night. Abaris was the bulwark of Egypt, but we could not keep the savages back. The city fell. The Governor and the soldiers were put to the sword, and I, with many more, was led away into captivity.

'For years and years I tended cattle in the great plains by the Euphrates. My master died, and his son grew old, but I was still as far from death as ever. At last I escaped upon a swift camel, and made my way back to Egypt. The Hyksos had settled in the land which they had conquered, and their own King ruled over the country. Abaris had been torn down, the city had been burned, and of the great temple there was nothing left save an unsightly mound. Everywhere the tombs had been rifled and the monuments destroyed. Of my Atma's grave no sign was left. It was buried in the sands of the desert, and the palm-trees which marked the spot had long disappeared. The papers of Parmes and the remains of the Temple of Thoth were either destroyed or scattered far and wide over the deserts of Syria. All search after them was vain.

'From that time I gave up all hope of ever finding the ring or discovering the subtle drug. I set myself to live as patiently as might be until the effect of the elixir should wear away. How can you understand how terrible a thing time is, you who have experience only of the narrow course which lies between the cradle and the grave! I know it to my cost, I who have floated down the whole stream of history. I was old when Ilium fell. I was very old when Herodotus came to Memphis. I was bowed down with years when the new gospel came upon earth. Yet you see me much as other men are, with the cursed elixir still sweetening my blood, and guarding me against that which I would court. Now at last, at last I have come to the end of it!

'I have travelled in all lands and I have dwelt with all nations. Every tongue is the same to me. I learned them all to help pass the weary time. I need not tell you how slowly they drifted by, the long dawn of modern civilisation, the dreary middle years, the dark times of barbarism. They are all behind me now, I have never looked with the eyes of love upon another woman. Atma knows that I have been constant to her.

'It was my custom to read all that the scholars had to say upon Ancient Egypt. I have been in many positions, sometimes affluent, sometimes poor, but I have always found enough to enable me to buy the journals which deal with such matters. Some nine months ago I was in San Francisco, when I read an account of some discoveries made in the neighbourhood of Abaris. My heart leapt into my mouth as I read it. It said that the excavator had busied himself in exploring some tombs recently unearthed. In one there had been found an unopened mummy with an inscription upon the outer case setting forth that it contained the body of the daughter of the Governor of the city in the days of Tuthmosis. It added that on removing the outer case there had been exposed a large platinum ring set with a crystal, which had been laid upon the breast of the embalmed woman. This, then was where Parmes had hid the ring of Thoth. He might well say that it was safe, for no Egyptian would ever stain his soul by moving even the outer case of a buried friend.

'That very night I set off from San Francisco, and in a few weeks I found myself once more at Abaris, if a few sand-heaps and crumbling walls may retain the name of the great city. I hurried to the Frenchmen who were digging there and asked them for the ring. They replied that both the ring and the mummy had been sent to the Boulak Museum at Cairo. To Boulak I went, but only to be told that Mariette Bey had claimed them and had shipped them to the Louvre. I followed them, and there at last, in the Egyptian chamber, I came, after close upon four thousand years, upon the remains of my Atma, and upon the ring for which I had sought so long.

'But how was I to lay hands upon them? How was I to have them for my very own? It chanced that the office of attendant was vacant. I went to the Director. I convinced him that I knew much about Egypt. In my eagerness I said too much. He remarked that a Professor's chair would suit me better than a seat in the Conciergerie. I knew more, he said, than he did. It was only by blundering, and letting him think that he had over-estimated my knowledge, that I prevailed upon him to let me move the few effects which I have retained into this chamber. It is my first and my last night here.

'Such is my story, Mr Vansittart Smith. I need not say more to a man of your perception. By a strange chance you have this night looked upon the face of the woman whom I loved in those far-off days. There were many rings with crystals in the case, and I had to test for the platinum to be sure of the one which I wanted. A glance at the crystal has shown me that the liquid is indeed within it, and that I shall at last be able to shake off that accursed health which has been worse to me than the foulest disease. I have nothing more to say to you. I have unburdened myself. You may tell my story or you may withhold it at your pleasure. The choice rests with you. I owe you some amends, for you have had a narrow escape of your life this night. I was a desperate man, and not to be baulked in my purpose. Had I seen you before the thing was done, I might have put it beyond your power to oppose me or to raise an alarm. This is the door. It leads into the Rue de Rivoli. Good night!'

The Englishman glanced back. For a moment the lean figure of Sosra the Egyptian stood framed in the narrow doorway. The next the door had slammed, and the heavy rasping of a bolt broke on the silent night.

It was on the second day after his return to London that Mr.

John Vansittart Smith saw the following concise narrative in the Paris correspondence of the *Times*:—

> *'Curious Occurrence in the Louvre. – Yesterday morning a strange discovery was made in the principal Egyptian Chamber. The ouvriers who are employed to clean out the rooms in the morning found one of the attendants lying dead upon the floor with his arms round one of the mummies. So close was his embrace that it was only with the utmost difficulty that they were separated. One of the cases containing valuable rings had been opened and rifled. The authorities are of opinion that the man was bearing away the mummy with some idea of selling it to a private collector, but that he was struck down in the very act by long-standing disease of the heart. It is said that he was a man of uncertain age and eccentric habits, without any living relations to mourn over his dramatic and untimely end.'*

THE EXTRAORDINARY CASE OF MR EBENSTAL

By D F Hannigan (fl. 1890s)

D F Hannigan trained as a barrister but made his name as a reviewer and as a scholar of French literature. He published a translation of Balzac's letters and, in the 1890s, became the first to translate Flaubert's novels, The Temptation of St Antony *and* Bouvard and Pécuchet, *into English. As his interest in Balzac and Flaubert might imply and ironically, given the subject of 'The Extraordinary Case of Mr Ebenstal', he was a great advocate of realism in fiction. In an essay published in 1890, he attacked those writers who pandered to the 'middle-class reader for whom the naked truth is unpalatable'. The contemporary English novelist he most admired was Thomas Hardy. Yet his own limited ventures into fiction were mostly the reverse of realistic. As well as the story below, he published another tale in* Ludgate Monthly *two months later, 'Old Doctor Rutherford', which took immortality as its subject matter. 'The Extraordinary Case of Mr Ebenstal' is certainly no lost masterpiece of genre fiction – indeed Hannigan's prose is fairly plodding – but it deserves attention for the sheer weirdness of its premise and for the light it unconsciously throws on some male attitudes to women in the last decade of the nineteenth century.*

Ludgate Monthly *August 1891*

I, Jacob Ackroyd, solicitor of Lincoln's Inn Fields, in the City of London, solemnly declare that the following narrative is true in substance and in fact:—

On 31 December last, I was seated in my private office, carefully perusing an exceedingly complicated deed, when Benjamin Wrayburn, my managing clerk, burst in upon me, rather abruptly.

I asked him, in a slightly irritable tone, what was the matter, and he replied, with a twinkle in his keen, grey eye, that a strange gentleman was waiting to see me, and had politely intimated that his business was of a most pressing and important character. I asked whether the gentleman had given his name, and Benjamin answered in the affirmative, adding that the new client's name was Mr Reuben Ebenstal.

I told him to send up Mr Ebenstal to me, without further delay, and putting aside the deed, I assumed the attitude of composure and vigilance with which I usually receive my clients.

Less than a minute had elapsed when a low tap at the door indicated that my client only wanted my permission to enter.

'Come in,' said I, in a tone of as much firmness as I could command.

The newcomer was a sallow-visaged man of about forty-five, attired in solemn black, and presenting altogether a somewhat semi-clerical appearance.

'Pray sit down, Mr Ebenstal,' said I, pointing towards a chair, and keeping my eyes fastened upon him all the time.

Mr Ebenstal, who appeared to be an unusually timid person, edged his way slowly towards the chair, deposited his hat beneath it, and cautiously balanced himself upon one corner of it, like a man who is afraid of sitting upon thistles.

I paused, expecting him to state his business, without further preliminaries; but, to my surprise, he only eyed me apprehensively, gasping like a man whose powers of articulation had been stricken with temporary paralysis.

For a few seconds we stared at one another in stony silence.

'I understand that you have called to see me on business of great importance?' said I, at last, compelled to take the lead.

'Ah! – ahem! – yes, business of importance,' said Mr Ebenstal, in a series of spasmodic jerks.

'Come, then, my worthy friend,' I urged, with growing impatience, 'let us hear what it is. You must know that this is a particularly busy hour with me.'

'Oh! Indeed, sir?' said Mr Ebenstal, evidently rather disconcerted. 'I am really very sorry to trouble you; but—' Here he checked himself suddenly, and seemed unable, for the moment, to go further.

'I must remind you, Mr Ebenstal,' said I, 'that my time is rather precious; and there is no necessity for this hesitation on your part. Remember that anything you tell me is a confidential communication.'

He coughed twice before he ventured to speak again. 'I beg your pardon, Mr Ackroyd,' he faltered. 'It is an extremely peculiar case, and I am at a loss how to lay the facts before you.'

'Oh! Nonsense,' said I. 'I have had a pretty long experience, and cases repeat themselves just like history. Even in the legal profession one realises the truth of the old adage that "there is nothing new under the sun."' Even these encouraging words did not seem to reassure Mr Ebenstal.

'You see, sir,' he said, drawing out his words with an air of painful irresolution, 'I am not what you would call a man of much imagination, nor have I much power of expression; and yet the matter I came to talk to you about is so extraordinary that anything I have ever read in a novel is commonplace compared with it.'

'You excite my curiosity,' said I, 'and yet you try my patience not a little, I must confess. Come, no matter how you tell it, commence, Mr Ebenstal. I'll be bound 'tis a matrimonial affair?'

A sickly smile, for an instant, flickered like a dying flame across Mr Ebenstal's colourless face.

'Well, yes, sir,' he replied, 'but I am inclined to think it is very different from the great mass of matrimonial affairs.'

'In what way?' I asked, in a tone which compelled him to give a direct answer.

'In this way, then, if I must tell the whole truth, Mr Ackroyd,' said my new client, as if he were nerving himself for a great effort, 'that I am seeking to obtain a dissolution of marriage on grounds which may appear to you unnatural, or incredible.'

'Unnatural? Incredible?' I repeated. 'Do you mean to say that you want to obtain a divorce, or perhaps a decree of nullity, without proper legal grounds? In that case, you know the thing is impossible.'

'It is not that,' said Mr Ebenstal. 'The circumstances can scarcely have ever arisen before. I am not six months married; and yet – and yet—'

'Yes, yes,' I cried, trying to dispel his timidity, 'pray go on, Mr Ebenstal.'

'Well, then, sir, if I must enter into my wretched history,' said Mr Ebenstal, after another interval of silence, during which he seemed to struggle with some painful emotion, 'I will tell it as best I can. As I was just observing, I am only six months married; but in that short space of time so many strange things have happened, that I feel as if a century had been added to my life. I remained a bachelor till I was considerably past my fortieth year. I had devoted myself almost entirely to business pursuits, and I had been tolerably successful. I had not mixed much in society – in fact, I had led a very secluded and rather austere life; but I was in the habit of making periodical visits to Germany, where I happen to have some blood-relations as well as some business connection. I am, I may tell you, partly of German extraction. Well, last spring, while I was staying with one of my kinsfolk, in the neighbourhood of the Black Forest, I met her who was destined to be my future wife. She was young, and exceedingly beautiful – so at least it seemed to me. Her name was Caroline Müller. She was, I discovered, an orphan, and had been brought up since she was a mere infant, by an eccentric old uncle, who allowed her to do as she pleased. He was not rich, but had quite enough to maintain himself and his niece without working at any trade, and, having nothing else to do, he amused himself by engaging in abstruse biological studies. He was supposed, in the locality where he lived, to have started some odd theory about man's relations to the lower animals, and for this reason he was considered a very rank type of materialist. Be that as it may, he taught some of his strange doctrines to his niece, whom he had educated himself; and, when I asked her to marry me, I was fully prepared to find in her one whose views on religion, and on life generally, were a little distorted. I was, however, too deeply enamoured of her to care much about this. Never, perhaps, was there a more devoted lover, and, though Caroline did not seem to care much for me, she was persuaded by her uncle to accept me. In this old man there was something artful, sinister, and mysterious, and I now believe he looked on me with secret satisfaction, as an excellent subject on which to exercise his accursed wiles; but 'tis only within the past few weeks that this explanation of his conduct suggested itself to my mind. I never entertained a doubt concerning either himself or his niece before my marriage, which took place in a little Jewish synagogue, not far from Johann Müller's house, on the borders of the Black Forest. Both uncle and niece professed the same faith as myself; but I now believe that their religious professions were really only a ruse to deceive me.'

'Excuse my interrupting you,' I interposed, 'but please do not mind telling me what you believe. Confine yourself to facts, or, at least, to what you assume to be actual occurrences.'

'I am coming to the most singular part of the transaction,' said Mr Ebenstal, in the same serious but unimpassioned style. 'After we were married, we travelled through Germany, and visited some of the chief cities in Holland and Belgium. When I told her that I lived in London – a fact which I had not hitherto touched upon – and that she should reside with me there, she appeared rather disappointed at first, and suggested that, at any rate, her uncle should accompany us to England, and reside with us as a regular member of the family. In my blind infatuation I assented to this proposal. I wrote to her uncle, and told him to meet us at Antwerp. It was not long ere he arrived there. I saw by his look of ill-disguised exultation that the arrangement had been planned beforehand between himself and Caroline; and yet I had not enough of manly determination to protest against it even at the eleventh hour. Ere we reached London, my eyes had been further opened to the dark and evil designs of this inhuman old wretch. He clung to me like a vampire; and, though he did not exactly seek to murder me, he evidently intended to live upon me, not only in a pecuniary sense, but physically and actually. Before he joined us, my health had been uniformly good; but, ever since, my face has entirely lost its colour, and I have rapidly been wasting away. It is only within the past few months that I have become the miserable hypochondriac I am now.'

He heaved a sigh, and beads of clammy perspiration started to his forehead.

'Oh! God!' he cried, suddenly, with an ejaculation such as he had not previously exhibited. 'I cannot tell you all.'

'Let me get you a glass of wine,' said I, starting up.

He made a faint protest; but I did not pretend to heed it.

As soon as I had poured out a glass of wine for my strange client, and urged him to drink it off, some signs of returning animation showed themselves on his sallow visage.

He raised the glass to his lips, and finished about half its contents.

'You feel better now, don't you?' said I; and, as the task of listening to Mr Ebenstal's story was slightly fatiguing, I thought I could not do better than pour out a glass of sherry for myself, too.

'Oh! Yes, thank you, Mr Ackroyd, I am much better,' was his reply. 'I was just telling you about – about—'

Again he hesitated, and got confused.

'You were speaking about your wife's uncle,' I observed emphatically.

'Oh! Of course, sir,' he returned. 'Thank you for reminding me of it, though, indeed, it is an unpleasant topic. He was a wicked man, Mr Ackroyd – a devil incarnate. He robbed me of every spark of energy I possessed. He found out all my business secrets – in fact, everything that I wished to keep concealed – and seemed to read my very thoughts.

'He made me a puppet in his hands, and, ere long, I could scarcely say that I was a free agent. He laughed scornfully at my moral prejudices, as he called them. He said his own opinion was that both Judaism and Christianity were living lies, and that all religion was a hollow mockery. He told me that neither he nor his niece believed in any existing creed, and he urged me to follow their example. Gradually, I began to abandon the religious practices I had always observed; and, as for Caroline, she seemed to have no conception of what was meant by the word "conscience". She seemed to me a lovely enigma for the first month of our marriage. I found in her mysterious faculties, which seemed to raise her either above or below humanity. But soon a new revelation dawned upon me. My beautiful wife, who, when she appeared – as she did, pretty often, at balls and public festivities – was looked upon as, at the same time, the handsomest and the most singular woman ever seen in London society, was truly a most peculiarly organised being. It was clear that she had not one feeling in common with me. She was daring, queenly, fascinating; but she had no capacity for love, no sympathy, no softness in her nature. Moreover, she was, if possible, a greater sceptic than her uncle – in fact, an atheist of the most uncompromising type. I was often shocked at her profanity, which amounted to actual impiousness. She spoke with irreverence, and even hatred, of the sacred name which Jew and Christian are bound to reverence – the great name of God. Towards me she exhibited not one particle of affection, and yet she never shrank from my caresses. But, one night, as we sat side by side, together – her uncle had retired – she burst into a fierce laugh, like that which might have come from some wild animal, at some words of endearment which I happened to utter, and, for the first time, I saw her protrude a hideous forked tongue. I drew back in sheer affright. She seemed to enjoy my discomfiture.'

'"Reuben Ebenstal," she exclaimed, "poor, foolish mortal! Do you know what it is you have wedded? Look! Look!"

'I did look; and what did I behold? Not a woman, surely; for those gleaming, golden scales, those snaky eyes, that hissing tongue, were not the attributes of womanhood! Then, with a sense of sickening horror, which no language can describe, I saw a fearful transformation take place in her entire appearance. The dress she wore – a rich and fashionable robe – seemed only to cling around the winding form of a creeping, bright-coloured species of animal – an appalling combination of woman and reptile! There was still loveliness, grace, and symmetry; but it was the loveliness, grace, and symmetry of a serpent. I fled from her side with a cry of despair. I rushed into the street. I tore my hair like a madman and, sobbing, asked myself, "What shall I do? In the name of Heaven, what shall I do?"

'After a struggle with myself, I grew calmer. The cool air of the night helped to restore my mind to its normal condition.

'"I will go and consult some eminent physician," I thought. "He may, perhaps, be able to throw some light on the mystery."

'I took heart of grace, as the hope of possible relief sprang up in my heart. What had just happened had for weeks before been shadowed forth by strange presentiments; and I had sufficient knowledge of physiology to be aware that there are such things as monsters – beings, which, though of human origin, could scarcely be said to be of human shape. This, however, afforded no adequate explanation of the difficulty. I resolved to seek an interview with Dr Charles Addison, who was one of the best authorities, at least in London, upon cases of deformity, or abnormal organisation. He had written a remarkable work on *Gynaecology*, which had been spoken of as one of the most striking and original contributions to medical philosophy. You see, Mr Ackroyd, I was, for a layman, rather fond of medical studies, and so I knew enough to enable me to pitch upon a man of established reputation.

'I found Dr Addison at home. He received me with the utmost cordiality. He listened to my account of the extraordinary occurrence of that evening. At first he laughed at me – then he took the matter more gravely. At length, he said, "Why should I not visit your wife tonight on the plea of her being, let us say, in a hysterical condition?"

'I caught at the suggestion eagerly.

'"Yes, yes, do come, doctor!" I cried. "Come for God's sake! I cannot live another hour in that house, unless you come and do something to help me!"

'He yielded to my appeal without further hesitation. We both walked across to my house together, and I opened the hall-door with a latch-key. I led the way up to my wife's room. The door was not locked, and so we managed to steal in on tiptoe.

'She was seated on an easy chair before a glowing fire. Her face shone resplendently. She wore a loose dressing-robe. It was hard at that moment to tell whether there was more of the woman or the serpent about her; but one thing I noticed – that her eyes had the peculiar snaky lustre which I had seen in them before I had, that very evening, rushed away from her in sheer terror.

'Ere Dr Addison had time to utter a single word, we both heard a step close behind us, and looking over my shoulder, I saw the evil face of Johann Müller.

'"Ah! *Mein Gott!*" he laughed. "What have we here? A strange man – yah, a physician, as I live!"

'"Yes, sir, I am a physician," said Dr Addison, with a stern bow, "and I have come, at her husband's request, to see this – this lady, who is, I understand, in anything but a good state of health."

'"You lie, Herr Doctor, you utter one infernal lie," said the old man, with his guttural German pronunciation. "She is well – she is very well; and it is her idiot of a husband whose head is turned. He does not appreciate the lovely creature he has married. He is a fool and a madman."

'The doctor cast a quick look of inquiry at me, scanning me half-doubtingly, half-wistfully. Then he directed his glance towards the old man's face.

'I looked also at Johann Müller. Did my senses deceive me or did I really see beads of flame in those sockets where his eyes had been?

'"Ah! Great God!" I suddenly burst out, "this, indeed, is not a man, but a demon!"

'I now could see his withered features lit up by a lurid glow.

'"Be it so, idiotic raver!" he said. "I am at any rate something more worthy of admiration and respect than a feeble thing like you. See you both," – addressing myself and the doctor at the same time – "I have here that which, for the present at least, removes me to a safe distance from such pestiferous wretches as Reuben Ebenstal. By and by, however, the hour of my vengeance shall come!"

'He drew forth from an inner coat pocket a long phial containing some curious, red fluid.

'"This," said he, "is a draught which no mortal hand has prepared. Behold! It transports me in one instant to the spirit-world!"

'He drank a small quantity of the contents of the phial, and then dropped it on the ground, where it was shattered to pieces. The result, indeed, seemed quite miraculous. Ere a word could be spoken, Johann Müller had vanished, as if by magic!

'Even the doctor looked amazed. He snatched up a fragment of the broken phial, but dropped it instantaneously with an exclamation of astonishment.

'"My God!" he cried, "it is as hot as a live coal!"

'Before I could say anything in reply, the figure, which had been reclining in the easy chair before the fire, sprang up suddenly, and with the snake-light in her eyes, Caroline glared around.

'"What! My uncle gone? My guardian, my protector gone?" she exclaimed – "Wretch! what have you done with him?" – and, with a menacing hiss, she flung herself upon me.

'Well for me, then, that I had Dr Addison beside me, for had he not interposed, that moment would, I believe, have been my last on earth. He dragged me bodily out of the room, and led me forth into the open air. It was frightful! I could almost feel the fangs of the serpent on my throat. Oh! God! Oh! Merciful God! and this was my wife!'

The poor wretch, at this point, was so completely choked by his overpowering emotions that his voice absolutely failed him. He stretched forth his hands for the glass, which was still half-filled with wine.

In spite of my professional training, my sympathies were aroused. I refilled the glass, and raised it to his lips.

'This is, indeed, a very strange affair,' I said to myself. 'It seems like a study in demonology.' Then, seeing that my client had recovered a little, I addressed him in this fashion: 'It certainly does look as if some devilish influence were at work, Mr Ebenstal; but I don't see how I can give you any legal assistance. In fact, I am afraid I can do nothing.'

'Nothing,' he repeated, with a look of pitiful disappointment. 'Why – why should I not be able, on the evidence I have given you, to dissolve this hellish marriage?'

'Well, you must know,' said I, very gravely, 'that the law has provided no machinery adapted to cases of this kind. It is presumed that unions of such an unnatural description are impossible. The law, at any rate, acts on that assumption. The only grounds for dissolving marriage are—'

'Hush! Hush!' broke in Mr Ebenstal, lifting up his bloodless forefinger. 'See! She is here! She – she has pursued me even to this place. Look at that! – Oh! Look at that, and tell me whether all I have said is not true – too, too true!'

He pointed towards the door. I turned my eyes in the direction indicated by Mr Ebenstal, and, unless it can be assumed that I was at that moment the victim of a temporary hallucination, I distinctly traced the shining figure, and the sinuous movements of a gliding body, with glittering scales, and heard the peculiar hiss, which is such a well-known characteristic of the serpent.

I should have been more, or less, than human to have remained unmoved by such an awful experience.

After a pause of some minutes, during which I felt rather stupefied, I turned towards my miserable client.

'Take courage, my friend!' I murmured. 'Whatever it was, it has disappeared! Don't lose heart! We may do something for you yet!'

But no response came from the lips of Mr Ebenstal. I now saw that his lips were blanched, and his teeth clenched together. His eyes glared at vacancy. He was beyond the reach, and beyond the help, of either law or physic!

A sense of duty has prompted me to publish the facts of this extraordinary case, as far as I have been able to collect them. I am not aware whether any next-of-kin of Mr Ebenstal can be found to pursue the investigation; but death has removed the seal of confidence imposed on me, and justice may require that guilt, even though hidden under mysterious forms, should be tracked out and punished. In any event, the transcendent interest of this case justifies me in placing the entire narrative before the public.

THE STORY OF THE GREY HOUSE

By E and H Heron
(pseudonyms of Kate Prichard [1851–1935] and Hesketh Prichard [1876–1922])

Hesketh Prichard led an extraordinarily adventurous life as an explorer and big-game hunter, travelling the world from Patagonia to Newfoundland and from Haiti to Norway. He was also a first-class cricketer and a brilliant marksman. During the First World War he was in charge of training snipers for the Western Front. Somehow, amidst all this other activity, he managed to find time to write fiction, often in collaboration with his mother Kate. Of the fiction Hesketh Prichard wrote on his own, the most interesting features 'November Joe', a Canadian backwoodsman and amateur detective who appears in a number of stories. Working with Kate, he produced tales of a Zorro-like figure named Don Q and, in the 1920s, one of them was turned into a Hollywood film starring Douglas Fairbanks. The Flaxman Low stories, which were the Prichards' first major successes were about an occult detective, and were originally published in Pearson's Magazine *in 1898 and 1899 before being collected in book form. Most of them are straightforwardly supernatural and are best categorised as ghost stories. However, 'The Story of the Grey House' is, as the Prichards point out in its first paragraph, a tale 'that seems to open up a new province of fantastic horror'.*

Pearson's Magazine, *May 1898*

Mr Flaxman Low declares that only on one occasion has he undertaken, unasked, the solving of a psychical mystery. To that case he always refers as the 'affair of the Grey House'. The house bears a different name in the annals of more than one scientific society, and much controversy has raged over the strange details of a story that seems to open up a new province of fantastic horror. Papers and treatises have been written about it in almost every European language, and many dismaying facts of a somewhat analogous nature have thus been brought to light.

There was some hesitation at first about laying this matter – backed as it is by an explanation, which, though terrible, is not altogether unsupported – before the public, but it has finally been decided to incorporate it in the present series.

During the dry summer of 1893 Mr Low happened to be staying in a lonely village on the coast of Devon. He was deeply immersed in some antiquarian work connected with the old Norse calendars, and therefore limited his acquaintance in the neighbourhood to one individual, a Dr Fremantle, who, beside being a medical man, was a botanist of some note.

One afternoon, when driving together, Mr Low and Dr Fremantle passed through a valley which nestled cup-like in the higher ground a few miles inland. As they passed along a deep, steep lane with overhanging hedges they caught a glimpse, through a break in the leaves, of a grey gable peeping out between the horizontal branches of a cedar.

Flaxman Low pointed it out to his companion.

'That's young Montesson's house,' answered Fremantle, 'and it bears a very sinister reputation. Nothing in your line, though,' with a smile. 'Indeed, no ghost would lend the same hideous associations to the place it now possesses as the result of a succession of mysterious murders that have occurred there.'

'The grounds seem neglected. I don't remember to have seen such rank growth anywhere.'

'Certainly not inside the British Isles,' returned Fremantle. 'The estate is left to take care of itself, partly because Montesson won't live there, partly because it is impossible to find labourers to work near the house. Our warm, damp climate and this sheltered position give rise to extraordinary luxuriance of growth. A stream runs along the bottom, and I expect all the low-lying land, where you see that belt of yellow African grass, is little better than a morass now.'

Fremantle drew up as they gained the top of the slope. From there they could overlook the tangle of vegetation, dimmed by a rising mist, which surrounded and almost hid the roof of the Grey House.

'Yes,' said Fremantle, in answer to an observation of Mr Low, 'Montesson's guardian, who lived here and looked after the property for him, turned the place into a subtropical garden. It used to be one of my chief pleasures to wander about here, but since my marriage my wife objects to my doing so, on account of the tales she has heard.'

'What is the danger?'

'Death!' replied Fremantle shortly.

'What form of death? Malaria?'

'No disease at all, my dear fellow. The persons who die at the Grey House are hanged by the neck until they are dead!'

'Hanged?' repeated Flaxman Low in surprise.

'Yes, hanged. Not only strangled but suspended, as the marks on the necks show. If there were any hint of a ghost in it you might investigate – Montesson would be only too grateful if you could fathom the mystery.'

'Tell me something more definite.'

'I'll tell you what has happened in my own knowledge. Montesson's father died some fifteen years ago and left him to the guardianship of a cousin named Lampurt, who, as I told you, was a horticulturist, and planted the place with a wonderful variety of foreign shrubs and flowers. Lampurt had a bad name in the county, and his appearance was certainly against him – a squint-eyed, pig-faced fellow, who sidled along like a crab, and could not look you in the face. He died first.'

'Was he hanged? Or did he hang himself?'

'Neither, in this case. He dropped in a kind of fit, right up in front of the house, while he was engaged in planting some new acquisition. Had it not been for the evidence of the persons who were present at the time, I should have said his death resulted from some tremendous mental shock. But the gardener and his relation, Mrs Montesson, agreed in saying that he was not exerting himself unduly, and that he had had no disturbing news. He was a healthy man and I could see no sufficient reason for his death. He was simply gardening, and had apparently pricked himself with a nail for he had a spot of blood upon his forefinger.

'After that all went well for a couple of years, when, during the summer holidays, the trouble began. Montesson must have been about sixteen at the time, and had a tutor with him. His mother and sister – a pretty girl rather older than himself – were also here. One morning the girl was found lying on the gravel under her window, quite dead. I was sent for, and, upon examination, discovered the extraordinary fact that she had been hanged!'

'Murder?'

'Of course, though we could find no trace of the murderer. The girl had been taken from her bedroom and hanged. Then the rope was removed and she was thrown in a heap under her window. The crime caused a tremendous sensation in the neighbourhood, and the police were busy for a long time, but nothing came of their inquiries.

'About a fortnight later, Platt, the tutor, sat up smoking at the open study window. In the morning he was found lying out over the sill. There could be no mistake as to how he met his death, for in addition to the deep line round his throat, his neck was broken as neatly as they could have done it at Newgate! As in the other case, there was nothing to show how he came by his death, no rope, no trace of footsteps or any struggle to lead one to suspect the presence of another person or persons. Yet from the facts it could not have been suicide.'

'I see you had some suspicion of your own,' said Flaxman Low.

'Well, yes, I had. But time has passed, and I now think I must have been mistaken. I must explain that the branches of the cedar you saw jut to within a few feet of the windows of the rooms occupied by Miss Montesson and Platt respectively at the time of death. I told you there were no traces of anyone having approached the house. It therefore struck me that some active person might have leaped from the cedar into the open windows and escaped in the same way, for the windows open vertically, and when both leaves are thrown back, there is a large aperture. But the murders were so purposeless and disconnected that they suggested irresponsible agency. I recollected Poe's story of the Rue Morgue, where, you remember, the crimes were committed by an ourang-outang. It seemed to me possible that Lampurt, who was of a morose and strange temper, might, among other things, have secretly imported an ape and turned it loose in the woods. I had a thorough search made in the park and grounds, but we found nothing, and I have long ago abandoned the theory.'

Low thought silently over the story for some time, then he asked for the dates of the three deaths. Fremantle answered categorically, and it appeared that all had taken place about the same season of the year – during summer, in fact. Upon this Mr Low made an offer to investigate the affair on psychical lines, if Montesson made no objection. In answer to this message Montesson took the next train down to Devon, and begged to be allowed to accompany Mr Low in his inquiries.

Flaxman Low quickly saw that Montesson might prove a very useful companion. He was a blond, heavily-built man, and plainly possessed of a strong will and temper. Low put aside his books and went off at once with Montesson to have a closer look at the Grey House while the daylight lasted.

It is difficult to give any adequate impression of the teeming exuberance of wild and tangled growth through which they had to cut their way. Young, lush, sappy leafage overlay and half disguised the dank rottenness of the older vegetation beneath. After wading more than breast-high through the matted reeds, below which the spreading stream was fast reducing the land to a swamp, they emerged into a fairly open space that had once been the lawn round the house.

Here brambles and lusty weeds now grew abundantly under the untended trees. Curious shrubs and plants flourished here and there. As they came up a stoat sneaked away by a narrow footpath, nettle-grown and caked with damp, which led past blackened bushes round the house. Otherwise the place was deserted, not a leaf seemed to move in the windless heat of the afternoon. The squat, grey face of the house was scarred across by a dark-leaved creeper, hung with orchid-like blossoms, a little to the left of which Low noticed the cedar mentioned by Dr Fremantle.

Low drew up at the weed-twisted, sunken little gate that gave upon the lawns and spoke for the first time.

'Tell me about it,' and he nodded towards the house.

Montesson repeated the story already told, but added further details. 'From here,' went on Montesson, 'you can see the exact spot where all these things took place. The upper of these two windows surrounded by the creeper and under the shadow of the cedar, belonged to my sister's room; the lower is that of the study where Platt died. The gravel path below ran the whole length of the house, but it is now over-grown. Has Fremantle told you of Lawrence?'

Low shook his head.

'I hate the very sight of the place!' said Montesson hoarsely. 'The mystery and the horror of it all seem in my blood. I can't forget! – My mother left on the day of Platt's death, and has never been here since. But when I came of age I resolved to make another attempt to live here, meaning to sift the past if I got the chance of doing so. I had the grounds cleared about the house, and after leaving Oxford, came down with a man of my own year, called Lawrence. We spent the Easter vacation here reading, and all went right enough. Meanwhile I had the house examined, thinking there might be a secret entrance or room, but nothing of the kind exists. This house is not haunted. Nothing has ever been seen or heard of a supernatural character – nothing but the same awful repetition of blind murder!'

After a few seconds he resumed.

'During the following summer Lawrence came down with me again. One hot evening, we were smoking as we walked up and down the gravel under the windows. It was bright moonlight, and I remember the heavy scent of those red flowers—' Montesson glanced round him strangely. 'I went in to fetch a cigar. It took me some minutes to find the box I wanted, and to light the cigar. When I came out, Lawrence lay crumpled up as if he had fallen from a height, and he was dead. Round his neck was the same bluish line I had seen in the two other cases. You can understand what it was to leave the man not five minutes before, in health and strength, and to come back to find him dead – hanged – to judge from appearances! But as usual, no trace of rope or struggle or murderer!'

After some further talk, Mr Low proposed to go into the house. It had evidently been deserted in haste. In the room once occupied by Miss Montesson, her girlish treasures still lay about, dusty, moth-eaten and discoloured. Montesson paused on the threshold. 'Poor little Fan! It's just as she left it!' he said hurriedly.

The cedar outside threw a gloomy shade into the room, and the fantastic red blossoms drooped motionless in the stagnant air.

'Was the window open when your sister was found?' inquired Low after he had examined the room.

'Yes, it was hot weather – early in August. This room has not been occupied since. After Platt's affair, I have always avoided this side of the house, so that it was only by chance Lawrence and I came round to this part of the lawn to smoke.'

'Then we may suppose that the danger, whatever it is, exists on this side of the house only?'

'So it seems,' replied Montesson.

'Your sister was last seen alive in this room? Platt in the room directly below? And your friend – what of him?'

'Lawrence was lying on the gravel path just under the study window. All of them have died under the shadow of the cedar. Did Fremantle give you his idea? Poor Lawrence's death disposed of that theory. No big ape could live in England all those five years in the open, and in any case it must have been seen some time in the interval.'

'I think so,' replied Low abstractedly. 'Now as to what we must do to try and get at the meaning of all this. Do you feel equal, considering all you have gone through in this house, do you feel equal to remaining here with me for a night or two?'

Montesson again glanced over his shoulder nervously.

'Yes,' he said. 'I know my nerves are not as stiff and steady as they should be, but I'll stand by you – especially as you would not find another man about here willing to run the risk. You see, it is not a ghost or any fanciful trouble, it means a real danger. Think over it, Mr Low, before you undertake so hazardous an attempt.'

Low looked into the blue eyes Montesson had fixed upon him. They were weary, anxious eyes, and, taken in combination with his compressed lips and square chin, told Low of the struggle this man constantly endured between his shaken nervous system and the strong will that mastered it.

'If you'll stand by me, I'll try to get to the bottom of it,' said Low.

'I wonder if I should allow you to risk your life in this way?' returned Montesson, passing his hand over his prematurely lined forehead.

'Why not? Besides it is my own wish. As for risking our lives – it is for the good of mankind.'

'I can't say I see it in that light,' said Montesson in surprise.

'If we lose our lives it will be in the effort to make another spot of earth clean and wholesome and safe for men to live on. Our duty to the public requires us to run a murderer to earth. Here we have a murderous power of some subtle kind; is it not quite as much our duty to destroy it if we can, even at risk to ourselves?'

The result of this conversation was an arrangement to pass the night at the Grey House. About ten o'clock they set out, intending to follow the path they had more or less successfully cleared for themselves in the afternoon. By Flaxman Low's advice, Montesson carried a long knife. The night was unusually hot and still, and lit only by a thin moon as they made their way along, stumbling over matted weeds and roots and literally feeling for the path, until they came to the little gate by the lawn. There they stopped a moment to look at the house, standing out among its strange sea of overgrowth, the dim moon low on the horizon, glinting palely upon the windows and over the deserted countryside. As they waited a nightbird hooted and flapped its way across the open.

At any moment they might be at hand-grips with the mysterious power of death which haunted the place. The warm lush-scented air and the sinister shadows seemed charged with some ominous influence. As they drew near the house Low perceived a sweet, heavy odour.

'What is it?' he asked.

'It comes from those scarlet flowers. It's unbearable! Lampurt imported the thing,' replied Montesson irritably.

'Which room will you spend the night in?' asked Low as they gained the hall.

Montesson hesitated. 'Have you ever heard the expression "grey with fear"?' he said, laughing in the dark. 'I'm that!'

Low did not like the laugh, it was only one remove, and that a very little one, from hysteria.

'We won't find out much unless we each remain alone and with open windows as they did,' said Low.

Montesson shook himself.

'No, I suppose not. *They* were each alone when – good night. I'll call if anything happens, and you must do the same for me. For heaven's sake, don't go to sleep!'

'And remember,' added Low, 'with your knife to cut at anything that touches you.' Then he stood at the study door and listened to Montesson's heavy steps as they passed up the stairs, for he had elected to pass the night in his sister's room. Low heard him walk across the floor above and throw wide the window.

When Mr Low turned into the study and tried to open the window there, he found it impossible to do so, as the creeper outside had fastened upon the woodwork, binding the sashes together. There was but one thing left for him to do, he must go outside and stand where Lawrence had stood on the fatal night. He let himself out softly and went round to the south side of the house.

There he paced up and down in the shadows for perhaps an hour.

In the deceptive, iridescent moonlight a pallid head seemed to wag at him from the gloom below the cedar, but, moving towards it, he grasped only the yellow bunched blossom of a giant ragwort. Then he stood still and looked up into the branches above; the gnarled black branches with their fringes of black sticky leaves. Fremantle's theory of the ape passing stealthily among them to spring upon his victims found a sudden horror of possibility in Low's mind. He imagined the girl awaking in the brute's cruel hands—

Out upon the quiet brooding of the night broke a scream – or rather a roar, a harsh, jagged, pulsating roar that ceased as abruptly as it had begun.

Without a moment's consideration, Mr Low seized the branch nearest to him and, swinging himself up into the tree, he climbed with a frantic effort towards the window of Montesson's room, from which he was almost sure the sound had come. Being an unusually active and athletic man he leaped from the branch towards the open window, and fell headlong in upon the floor. As he did so, something seemed to pass him, something swift and sinuous that might have been a snake, and disappear out of the window!

Remembering a candle on the toilet table, he lit it when he regained his feet and looked about him.

Montesson lay on the floor, 'crumpled up' as he had himself described Lawrence's position. Low recalled this with misgiving as he hurried to his side. A dark smear like blood was on Montesson's cheek, but though unconscious, he was still alive. Low lifted him on to the bed and did what he could to rouse him, but without success. He lay rigid, breathing the slow, almost imperceptible respiration of deep stupor.

Low was about to go to the window, when the candle suddenly went out, and he was left in the increasing darkness, to all intents alone, to face an unknown though tangible assailant.

Silence had again fallen upon the house – that is, the silence of night, and woodlands, and many-folded leafage, and the things that go by night. He stood by the window and listened. His senses were acute and throbbing: he felt as if he could hear for miles. The scent of the scarlet blossoms rose like deadening fumes into his brain, and he drew away from the window, and, feeling strangely spent, threw himself upon a couch. Then he drew out the knife at his belt and strung himself up to watchfulness with an effort.

He knew that the attack he had to expect would be likely to come from the direction of the window. He saw the faint, swimming moonlight that fell through the leaves and tendrils of the creeper fade slowly away. Probably clouds were coming up over the sky, for the steamy heat was even more oppressive.

The low window-sill was scarcely more than a foot above the floor, and presently he fancied something was moving along the carpet among the entangling shadows of the leaves, but the darkness was now intensified, and he could not be sure. Montesson's breathing had become quieter. It was the dead hour of the night; hardly a sound was to be heard.

Suddenly Low felt a soft touch upon his knee. His whole consciousness had been so absorbed in the act of listening that this unexpected appeal to another sense startled him. Here and there, rapid, soft, and light, the touches passed over his body. It might have been some animal nosing about him in the dark. Then a smooth, cold touch fell upon his cheek.

Low sprang up, and slashed about him in the darkness with his knife.

In that instant the thing closed with him – a flexuous, snaky thing that flung its coils about his limbs and body in one swift spring like a curling whiplash!

Flaxman Low was all but helpless in the winding grasp of what? – The tentacles of some strange creature? Or was it some great snake, this sentient thing that was feeling for his throat? There was not an instant to lose. The knife was pressed against his body; with a violent effort he drew it sharply, edge outwards, against the tightening coils. A spurt of clammy fluid fell upon his hand, and the thing loosed and fell away from him into the stifling gloom.

In the morning, Montesson came to himself in one of the lower rooms at the other side of the house. Fremantle was beside him.

'What's the matter?' he asked. 'Ah, I remember now. There's Low. It has beaten us again, Fremantle! It is hopeless. I don't know what happened – I was not asleep, when I found myself seized, lifted up, drawn towards the window, and strangled by living ropes. Look at Low!' he went on harshly, raising himself. 'Why, man, you're all over blood!'

Flaxman Low glanced down at his hands.

'Looks like it,' he said.

'It has beaten even you, Low!' went on Montesson. 'There is something much more terrible and tangible than a ghost in this cursed house! See here!'

He pulled down his collar. A faint bluish circle with suffused dots was drawn round his throat.

'It is some deadly species of snake,' exclaimed Fremantle.

Low sat down astride a chair thoughtfully.

'I'm sorry to disagree with both of you. But I am inclined to think it is not a snake, and on the other hand I fancy it has a great deal to do with what we may roughly call a ghost. The whole evidence points in only one direction.'

'You mustn't let your prejudice in favour of psychical problems run away with your reason,' said Fremantle drily. 'Has a ghost actual, palpable power? – To go further, has it blood?'

Montesson, who had been looking at his neck in the glass, turned quickly. 'It's some horrible thing in nature! Something between a snake and an octopus! What do you say to it, Low?'

Low looked up gravely.

'In spite of Fremantle's objections, the steps from beginning to end are very clear.'

Fremantle and Montesson exchanged a glance of incredulity.

'My dear fellow, much learning has warped your mind,' said Fremantle with an embarrassed laugh.

'First of all,' continued Low, 'we know where all the deaths have occurred.'

'To speak precisely, they have all occurred in different places,' interposed Fremantle.

'True; but within a strictly limited area. The slight differences have been of material help to me. In all cases they have occurred in the vicinity of one thing.'

'The cedar!' cried Montesson, with some excitement.

'That was my first idea – now I refer to the wall. Will you tell me the probable weight of Lawrence and Platt at the date of death?'

'Platt was a small man – perhaps under nine stone. Lawrence, though much taller, was thin, and could not have weighed more than eleven. As for poor little Fan, she was only a slip of a girl.'

'Three people have been killed – one has escaped. In what way do you differ from the others, Montesson?' asked Low.

'If you mean I'm heavier, I certainly am. I scale something like fifteen. But what has that to do with it?'

'Everything. The coils have evidently not sufficient compressive power to destroy life by strangulation simply – there must be suspension as well. You were simply too heavy for them to tackle.'

'Coils of what?'

'Of this.' Low held up a tapering, reddish-brown tendon or line, which had red curved triangular teeth set on it at intervals.

The two other men stared at this object, and then Montesson burst out: 'The creeper on the wall!' he said, in a tone of disappointment. 'It couldn't be! Besides, has a plant blood?'

'Let us go and look at it,' said Low. 'This creeper has never been cut because it withers away every winter to the ground and grows again in the spring. Look here!' He took out his knife and cut a leathery shoot. A crimson stain spurted out on his cuff. 'The only person, as far as I can gather, who cut this plant was Mr Lampurt in nailing it to the wall. He died of shock when he saw the red stain on his finger, as he knew something of its deadly properties. But though stupefying – as your condition last night proved, Montesson – they are not fatal. Even to stupefy they must get into the blood. Now the deaths have all occurred within reach of the tendrils of this plant. And all have happened at the same season of the year, that is to say, at the time when it attains its full annual strength and growth. Another point in favour of Montesson's escape was the dryness of the season. The growth is not quite so good as usual this summer, is it?'

'No, the tendrils are thinner – a good deal thinner and smaller.'

'Just so. Therefore your weight saved you, though you were stupefied by the punctures of the thorns. I feared that, and warned you to use your knife.'

'But the brain of the thing?' cried Fremantle. 'Why, man, has a plant will and knowledge and malevolence?'

'Not of itself, as I believe,' answered Low. 'Perhaps you will prefer to attribute much to the long arm of coincidence, but the explanation I can offer is one that has long been held by occultists in other countries. Pythagoras and others have taught that the forms of incarnation change as the soul raises or debases itself during each spell of Life. Connect with this the belief of the Brahmins, and I may add of various African tribes, that an earth-bound spirit, at the moment of a premature or sudden death, may pass into plants or trees of certain species, by virtue of an inherent attraction possessed by these plants for such entities. To go further, it is said that these degraded souls have intervals during which they have power of voluntary action to do good or evil, and such action has influence on their future incarnations.'

'What do you mean? What do you intend us to believe?' Montesson said, and stopped.

'It is hard to put it into words in these latter days of unbelief,' said Low, 'but the evidence goes to show that a man – presumably not a good man – dies a sudden death near this plant, even inoculated with its sap. Fremantle knows this plant to be a Malayan creeper, belonging to a family that possess strange powers and properties. I may recall the old story of the upas tree, and more lately still the murder tree discovered near Kolwe, in East Africa, by Herr Boltze. There are also other instances.'

'It is incredible!' said Fremantle almost angrily.

'I don't ask you to believe it,' said Flaxman Low quietly. 'I only tell you such beliefs exist. Montesson can do something towards proving my theory. Let him have the plant destroyed, and judge by results.'

The tendril of the creeper severed by Mr Low in his struggle was presented by him to the authorities at Kew.

Mr Montesson has acted upon Mr Flaxman Low's suggestions. The Grey House is now occupied and safe, and it is a strange fact that no plant, not even the hardy ivy, will live where the red-blossomed creeper once grew.

THE LIZARD

By C J Cutcliffe Hyne (1866–1944)

C J Cutcliffe Hyne was a prolific and popular writer from the 1890s to the 1930s, particularly well-known for his stories of the roguish adventurer Captain Kettle, which were sufficiently popular to warrant the making of a silent film featuring the character in the early 1920s. Unfortunately, read today, the Captain Kettle tales are marred by racism and the prejudices of the day. Much of Hyne's work has now been forgotten, although The Lost Continent *has been regularly reprinted in the century and more since it was first published in 1899, and has some claims to being the classic novel of the lost civilisation of Atlantis. Other novels, such as* The New Eden *(a scientist places a young man and woman on a remote island to test his theories) and* Abbs, His Story Through Many Ages *(a variant of the legend of the Wandering Jew), have not been so lucky. Hyne began his career as a writer in his early twenties and his very first novel,* Beneath Your Very Boots, *published in 1889, focuses, like 'The Lizard', on a man who finds more than he expected when he goes caving. In the novel, Hyne's hero encounters an entire civilisation in the depths of the earth; in the short story, the narrator discovers a long-hibernating monster.*

The Strand Magazine *June 1898*

It is not in the least expected that the general public will believe the statements which will be made in this paper. They are written to catch the eye of Mr Wilfred Cecil Cording (or Cordy) if he still lives, or in the event of his death to carry some news of his last movements to any of his still existing friends and relations. Further details may be had from me (by any of these interested people) at Poste Restante, Kettlewell, Wharfedale, Yorkshire. My name is Chesney, and I am sufficiently well known there for letters to be forwarded to wherever I may be at the moment.

The matters in question happened two years ago on the last day of August. I had a small, high-ground shoot near Kettlewell, but that morning all the upper parts of the hill were thick with dense mist, and shooting was out of the question. However, I had been going it pretty hard since the Twelfth, and was not sorry for an off-day, the more so as there was a newly-found cave in the neighbourhood which I was anxious to explore thoroughly. Incidentally I may mention that cave-hunting and shooting were my only two amusements.

It was my keeper who brought me news to the inn about the impossibility of shooting, and I suggested to him that he should come with me to inspect the cave. He made some sort of excuse – I forget what – and I did not press the matter further. He was a Kettlewell native, and the dalesmen up there look upon the local caves with more awe than respect. They will not own up to believing in bogles, but I fancy their creed runs that way. I used to have a contempt for their qualms, but latterly I have somehow or other learned to respect them.

I had taken unwilling helpers cave-hunting with me before, and found them such a nuisance that I had made up my mind not to be bothered with them again; so, as I say, I did not press for the keeper's society, but took candles, matches in a bottle, some magnesium wire, a small coil of rope, and a large flask of whisky, and set off alone.

The clouds above were wet, and a fine rain fell persistently. I tramped off along one of the three main roads that lead from the village, but which road it was had better remain hidden for the present. And in time I got off this road and cut over the moor.

What I was looking for was a fresh scar on the hillside, caused by a roof-fall in one of the countless caves which honeycomb this limestone district; and, although I had got my bearings pretty accurately, the fog was so thick up there that I had to take a good dozen casts before I hit upon the place.

I had not seen it since the 10th of August, when I first stumbled across it by accident whilst I was going over the hill to see how the birds promised for the following Twelfth; and I was a good deal annoyed to find by the boot-marks that quite a lot of people had visited it in the interval. However, I hoped that the larger part of these were made by shepherds, and perhaps by my own keepers, and, remembering their qualms, trusted that I might find the interior still untampered with.

The cave was easy enough to enter. There was a funnel-shaped slide of peat-earth and mud and clay to start with, well pitted with boot-marks; and then there was a tumbled wall of boulders, slanting inwards, down which I crawled face uppermost till the light behind me dwindled. The way was getting pretty murky, so I lit up a candle to avoid accidents, stepped knee-deep into a lively stream of water, and went briskly ahead. It was an ordinary enough limestone cave so far, with inferior stalactites, and a good deal of wet everywhere. It did not appear to have been disturbed, and I stepped along cheerfully.

Presently I got a bit of a shock. The roof above began to droop downwards, slowly but relentlessly. It seemed as though my way was soon going to be blocked. However, the water beneath deepened, and so I waded along to inspect as far on as possible. It was a cold job, for the water was icy, but then I am a bit of an enthusiast about cave-hunting, and it takes more than a trifle of discomfort to stop me.

The roof came down and down till I was forced into the water up to my chin, and the air, too, was none of the best. I was beginning to get disappointed; it looked as if I had got wet through to the bone with freezing cold cave-water for no adequate result.

However, there is no accounting for the freaks of caves. Just when I fancied I was at the end of my tether, up went the roof again; I was able to stand erect once more; and a dozen yards farther on I came out on to dry rock, and was able to have a rest and a drop of whisky. The roof had quite disappeared to candle-light overhead, so I burned a foot of magnesium wire for a better inspection. It was really a magnificent cave.

But I did not stop to make any accurate measurements or drawings then, and, for reasons which will appear, I have not been near to do so since. I was too cold to care for prolonged admiration, and I wanted to (so to speak) annex the whole of the cave's main contours before I took my departure. I was first man in, and wished to be able to describe the whole of my find. There is a certain keen emulation about these matters amongst cave-hunters.

So I walked on over the flat floor of rock, stepping over and through pools, and round boulders, and dodging round stalactites, which hung from the unseen roof above, and slipping between slimy palings of stalagmite which sprouted from the floor. And then I came to a regular big subterranean tarn, which stretched right across the cavern.

Spaces were big here, and the candle did little to show them.

It burned brightly enough, and that pleased me: one has to be very careful in cave-hunting about foul air, because once overcome by that, it means certain death. The air in this cave, however, did not altogether pass muster; there was something new about it, and anything new in cave smells is always suspicious. It wasn't the smell of peat, or iron, or sandstone, or limestone, or fungus, though all these are common enough in caves; it was a sort of faint musky smell; and I had got an idea that it was in flavour rather sickly. It is hard to define these things, but that smell, although it might very possibly lead to a new discovery, somehow did not cheer me. In fact, at times, when I inhaled a deeper breath of it than usual, it came very near to making my flesh creep.

However, hesitations of this kind are not business. I nipped off another foot of magnesium wire, lit it at the candle, and held the flaming end high above my head. Before me the water of the tarn lay motionless as a mirror of black glass; the sides vignetted away into alleys and bays; the roof was a groined and fretted dome, far overhead; and at the farther side was a beach of white tumbled limestone.

I pitched a stone into the black water, and the mirror broke (I was pleased to think) for the first time during a million years into ripples. Yes, it's worth even a year of hard cave-hunting to do a thing like that.

The stone sank with a luscious pop. The water was very deep. But I was wet to the neck already, and didn't mind a swim. So with a lump of clay I stuck one candle in my cap, set up a couple more on the dry rock as a lighthouse to guide my return, lowered myself into the black water, and struck out. The smell of musk oppressed me, and I fancied it was growing more pronounced. So I didn't dawdle. Roughly, I guessed the pool to be some thirty-five yards across. I landed amongst the white broken limestone on the farther side, with a shiver and a scramble, and there was no doubt about the smell of musk now; it was strong enough to make me cough. But when I had stood up, got the candle in my hand again, and peered about through the dark, a thrill came through me as I thought I guessed at the cause. A dozen yards farther on amongst the tumbled stone was a broken 'cast', where some monstrous uncouth animal had been entombed in the forgotten ages of the past, and mouldered away and left only the outer shell of its form and shape. For ages this, too, had endured; indeed, it had only been violated by the eroding touch of the water and some earth tremor within the last few days; perhaps at the same time that the 'slip' was made in the moor far above, which gave an entrance to the caves.

The 'cast' was half full of splintered rubbish, but even as it was, I could see the contour of its sides in many places, and with care the debris could be scooped out, and a workman could with plaster of Paris make an exact model of this beast, which had been lost to the world's knowledge for so many weary millions of years. It had been some sort of a lizard or a crocodile, and, in fancy, I was beginning to picture its restored shape posed in the National Museum, with my name underneath as discoverer, when my eye fell on something amongst the rubble which brought me to earth with a jar. I stooped and picked it up. It was a common white-handled penknife, of the variety sold by stationers for a shilling. On one side of it was the name of Wilfred Cecil Cording (or Cordy), scratched apparently with a nail. The work was neat enough to start with, but the engraver had wearied with his job; and the 'Cecil' was slipshod, and the surname too scratchy to be certain about.

On the hot impulse of the moment, I threw the knife far from me into the black water, and swore. It is more than a bit unpleasant for an explorer who has made a big discovery to find that he has been forestalled. But since then I have more than once regretted the hard things I said against Cording (if that is his name) in the heat of my first passion. If the man is alive, I apologise to him. If, as I strongly suspect, he came to a horrible end there in the cave, I tender my regrets to his relatives.

I looked upon the cast of the saurian now with the warmth of discovery quite gone. I was conscious of cold, and, moreover, the musky smell of the place was vastly unpleasant. And I think I should straightway have gone back to daylight and a change of clothes down in Kettlewell, but for one thing. I seemed somehow or other to trace on the rock beneath me the outline of another cast. It was hazy, as a thing of the kind would be if seen through the medium of sparsely transparent limestone, and by the light of a solitary paraffin wax candle. I kicked at it petulantly.

Some flakes of stone shelled off, and I distinctly heard a more extensive crack. I kicked again, harder – with all my might, in fact. More flakes shelled away, and there was a little volley of cracks this time. It did not feel like kicking against stone. It was like kicking against something that gave. And I could have sworn that the musky smell increased. I felt a curious glow coming over me that was part fright, part excitement, part, I fancy, nausea; but plucked up my courage and held my breath, and kicked again, and again, and again. The laminae of limestone flew up in tinkling showers. There was no doubt about there being something springy underneath now, and that it was the dead carcass of another lizard I hadn't a doubt. Here was luck, here was a find. Here was I the discoverer of the body of a prehistoric beast, preserved in the limestone down through all the ages, just as mammoths have been preserved in Siberian ice.

The quarrying of my boot heel was too slow for me. I stuck my candle by its clay socket to a rock, and picked up a handy boulder and beat away the sheets of the stone with that; and all the time I toiled, the springiness of the carcass beneath distinctly helped me. The smell of musk nearly made me sick, but I stuck to the work. There was no doubt about it now. More than once I barked my knuckles against the harsh, scaly skin of the beast itself – against the skin of this anachronism, which ought to have perished body and bones ten million years ago. I remember wondering whether they would make me a baronet for the discovery. They do make scientific baronets nowadays for the bigger finds.

Then of a sudden I got a start: I could have sworn the dead flesh moved beneath me.

But I shouted aloud at myself in contempt. 'Pah!' I said. 'Ten million years: the ghost is rather stale by this!' And I set to work afresh, beating away the stone which covered the beast from my sight.

But again I got a start, and this time it was a more solid one. After I had delivered my blow, and whilst I was raising my weapon for another, a splinter of stone broke away as if pressed up from below, flipped up in the air, and tinkled back to a standstill. My blood chilled, and for a moment the loneliness of that unknown cave oppressed me. But I told myself that I was an old hand; that this was childishness; and, in fact, pulled myself together. I refused to accept the hint. I deliberately put the candle so as to throw a better light, swallowed back my tremors, and battered afresh at the laminated rock.

Twice more I was given warnings, and disregarded them in the name of what I was pleased to call cold common reason; but the third time I dropped the battering stone as though it burnt me, and darted back with the most horrible shock of terror which (I make bold to say) any man could endure and still retain his senses.

There was no doubt about it – the beast was actually moving.

Yes, moving and alive. It was writhing, and straining, and struggling to leave its rocky bed, where it had lain quiet through all those countless cycles of time, and I watched it in a very petrification of terror. Its efforts threw up whole basketfuls of splintered stone at a time. I could see the muscles of its back ripple at each effort. I could see the exposed part of its body grow in size every time it wrenched at the walls of that semi-eternal prison.

Then, as I looked, it doubled up its back like a bucking horse, and drew out its stumpy head and long feelers, giving out the while a thin, small scream like a hurt child; and then with another effort it pulled out its long tail and stood upon the debris of the limestone, panting with a new-found life.

I gazed upon it with a sickly fascination. Its body was about the bigness of two horses. Its head was curiously short, but the mouth opened back almost to the forearm; and sprouting from the nose were two enormous feelers, or antennae, each at least six feet long, and tipped with fleshy tendrils like fingers, which opened and shut tremulously. Its four legs were jointless, and ended in mere club-feet, or callosities; its tail was long, supple, and fringed on the top with a saw-like row of scales. In colour, it was a bright grass-green, all except the feelers, which were of a livid blue. But mere words go poorly for a description, and the beast was outside the vocabulary of today. It conveyed, somehow or other, a horrible sense of deformity, which made one physically ill to look upon it.

But worst of all was the musky smell. That increased till it became well-nigh unendurable, and though I half-strangled myself to suppress a sound, I had to yield at last and give my feelings vent. The beast heard me. I could not see that it had any ears, but anyway it distinctly heard me. Worse, it hobbled round clumsily with its jointless legs, and waved its feelers in my direction. I could not make out that it had any eyes – anyway, they did not show distinct from the rough skin of its head; its sensitiveness seemed to lie in those fathom-long feelers and in the fleshy fingers which twitched and grappled at the end of them.

Then it opened its great jaws – which hinged, as I said, down by the forearm – and yawned cavernously, and came towards me. It seemed to have no trace of fear or hesitation. It hobbled clumsily on, exhibiting its monstrous deformity in every movement, and preceded always by those hateful feelers, which seemed to be endued with an impish activity.

For a while I stayed in my place, too paralysed by horror at this awful thing I had dragged up from the forgotten dead, to move or breathe. But then one of its livid blue feelers – a hard, armoured thing like a lobster's – touched me, and the fleshy fingers at the end of it pawed my face and burned me like nettles. I leaped into movement again. The beast was hungry after its fast of ten million years; it was trying to make me its prey: those fearful jaws—

I turned and ran.

It followed me. In the feeble light of the one solitary candle I could see it following accurately in my track, with the waving feelers and their twitching fingers preceding it. It had pace, too. Its gait, with those clumsy, jointless legs, reminded one of a barrel-bellied sofa suddenly endowed with life, and careering over rough ground. But it distinctly had pace, and what was worse, the pace increased. At first it had the rust of those eternal ages to work out of its cankered joints; but this stiffness passed away, and presently it was following me with a speed equal to my own.

If this huge green beast had shown anger, or eagerness, or any of those things, it would have been less horrible; but it was absolutely unemotional in its hunt, and this helped to paralyse me; and in the end, when it drove me into a *cul-de-sac* amongst the rocks, I was very near surrendering myself through sheer terror to what seemed the inevitable. I wondered dully whether there had been another beast entombed beside it, and whether that had eaten the man who owned the penknife.

But the idea warmed me up. I had a stout knife in my own pocket, and after some fumbling got it out and opened the blade. The feelers with their fringe of fumbling fingers were close to me: I slashed at them viciously, and felt my knife grate against their armour. I might as well have hacked at an iron rail.

Still, the attempt did me good. There is an animal love for fighting stowed away in the bottom of all of us somewhere, and mine woke then. I don't know that I expected to win; but I did intend to do the largest possible amount of damage before I was caught. I made a rush, stepped with one foot on the beast's creeping back, and leaped astern of him; and the beast gave its thin, small, whistling scream, and turned quickly in chase after me.

The pace was getting terrific. We doubled, and turned, and sprawled, and leapt amongst the slimy boulders, and every time we came to close quarters I stabbed at the beast with my knife, but without ever finding a joint in its armour. The tough skin gave to the weight of the blows, it is true, but it was like stabbing with a stick upon leather.

It was clear, though, that this could not go on. The beast grew in strength and activity, and probably in dumb anger, though actually it was unemotional as ever; but I was every moment growing more blown and more bruised and more exhausted.

At last I tripped and fell. The beast with its clumsy waddle shot past me before it could pull up, and in desperation I threw one arm and my knees around its grass-green tail, and with my spare hand drove the knife with the full of my force into the underneath part of its body.

That woke it at last. It writhed, and it plunged, and it bucked with a frenzy that I had never seen before, and its scream grew in piercingness till it was strong as the whistle of a steam-engine. But still I hung doggedly on to my place, and planted my vicious blows. The great beast doubled and tried to reach me; it flung its livid blue feelers backwards in vain efforts: I was beyond its clutch. And then, with my weight still on its back, it gave over dancing about the floor of the cavern, and set off at its hobbling gait directly for the water.

Not till it reached the brink did I slip off; but I saw it plunge in; I saw it swim strongly with its tail; and then I saw it dive and disappear for good.

And what next? I took to the water too, and swam as I had never swum before – swam for dear life to the opposite side. I knew that if I waited to cool my thoughts I should never pluck up courage for the attempt. It was then or not at all. It was risk the horrors of that passage, or stay where I was and starve – and be eaten.

How I got across I do not know. How I landed I cannot tell. How I got down the windings of the cave and through that water-alley is more than I can say. And whether the beast followed me I do not know either. I got to daylight again somehow, staggering like a drunken man. I struggled down off the moor, and on to the village, and noted how the people ran from me. At the inn the landlord cried out as though I had been the plague. It seemed that the musky smell that I brought with me was unendurable, though, by this time, the mere detail of a smell was far beneath my notice. But I was stripped from my stinking clothes, and washed, and put to bed, and a doctor came and gave me an opiate; and when twelve hours later wakefulness came to me again, I had the sense to hold my tongue. All the village wanted to know from whence came that hateful odour of musk, but I said, stupidly, I did not know. I said I must have fallen into something.

And there the matter ends for the present. I go no more cave-hunting, and I offer no help to those who do. But if the man who owned that white-handled penknife is alive, I should like to compare experiences with him; and if, as I strongly suspect, he is dead, these pages may be of interest to his relatives. He was not known in Kettlewell or any of the other villages where I inquired, but he could very well have come over the hills from Pateley Bridge way. 'Cording' was the name scratched on the knife, or 'Cordy', I could not be sure which; and, as I have said, mine is Chesney, and I can be heard of at the Kettlewell post-office, though I have given up the shooting on the moor near there. Somehow, the air of the district sickens me. There seems to be a taint in it.

THE DANCING PARTNER

By Jerome K Jerome (1859–1927)

Born in Walsall, Jerome K Jerome moved with his family to London as a boy and was educated at a grammar school in Marylebone. As a young man, he had a succession of jobs, from railway clerk and schoolteacher to actor in a touring repertory company, before choosing to become a journalist, producing essays and comic pieces for a number of weekly and monthly magazines. He is best remembered today for Three Men in a Boat, *a classic work of English comic fiction, in which a trio of middle-class Englishmen bumble their way through a boating holiday on the Thames. However, Jerome was a writer with plenty of other achievements to his name.* Three Men on the Bummel, *the sequel to his most famous book, in which the same three hapless heroes take a cycling tour through Germany, is almost as funny as its predecessor; several of his plays were London stage successes in their day; and his autobiography remains well worth reading. In the 1890s, he was also the joint editor, with Robert Barr, of* The Idler, *in the pages of which 'The Dancing Partner' first appeared. This tale of an automaton escaping the control of its maker, with catastrophic consequences, is part of a sequence of interconnected stories published in the magazine, which explains the somewhat abrupt way in which the narrative begins.*

The Idler *March 1893*

'This story,' commenced MacShaugnassy, 'comes from Furtwangen, a small town in the Black Forest. There lived there a very wonderful old fellow named Nicholaus Geibel. His business was the making of mechanical toys, at which work he had acquired an almost European reputation. He made rabbits that would emerge from the heart of a cabbage, flop their ears, smooth their whiskers, and disappear again; cats that would wash their faces, and mew so naturally that dogs would mistake them for real cats, and fly at them; dolls, with phonographs concealed within them, that would raise their hats and say, "Good morning; how do you do?", and some that would even sing a song.

'But he was something more than a mere mechanic; he was an artist. His work was with him a hobby, almost a passion. His shop was filled with all manner of strange things that never would, or could, be sold – things he had made for the pure love of making them. He had contrived a mechanical donkey that would trot for two hours by means of stored electricity, and trot, too, much faster than the live article, and with less need for exertion on the part of the driver; a bird that would shoot up into the air, fly round and round in a circle, and drop to earth at the exact spot from where it started; a skeleton that, supported by an upright iron bar, would dance a hornpipe; a life-size lady doll that could play the fiddle; and a gentleman with a hollow inside who could smoke a pipe and drink more lager beer than any three average German students put together, which is saying much.

'Indeed, it was the belief of the town that old Geibel could make a man capable of doing everything that a respectable man need want to do. One day he made a man who did too much, and it came about in this way:

'Young Doctor Follen had a baby, and the baby had a birthday. Its first birthday put Doctor Follen's household into somewhat of a flurry, but on the occasion of its second birthday, Mrs Doctor Follen gave a ball in honour of the event. Old Geibel and his daughter Olga were among the guests.

'During the afternoon of the next day some three or four of Olga's bosom friends, who had also been present at the ball, dropped in to have a chat about it. They naturally fell to discussing the men, and to criticising their dancing. Old Geibel was in the room, but he appeared to be absorbed in his newspaper, and the girls took no notice of him.

'"There seem to be fewer men who can dance at every ball you go to," said one of the girls.

'"Yes, and don't the ones who can give themselves airs," said another. "They make quite a favour of asking you."

'"And how stupidly they talk," added a third. "They always say exactly the same things: 'How charming you are looking tonight.' 'Do you often go to Vienna? Oh, you should, it's delightful.' 'What a charming dress you have on.' 'What a warm day it has been.' 'Do you like Wagner?' I do wish they'd think of something new."

'"Oh, I never mind how they talk," said a fourth. "If a man dances well, he may be a fool for all I care."

'"He generally is," slipped in a thin girl, rather spitefully.

'"I go to a ball to dance," continued the previous speaker, not noticing the interruption. "All I ask of a partner is that he shall hold me firmly, take me round steadily, and not get tired before I do."

'"A clockwork figure would be the thing for you," said the girl who had interrupted.

'"Bravo!" cried one of the others, clapping her hands. "What a capital idea!"

'"What's a capital idea?" they asked.

'"Why, a clockwork dancer, or, better still, one that would go by electricity and never run down."

'The girls took up the idea with enthusiasm.

'"Oh, what a lovely partner he would make," said one. "He would never kick you, or tread on your toes."

'"Or tear your dress," said another.

'"Or get out of step."

'"Or get giddy and lean on you."

'"And he would never want to mop his face with his handkerchief. I do hate to see a man do that after every dance."

'"And wouldn't want to spend the whole evening in the supper room."

'"Why, with a phonograph inside him to grind out all the stock remarks, you would not be able to tell him from a real man," said the girl who had first suggested the idea.

'"Oh, yes, you would," said the thin girl. "He would be so much nicer."

'Old Geibel had laid down his paper, and was listening with both his ears. On one of the girls glancing in his direction, however, he hurriedly hid himself again behind it.

'After the girls were gone, he went into his workshop, where Olga heard him walking up and down, and every now and then chuckling to himself; and that night he talked to her a good deal about dancing and dancing men – asked what they usually said and did – what dances were most popular – what steps were gone through, with many other questions bearing on the subject.

'Then for a couple of weeks he kept much to his factory, and was very thoughtful and busy, though prone at unexpected moments to break into a quiet low laugh, as if enjoying a joke that nobody else knew of.

'A month later another ball took place in Furtwangen. On this occasion it was given by old Wenzel, the wealthy timber merchant, to celebrate his niece's betrothal, and Geibel and his daughter were again among the invited.

'When the hour arrived to set out, Olga sought her father. Not finding him in the house, she tapped at the door of his workshop. He appeared in his shirt-sleeves, looking hot but radiant.

'"Don't wait for me," he said. "You go on. I'll follow you. I've got something to finish."

'As she turned to obey he called after her, "Tell them I'm going to bring a young man with me – such a nice young man, and an excellent dancer. All the girls will like him." Then he laughed and closed the door.

'Her father generally kept his doings secret from everybody, but she had a pretty shrewd suspicion of what he had been planning, and so, to a certain extent, was able to prepare the guests for what was coming. Anticipation ran high, and the arrival of the famous mechanist was eagerly awaited.

'At length the sound of wheels was heard outside, followed by a great commotion in the passage, and old Wenzel himself, his jolly face red with excitement and suppressed laughter, burst into the room and announced in stentorian tones:

'"Herr Geibel – and a friend!"

'Herr Geibel and his "friend" entered, greeted with shouts of laughter and applause, and advanced to the centre of the room.

'"Allow me, ladies and gentlemen," said Herr Geibel, "to introduce you to my friend. Lieutenant Fritz. Fritz, my dear fellow, bow to the ladies and gentlemen."

'Geibel placed his hand encouragingly on Fritz's shoulder, and the lieutenant bowed low, accompanying the action with a harsh clicking noise in his throat, unpleasantly suggestive of a death rattle. But that was only a detail.

'"He walks a little stiffly." (Old Geibel took his arm and walked him forward a few steps. He certainly did walk stiffly.) "But then, walking is not his forte. He is essentially a dancing man. I have only been able to teach him the waltz as yet, but at that he is faultless. Come, which of you ladies may I introduce him to as a partner? He keeps perfect time; he never gets tired; he won't kick you or tread on your dress; he will hold you as firmly as you like, and go as quickly or as slowly as you please; he never gets giddy; and he is full of conversation. Come, speak up for yourself, my boy."'

'The old gentleman twisted one of the buttons at the back of his coat, and immediately Fritz opened his mouth, and in thin tones that appeared to proceed from the back of his head, remarked suddenly, "May I have the pleasure?" and then shut his mouth again with a snap.

'That Lieutenant Fritz had made a strong impression on the company was undoubted, yet none of the girls seemed inclined to dance with him. They looked askance at his waxen face, with its staring eyes and fixed smile, and shuddered. At last old Geibel came to the girl who had conceived the idea.

'"It is your own suggestion, carried out to the letter," said Geibel. "An electric dancer. You owe it to the gentleman to give him a trial."

'She was a bright, saucy little girl, fond of a frolic. Her host added his entreaties, and she consented.

'Herr Geibel fixed the figure to her. Its right arm was screwed round her waist, and held her firmly; its delicately-jointed left hand was made to fasten itself upon her right. The old toymaker showed her how to regulate its speed, and how to stop it, and release herself.

'"It will take you round in a complete circle," he explained. "Be careful that no one knocks against you, and alters its course."

'The music struck up. Old Geibel put the current in motion, and Annette and her strange partner began to dance.

'For a while everyone stood watching them. The figure performed its purpose admirably. Keeping perfect time and step, and holding its little partner tight, clasped in an unyielding embrace, it revolved steadily, pouring forth at the same time a constant flow of squeaky conversation, broken by brief intervals of grinding silence.

'"How charming you are looking tonight," it remarked in its thin, far-away voice. "What a lovely day it has been. Do you like dancing? How well our steps agree. You will give me another, won't you? Oh, don't be so cruel. What a charming gown you have on. Isn't waltzing delightful? I could go dancing for ever – with you. Have you had supper?"

'As she grew more familiar with the uncanny creature, the girl's nervousness wore off, and she entered into the fun of the thing.

'"Oh, he's just lovely," she cried, laughing. "I could go on dancing with him all my life."

'Couple after couple now joined them, and soon all the dancers in the room were whirling round behind them. Nicholaus Geibel stood looking on, beaming with childish delight at his success.

'Old Wenzel approached him, and whispered something in his ear. Geibel laughed and nodded, and the two worked their way quietly towards the door.

'"This is the young people's house tonight," said Wenzel, as soon as they were outside. "You and I will have a quiet pipe and a glass of hock, over in the counting-house."

'Meanwhile the dancing grew more fast and furious. Little Annette loosened the screw regulating her partner's rate of progress, and the figure flew round with her swifter and swifter. Couple after couple dropped out exhausted, but they only went the faster, till at length they remained dancing alone.

'Madder and madder became the waltz. The music lagged behind: the musicians, unable to keep pace, ceased, and sat staring. The younger guests applauded, but the older faces began to grow anxious.

'"Hadn't you better stop, dear?" said one of the women. "You'll make yourself so tired."

'But Annette did not answer.

'"I believe she's fainted," cried out a girl who had caught sight of her face as it was swept by.

'One of the men sprang forward and clutched at the figure, but its impetus threw him down on to the floor, where its steel-cased feet laid bare his cheek. The thing evidently did not intend to part with its prize easily.

'Had anyone retained a cool head, the figure, one cannot help thinking, might easily have been stopped. Two or three men acting in concert might have lifted it bodily off the floor, or have jammed it into a corner. But few human heads are capable of remaining cool under excitement. Those who are not present think how stupid must have been those who were; those who are reflect afterwards how simple it would have been to do this, that, or the other, if only they had thought of it at the time.

'The women grew hysterical. The men shouted contradictory directions to one another. Two of them made a bungling rush at the figure, which had the result of forcing it out of its orbit in the centre of the room, and sending it crashing against the walls and furniture. A stream of blood showed itself down the girl's white frock, and followed her along the floor. The affair was becoming horrible. The women rushed screaming from the room. The men followed them.

'One sensible suggestion was made: "Find Geibel – fetch Geibel."

'No one had noticed him leave the room, no one knew where he was. A party went in search of him. The others, too unnerved to go back into the ball-room, crowded outside the door and listened.

They could hear the steady whirr of the wheels upon the polished floor as the thing spun round and round; the dull thud as every now and again it dashed itself and its burden against some opposing object and ricocheted off in a new direction.

'And everlastingly it talked in that thin ghostly voice, repeating over and over the same formula: "How charming you are looking tonight. What a lovely day it has been. Oh, don't be so cruel. I could go on dancing for ever – with you. Have you had supper?"

'Of course they sought for Geibel everywhere but where he was. They looked in every room in the house, then they rushed off in a body to his own place, and spent precious minutes in waking up his deaf old housekeeper. At last it occurred to one of the party that Wenzel was missing also, and then the idea of the counting-house across the yard presented itself to them, and there they found him.

'He rose up, very pale, and followed them; and he and old Wenzel forced their way through the crowd of guests gathered outside, and entered the room, and locked the door behind them.

'From within there came the muffled sound of low voices and quick steps, followed by a confused scuffling noise, then silence, then the low voices again.

'After a time the door opened, and those near it pressed forward to enter, but old Wenzel's broad shoulders barred the way.

'"I want you – and you, Bekler," he said, addressing a couple of the elder men. His voice was calm, but his face was deadly white. "The rest of you, please go – get the women away as quickly as you can."

'From that day old Nicholaus Geibel confined himself to the making of mechanical rabbits, and cats that mewed and washed their faces.'

THE DEVIL'S MANUSCRIPT

By S Levett-Yeats (1858–1916)

Sidney Kilner Levett-Yeats came from a family with deep connections to British India (his father was a senior civil servant in the Raj) and he began his own career as an officer in the Punjab Light Horse. He then followed his father into the Indian civil service, spending more than a decade working in the Public Works Department of the Punjab. During this time, he took to writing fiction in his spare time and his work became sufficiently popular (and lucrative) that he was able to give up the day job and concentrate on his writing. He moved from India back to Britain and published a number of novels in the 1890s and 1900s. Like Rudyard Kipling, with whom he was sometimes compared, Levett-Yeats wrote tales set in the India he knew well, but his greatest successes came with historical adventure novels such as The Chevalier d'Auriac, *set in Renaissance France, and* The Honour of Savelli, *a story of intrigue and romance in Italy during the heyday of the Borgias.* The Heart of Denise and Other Tales, *from which 'The Devil's Manuscript' is taken, is a collection of novellas and short stories. Most of these are, like the majority of Levett-Yeats's works, set either in India or in the past but this particular tale strays into the realms of the 'weird' with its intriguing variation on the well-worn theme of a man making a Faustian pact with the Devil.*

First published in The Heart of Denise and Other Tales, *1899*

I: THE BLACK PACKET

'M De Bac? De Bac? I do not know the name.'

'Gentleman says he knows you, sir, and has called on urgent business.'

There was no answer, and John Brown, the ruined publisher, looked about him in a dazed manner. He knew he was ruined; tomorrow the world would know it also, and then – beggary stared him in the face, and infamy too. For this the world would not care. Brown was not a great man in 'the trade', and his name in the *Gazette* would not attract notice; but his name, as he stood in the felon's dock, and the ugly history a cross-examination might disclose, would probably arouse a fleeting interest, and then the world would go on with a pitiless shrug of its shoulders. What does it matter to the moving wave of humanity if one little drop of spray from its crest is blown into nothing by the wind? Not a jot. But it was a terrible business for the drop of spray, otherwise John Brown, publisher. He was at his best not a good-looking man, rather mean-looking than otherwise, with a thin, angular face, eyes as shifty as a jackal's, and shoulders shaped like a champagne-bottle. As the shadow of coming ruin darkened over him, he seemed to shrink and look meaner than ever. He had almost forgotten the presence of his clerk. He could think of nothing but the morrow, when Simmonds's voice again broke the stillness.

'Shall I say you will see him, sir?'

The question cut sharply into the silence, and brought Brown to himself. He had half a mind to say 'No.' In the face of the coming tomorrow, business, urgent or otherwise, was nothing to him. Yet, after all, there could be no harm done in receiving the man. It would, at any rate, be a distraction, and, lifting his head, Brown answered, 'Yes, I will see him, Simmonds.'

Simmonds went out, closing the green baize door behind him. There was a delay of a moment, and M De Bac entered – a tall, thin figure, bearing an oblong parcel, packed in shiny, black paper, and sealed with flame-coloured wax.

'Good-day, Mr Brown,' and M De Bac, who, for all his foreign name, spoke perfect English, extended his hand.

Brown rose, put his own cold fingers into the warm grasp of his visitor, and offered him a seat.

'With your permission, Mr Brown, I will take this other chair. It is nearer the fire. I am accustomed to warm climates, as you doubtless perceive,' and De Bac, suiting his action to his words, placed his packet on the table, and began to slowly rub his long, lean fingers together. The publisher glanced at him with some curiosity. M De Bac was as dark as an Italian, with clear, resolute features, and a moustache, curled at the ends, thick enough to hide the sarcastic curve of his thin lips. He was strongly if sparely built, and his fiery black eyes met Brown's gaze with a look that ran through him like a needle.

'You do not appear to recognise me, Mr Brown?' – De Bac's voice was very quiet and deep-toned.

'I have not the honour—' began the publisher; but his visitor interrupted him.

'You mistake. We are quite old friends; and in time will always be very near each other. I have a minute or two to spare,' – he glanced at a repeater – 'and will prove to you that I know you. You are John Brown, that very religious young man of Battersea, who, twelve years ago, behaved like a blackguard to a girl at Homerton, and sent her to – but no matter. You attracted my attention then; but, unfortunately, I had no time to devote to you. Subsequently, you effected a pretty little swindle – don't be angry, Mr Brown – it *was* very clever. Then you started in business on your own account, and married. Things went well with you; you know the art of getting at a low price, and selling at a high one. You are a born "sweater". Pardon the word. You know how to keep men down like beasts, and go up yourself. In doing this, you did me yeoman's service, although you are even now not aware of this. You had one fault, you have it still, and had you not been a gambler you might have been a rich man. Speculation is a bad thing, Brown – I mean gambling speculation.'

Brown was an Englishman, and it goes without saying that he had courage. But there was something in De Bac's manner, some strange power in the steady stare of those black eyes, that held him to his seat as if pinned there.

As De Bac stopped, however, Brown's anger gave him strength. Every word that was said was true, and stung like the lash of a whip. He rose white with anger.

'Sir!' he began with quivering lips, and made a step forward. Then he stopped. It was as if the sombre fire in De Bac's gaze withered his strength. An invisible hand seemed to drag him back into his seat and hold him there.

'You are hasty, Mr Brown,' and De Bac's even voice continued. 'You are really very rash. I was about to tell you a little more of your history, to tell you you are ruined, and tomorrow everyone in London – it is the world for you, Brown – will know you are a beggar, and many will know you are a cheat.'

The publisher swore bitterly under his breath.

'You see, Mr Brown,' continued his strange visitor, 'I know all about you, and you will be surprised, perhaps, to hear that you deserve help from me. You are too useful to let drift. I have therefore come to save you.'

'Save me?'

'Yes. By means of this manuscript here,' he pointed to the packet, 'which you are going to publish.'

Brown now realised that he was dealing with a lunatic. He tried to stretch out his arm to touch the bell on the table; but found that he had no power to do so. He made an attempt to shout to Simmonds; but his tongue moved inaudibly in his mouth. He seemed only to have the faculty of following De Bac's words, and of answering them. He gasped out, 'It is impossible!'

'My friend,' – and De Bac smiled mirthlessly – 'you will publish that manuscript. I will pay. The profits will be yours. It will make your name, and you will be rich. You will even be able to build a church.'

'Rich!' Brown's voice was very bitter. 'M De Bac, you said rightly. I am a ruined man. Even if you were to pay for the publication of that manuscript I could not do it now. It is too late. There are other houses. Go to them.'

'But not other John Browns. You are peculiarly adapted for my purpose. Enough of this! I know what business is, and I have many things to attend to. You are a small man, Mr Brown, and it will take little to remove your difficulties. See! Here are £1,000. They will free you from your present troubles,' and De Bac tossed a pocketbook on the table before Brown. 'I do not want a receipt,' he went on. 'I will call tomorrow for your final answer, and to settle details. If you need it I will give you more money. This hour – twelve – will suit me. *Adieu*!' He was gone like a flash, and Brown looked around in blank amazement. He was as if suddenly aroused from a dream.

He could hardly believe the evidence of his senses, although he could see the black packet, and the neat leather pocket-book with the initials 'L. De B.' let in in silver on the outside. He rang his bell violently, and Simmonds appeared.

'Has M De Bac gone?'

'I don't know, sir. He didn't pass out through the door.'

'There is no other way. You must have been asleep.'

'Indeed I was not, sir.'

Brown felt a chill as of cold fingers running down his backbone, but pulled himself together with an effort. 'It does not matter, Simmonds. You may go.'

Simmonds went out scratching his head. 'How the demon did he get out?' he asked himself. 'Must have been sleeping after all. The guv'nor seems a bit dotty today. It's the smash coming – sure.'

He wrote a letter or two, and then taking his hat, sallied forth to an aerated bread-shop for his cheap and wholesome lunch, for Simmonds was a saving young man, engaged to a young lady living out Camden Town way. Simmonds perfectly understood the state of affairs, and was not a little anxious about matters, for the mother of his fiancée, a widow who let lodgings, had only agreed to his engagement after much persuasion; and if he had to announce the fact that, instead of 'thirty bob a week', as he put it, his income was nothing at all, there would be an end of everything.

'M'ria's all right,' he said to his friend Wilkes, in trustful confidence as they sat over their lunch, 'but that old torpedo' – by which name he designated his mother-in-law-elect – 'she'll raise Cain if there's a smash-up.'

In the meantime, John Brown tore open the pocket-book with shaking hands, and, with a crisp rustling, a number of new bank-notes fell out, and lay in a heap before him. He counted them one by one. They totalled a thousand pounds exactly. He was a small man, M De Bac had said so truly, if a little rudely, and the money was more than enough to stave off ruin. De Bac had said, too, that if needed he would give him more, and then Brown fell to trembling all over. He was like a man snatched from the very jaws of death. At Battersea he wore a blue ribbon; but now he went to a cabinet, filled a glass with raw brandy, and drained it at a gulp. In a minute or so the generous cordial warmed his chilled blood, and picking up the notes, he counted them again, and thrust them into his breast-pocket. After this he paced the room up and down in a feverish manner, longing for the morrow, when he could settle up the most urgent demands against him. Then, on a sudden, a thought struck him. It was almost as if it had been whispered in his ear. Why trouble at all about matters? He had a clear thousand with him, and in an hour he could be out of the country! He hesitated, but prudence prevailed. Extradition laws stretched everywhere; and there was another thing – that extraordinary madman, De Bac, had promised more money on the morrow. After all, it was better to stay.

As he made this resolve his eyes fell on the black packet on the table. The peculiar colour of the seals attracted his attention. He bent over them, and saw that the wax bore an impress of a V-shaped shield, within which was set a trident. He noticed also that the packet was tied with a silver thread. His curiosity was excited. He sat down, snipped the threads with a penknife, tore off the black paper covering, flung it into the fire, and saw before him a bulky manuscript exquisitely written on very fine paper. A closer examination showed that it was a number of short stories. Now Brown was in no mood to read; but the title of the first tale caught his eye, and the writing was so legible that he had glanced over half a dozen lines before he was aware of the fact. Those first half-dozen lines were sufficient to make him read the page, and when he had read the page the publisher felt he was before the work of a genius.

He was unable to stop now; and, with his head resting between his hands, he read on tirelessly. Simmonds came in once or twice and left papers on the table, but his master took no notice of him. Brown forgot all about his lunch and turning over page after page, read as if spellbound. He was a business man, and was certain the book would sell in thousands. He read as one inspired to look into the author's thoughts and see his design. Short as the stories were, they were titanic fragments, and every one of them taught a hideous lesson of corruption. Some of them, cloaked in a religious garb, breathed a spirit of pitiless ferocity; others were rich with the sensuous odours of an Eastern garden; others, again, were as the tender green of moss hiding the treacherous deeps of a quicksand; and all of them bore the hallmark of genius. They moved the man sitting there to tears, they shook him with laughter, they seemed to rock his very soul asleep; but through it all he saw, as the mariner views the beacon fire on a rocky coast, the deadly plan of the writer. There was money in them – thousands – and all was to be his. Brown's sluggish blood was running to flame, a strange strength glowed in his face, and an uncontrollable admiration for De Bac's evil power filled him. The book, when published, might corrupt generations yet unborn; but that was nothing to Brown. It meant thousands for him, and an eternal fame to De Bac. He did not grudge the writer the fame as long as he kept the thousands.

'By Heaven!' and he brought his fist down on the table with a crash. 'The man may be a lunatic; but he is the greatest genius the world ever saw – or he is the devil incarnate.'

And somebody laughed softly in the room.

The publisher looked up with a start, and saw Simmonds standing before him.

'Did you laugh, Simmonds?'

'No, sir!' replied the clerk with a surprised look.

'Who laughed then?'

'There is no one here but ourselves, sir – and I didn't laugh.'

'Did you hear nothing?'

'Nothing, sir.'

'Strange!' and Brown began to feel chill again.

'What time is it?' he asked with an effort.

'It is half-past six, sir.'

'So late as that? You may go, Simmonds. Leave me the keys. I will be here for some time. Good-evening.'

'Mad as a coot,' muttered Simmonds to himself. 'Must break the news to M'ria tonight. Oh, Lor'!' and his eyes were very wet as he went out into the Strand, and got into a blue omnibus.

When he was gone, Brown turned to the fire, poker in hand. To his surprise he saw that the black paper was still there, burning red hot, and the wax of the seals was still intact – the seals themselves shining like orange glow-lights. He beat at the paper with the poker; but instead of crumbling to ashes it yielded passively to the stroke, and came back to its original shape. Then a fury came on Brown. He raked at the fire, threw more coals over the paper, and blew at the flames with his bellows until they roared up the chimney; but still the coppery glare of the packet-cover never turned to the grey of ashes. Finally, he could endure it no longer, and, putting the manuscript into the safe, turned off the electric light, and stole out of his office like a thief.

II: THE RED TRIDENT

When Beggarman, Bowles & Co., of Providence Passage, Lombard Street, called at 11 o'clock on the morning following De Bac's visit, their representative was not a little surprised to find the firm's bills met in hard cash, and Simmonds paid him with a radiant face. When the affair was settled, the clerk leant back in his chair, saying half-aloud to himself, 'By George! I am glad after all M'ria did not keep our appointment in the Camden Road last night.' Then his face began to darken. 'Wonder where she could have been, though?' His thoughts ran on: 'Half sorry I introduced her to Wilkes last Sunday at Victoria Park. Wilkes ain't half the man I am though,' and he tried to look at himself in the window-pane, 'but he has two pound ten a week – Lord! There's the guv'nor ringing.' He hurried into Brown's room, received a brief order, and was about to go back when the publisher spoke again.

'Simmonds!'

'Sir.'

'If M De Bac calls, show him in at once.'

'Sir,' and the clerk went out.

Left to himself, Brown tried to go on with the manuscript; but was not able to do so. He was impatient for the coming of De Bac, and kept watching the hands of the clock as they slowly travelled towards 12. When he came to the office in the morning Brown had looked with a nervous fear in the fireplace, half expecting to find the black paper still there; and it was a considerable relief to his mind to find it was not. He could do nothing, not even open the envelopes of the letters that lay on his table. He made an effort to find occupation in the morning's paper. It was full of some absurd correspondence on a trivial subject, and he wondered at the thousands of fools who could waste time in writing and in reading yards of print on the theme of

'Whether women should wear neckties'. The ticking of the clock irritated him. He flung the paper aside, just as the door opened and Simmonds came in. For a moment Brown thought he had come to announce De Bac's arrival; but no – Simmonds simply placed a square envelope on the table before Brown.

'Pass-book from Bransom's, sir, just come in,' and he went out.

Brown took it up mechanically, and opened the envelope. A typewritten letter fell out with the pass-book. He ran his eyes over it with astonishment. It was briefly to inform him that M De Bac had paid into Brown's account yesterday afternoon the sum of five thousand pounds, and that, adjusting overdrafts, the balance at his credit was four thousand seven hundred and twenty pounds thirteen shillings and three pence. Brown rubbed his eyes. Then he hurriedly glanced at the pass-book. The figures tallied – there was no error, no mistake. He pricked himself with his penknife to see if he was awake, and finally shouted to Simmonds.

'Read this letter aloud to me, Simmonds,' he said.

Simmonds's eyes opened, but he did as he was bidden, and there was no mistake about the account.

'Anything else, sir?' asked Simmonds when he had finished.

'No – nothing,' and Brown was once more alone. He sat staring at the figures before him in silence, almost mesmerising himself with the intentness of his gaze.

'My God!' he burst out at last, in absolute wonder.

'Who is your God, Brown?' answered a deep voice.

'I – I – M De Bac! How did you come?'

'I did not drop down the chimney,' said De Bac with a grin. 'Your clerk announced me in the ordinary way, but you were so absorbed you did not hear. So I took the liberty of sitting in this chair, and awaiting your return to earthly matters. You were dreaming, Brown – by the way, who is your God?' he repeated with a low laugh.

'I –I do not understand, sir.'

'Possibly not, possibly not. I wouldn't bother about the matter. Ah! I see Bransom's have sent you your pass-book! Sit down, Brown. I hate to see a man fidgeting about – I paid in that amount yesterday on a second thought. It is enough – eh?'

Brown's jackal eyes contracted. Perhaps he could get more out of De Bac? But a look at the strong impassive face before him frightened him.

'More than enough, sir,' he stammered; and then, with a rush, 'I am grateful – anything I can do for you?'

'Oh! I know, I know, Brown – by the way, you do not object to smoke?'

'Certainly not. I do not smoke myself.'

'In Battersea, eh?' And De Bac, pulling out a silver cheroot case, held it out to Brown. But the publisher declined.

'Money wouldn't buy a smoke like that in England,' remarked De Bac, 'but as you will. I wouldn't smoke if I were you. Such abstinence looks respectable and means nothing.' He put a cigar between his lips, and pointed his forefinger at the end. To Brown's amazement an orange-flame licked out from under the fingernail, and vanished like a flash of lightning; but the cigar was alight, and its fragrant odour filled the room. It reached even Simmonds, who sniffed at it like a buck scenting the morning air.

'By George!' he exclaimed in wonder, 'what baccy!'

M De Bac settled himself comfortably in his chair, and spoke with the cigar between his teeth. 'Now you have recovered a little from your surprise, Brown, I may as well tell you that I never carry matches. This little scientific discovery I have made is very convenient, is it not?'

'I have never seen anything like it.'

'There are a good many things you have not seen, Brown – but to work. Take a pencil and paper and note down what I say. You can tell me when I have done if you agree or not.'

Brown did as he was told, and De Bac spoke slowly and carefully.

'The money I have given you is absolutely your own, on the following terms. You will publish the manuscript I left with you, enlarge your business, and work as you have hitherto worked – as a "sweater". You may speculate as much as you like. You will not lose. You need not avoid the publication of religious books, but you must never give in charity secretly. I do not object to a big cheque for a public object, and your name in all the papers. It will be well for you to hound down the vicious. Never give them a chance to recover themselves. You will be a legislator. Strongly uphold all those measures which, under a moral cloak, will do harm to mankind. I do not mention them. I do not seek to hamper you with detailed instructions. Work on these general lines, and you will do what I want. A word more. It will be advisable whenever you have a chance to call public attention to a great evil which is also a vice. Thousands who have never heard of it before will hear of it then – and human nature is very frail. You have noted all this down?'

'I have. You are a strange man, M De Bac.'

M De Bac frowned, and Brown began to tremble.

'I do not permit you to make observations about me, Mr Brown.'

'I beg your pardon, sir.'

'Do not do so again. Will you agree to all this? I promise you unexampled prosperity for ten years. At the end of that time I shall want you elsewhere. And you must agree to take a journey with me.'

'A long one, sir?' Brown's voice was just a shade satirical.

M De Bac smiled oddly. 'No – in your case I promise a quick passage. These are all the conditions I attach to my gift of six thousand pounds to you.'

Brown's amazement did not blind him to the fact of the advantage he had, as he thought, over his visitor. The six thousand pounds were already his, and he had given no promise. With a sudden boldness he spoke out.

'And if I decline?'

'You will return me my money, and my book, and I will go elsewhere.'

'The manuscript, yes – but if I refuse to give back the money?'

'Ha! ha! ha!' M De Bac's mirthless laugh chilled Brown to the bone. 'Very good, Brown – but you won't refuse. Sign that like a good fellow,' and he flung a piece of paper towards Brown, who saw that it was a promissory note, drawn up in his name, agreeing to pay M De Bac the sum of six thousand pounds on demand.

'I shall do no such thing,' said Brown stoutly.

M De Bac made no answer, but calmly touched the bell. In a half-minute Simmonds appeared.

'Be good enough to witness Mr Brown's signature to that document,' said De Bac to him, and then fixed his gaze on Brown. There was a moment of hesitation, and then – the publisher signed his name, and Simmonds did likewise as a witness. When the latter had gone, De Bac carefully put the paper by in a letter-case he drew from his vest pocket.

'Your scientific people would call this an exhibition of odic force, Brown – eh?'

Brown made no answer. He was shaking in every limb, and great pearls of sweat rolled down his forehead.

'You see, Brown,' continued De Bac, 'after all you are a free agent. Either agree to my terms and keep the money, or say you will not, pay me back, receive your note-of-hand, and I go elsewhere with my book. Come – time is precious.'

And from Brown's lips there hissed a low 'I agree.'

'Then that is settled,' and De Bac rose from his chair. 'There is a little thing more – stretch out your arm like a good fellow – the right arm.'

Brown did so; and De Bac placed his forefinger on his wrist, just between what palmists call 'the lines of life'. The touch was as that of a red-hot iron, and with a quick cry Brown drew back his hand and looked at it. On his wrist was a small red trident, as cleanly marked as if it had been tattooed into the skin. The pain was but momentary; and, as he looked at the mark, he heard De Bac say, 'Adieu once more, Brown. I will find my way out – don't trouble to rise.' Brown heard him wish Simmonds an affable 'Good-day,' and he was gone.

III: THE MARK OF THE BEAST

It was early in the spring that Brown published *The Yellow Dragon* – as the collection of tales left with him by De Bac was called – and the success of the book surpassed his wildest expectations. It became the rage. There were the strangest rumours afloat as to its authorship, for no one knew De Bac, and the name of the writer was supposed to be an assumed one. It was written by a clergyman; it was penned by a schoolgirl; it had employed the leisure of a distinguished statesman during his retirement; it was the work of an ex-crowned head. These, and such-like statements, were poured forth one day, to be contradicted the next. Wherever the book was noticed, it was either with the most extravagant praise or the bitterest rancour. But friend and foe were alike united on one thing – that of ascribing to its unknown author a princely genius. The greatest of the reviews, after pouring on *The Yellow Dragon* the vials of its wrath, concluded with these words of unwilling praise: 'There is not a sentence of this book which should ever have been written, still less published; but we do not hesitate to say that, having been written and given to the world, there is hardly a line of this terrible work which will not become immortal – to the misery of mankind.'

Be this as it may, the book sold in tens of thousands, and Brown's fortune was assured. In ten years a man may do many things; but during the ten years that followed the publication of *The Yellow Dragon*, Brown did so many things that he astonished 'the city', and it takes not a little to do that. It was not alone the marvellous growth of his business – although that advanced by leaps and bounds until it overshadowed all others – it was his wonderful luck on the Stock Exchange. Whatever he touched turned to gold. He was looked upon as the Napoleon of finance. His connection with *The Yellow Dragon* was forgotten when his connection with the yellow sovereign was remembered. He had a palace in Berkshire; another huge pile owned by him overlooked Hyde Park. He was a county member and a cabinet-minister. He had refused a peerage and built a church. Could ambition want more? He had clean forgotten De Bac. From him he had heard no word, received no sign, and he looked upon him as dead. At first, when his eyes fell on the red trident on his wrist, he was wont to shudder all over; but as years went on he became accustomed to the mark, and thought no more of it than if it had been a mole. In personal appearance he was but little changed, except that his hair was thin and grey, and there was a bald patch on the top of his head. His wife had died four years ago, and he was now contemplating another marriage – a marriage that would ally him with a family dating from the Confessor.

Such was John Brown, when we meet him again ten years after De Bac's visit, seated at a large writing-table in his luxurious office. A clerk standing beside him was cutting open the envelopes of the morning's post, and placing the letters one by one before his master.

It is our friend Simmonds – still a young man, but bent and old beyond his years, and still on 'thirty bob' a week. And the history of Simmonds will show how Brown carried out De Bac's instructions.

When *The Yellow Dragon* came out and business began to expand, Simmonds, having increased work, was ambitious enough to expect a rise in his salary, and addressed his chief on the subject. He was put off with a promise, and on the strength of that promise Simmonds, being no wiser than many of his fellows, married M'ria; and husband and wife managed to exist somehow with the help of the mother-in-law. Then the mother-in-law died, and there was only the bare thirty shillings a week on which to live, to dress, to pay Simmonds's way daily to the city and back, and to feed more than two mouths – for Simmonds was amongst the blessed who have their quivers full. Still the expected increase of pay did not come. Other men came into the business and passed over Simmonds. Brown said they had special qualifications. They had; and John Brown knew Simmonds better than he knew himself. The other men were paid for doing things Simmonds could not have done to save his life; but he was more than useful in his way. A hundred times it was in the mind of the wretched clerk to resign his post and seek to better himself elsewhere. But he had given hostages to fortune. There was M'ria and her children, and M'ria set her face resolutely against risk. They had no reserve upon which to fall back, and it was an option between partial and total starvation. So 'Sim', as M'ria called him, held on and battled with the wolf at the door, the wolf gaining ground inch by inch. Then illness came, and debt, and then – temptation. 'Sim' fell, as many a better man than he has fallen.

Brown found it out, and saw his opportunity to behave generously, and make his generosity pay. He got a written confession of his guilt from Simmonds, and retained him in his service for ever on thirty shillings a week. And Simmonds's life became such as made him envy the lot of a Russian serf, of a Siberian exile, of a negro in the old days of the sugar plantations. He became a slave, a living machine who ground out his daily hours of work; he became mean and sordid in soul, as one does become when hope is extinct. Such was Simmonds as he cut open the envelopes of Brown's letters, and the great man, reading them quickly, endorsed them with terse remarks in blue pencil, for subsequent disposal by his secretary. A sudden exclamation from the clerk, and Brown looked up.

'What is it?' he asked sharply.

'Only this, sir,' and Simmonds held before Brown's eyes a jet-black envelope; and as he gazed at it, his mind travelled back ten years, to that day when he stood on the brink of public infamy and ruin, and De Bac had saved him. For a moment everything faded before Brown's eyes, and he saw himself in a dingy room, with the gaunt figure of the author of *The Yellow Dragon*, and the maker of his fortune, before him.

'Shall I open it, sir?' Simmonds's voice reached him as from a far distance, and Brown roused himself with an effort.

'No,' he said. 'Give it to me, and go for the present.'

When the bent figure of the clerk had passed out of the room, Brown looked at the envelope carefully. It bore a penny stamp and the impress of the postmark was not legible. The superscription was in white ink, and it was addressed to Mr John Brown. The 'Mr' on the letter irritated Brown, for he was now The Right Hon'ble John Brown, and was punctilious on that score. He was so annoyed that at first he thought of casting the letter unopened into the wastepaper basket beside him, but changed his mind, and tore open the cover. A note-card discovered itself. The contents were brief and to the point:

'Get ready to start. I will call for you at the close of the day. L. De B.'

For a moment Brown was puzzled, then the remembrance of his old compact with De Bac came to him. He fairly laughed. To think that he, The Right Hon'ble John Brown, the richest man in England, and one of the most powerful, should be written to like that! Ordered to go somewhere he did not even know! Addressed like a servant! The cool insolence of the note amused Brown first, and then he became enraged. He tore the note into fragments and cast it from him. 'Curse the madman,' he said aloud, 'I'll give him in charge if he annoys me.' A sudden twinge in his right wrist made him hurriedly look at the spot. There was a broad pink circle, as large as a florin, around the mark of the trident, and it smarted and burned as the sting of a wasp. He ran to a basin of water and dipped his arm in to the elbow; but the pain became intolerable, and, finally, ordering his carriage, he drove home. That evening there was a great civic banquet in the city, and amongst the guests was The Right Hon'ble John Brown.

All through the afternoon he had been in agony with his wrist, but towards evening the pain ceased as suddenly as it had come on, and Brown attended the banquet, a little pale and shaken, but still himself. On Brown's right hand sat the Bishop of Browboro', on his left a most distinguished scientist, and amongst the crowd of waiters was Simmonds, who had hired himself out for the evening to earn an extra shilling or so to eke out his miserable subsistence. The man of science had just returned from Mount Atlas, whither he had gone to observe the transit of Mercury, and had come back full of stories of witchcraft. He led the conversation in that direction, and very soon the Bishop, Brown, and himself were engaged in the discussion of *diablerie*. The Bishop was a learned and a saintly man, and was a 'believer'; the scientist was puzzled by what he had seen, and Brown openly scoffed.

'Look here!' and pulling back his cuff, he showed the red mark on his wrist to his companions. 'If I were to tell you how that came here, you would say the devil himself marked me.'

'I confess I am curious,' said the scientist; and the Bishop fixed an inquiring gaze upon Brown. Simmonds was standing behind, and unconsciously drew near. Then the man, omitting many things, told the history of the mark on his wrist. He left out much, but he told enough to make the scientist edge his chair a little further from him, and a look of grave compassion, not untinged with scorn, to come into the eyes of the Bishop. As Brown came to the end of his story, he became unnaturally excited, he raised his voice, and, with a sudden gesture, held his wrist close to the Bishop's face. 'There!' he said. 'I suppose you would say the devil did that?'

And as the Bishop looked, a voice seemed to breathe in his ear: '*And he caused all ... to receive a mark in their right hand, or in their foreheads.*' It was as if his soul was speaking to him and urging him to say the words aloud. He did not; but with a pale face gently put aside Brown's hand. 'I do not know, Mr Brown – but I think you are called upon for a speech.'

It was so; and, after a moment's hesitation, Brown rose. He was a fluent speaker, and the occasion was one with which he was peculiarly qualified to deal. He began well; but as he went on those who looked upon him saw that he was ghastly pale, and that the veins stood out on his high forehead in blue cords. As he spoke he made some allusion to those men who have risen to eminence from an obscure position. He spoke of himself as one of these, and then began to tell the story of *The Devil's Manuscript*, as he called it, with a mocking look at the Bishop. As he went on he completely lost command over himself, and the story of the manuscript became the story of his life. He concealed nothing, he passed over nothing. He laid all his sordid past before his hearers with a vivid force. His listeners were astonished into silence; perhaps curiosity kept them still. But, as the long tale of infamy went on, some, in pity for the man, and believing him struck mad, tried to stop him, but in vain. He came at last to the incident of the letter, and told how De Bac was to call for him tonight.

'The Bishop of Browboro',' he said with a jarring laugh, 'thought De Bac was the fiend himself,' but he (Brown) knew better; he – he stopped, and, with a half-inarticulate cry, began to back slowly from the table, his eyes fixed on the entrance to the room. And now a strange thing happened. There was not a man in the room who had the power to move or to speak; they were as if frozen to their seats; as if struck into stone. Some were able to follow Brown's glance, but could see nothing. All were able to see that in Brown's face was an awful fear, and that he was trying to escape from a horrible presence which was moving slowly towards him, and which was visible to himself alone. Inch by inch Brown gave way, until he at last reached the wall, and stood with his back to it, with his arms spread out, in the position of one crucified. His face was marble white, and a dreadful terror and a pitiful appeal shone in his eyes. His blue lips were parted as of one in the dolours of death.

The silence was profound.

There were strong men there; men who had faced and overcome dangers, who had held their lives in their hands, who had struggled against desperate odds and won; but there was not a man who did not now feel weak, powerless, helpless as a child before that invisible, advancing terror that Brown alone could see. They could move no hand to aid, lift no voice to pray. All they could do was to wait in that dreadful silence and to watch. Time itself seemed to stop. It was as if the stillness had lasted for hours.

Suddenly Brown's face, so white before, flushed a crimson-purple, and with a terrible cry he fell forward on the polished woodwork of the floor.

As he fell, it seemed as if the weight which held all still was on the moment removed, and they were free. With scared faces they gathered around the fallen man and raised him. He was quite dead; but on his forehead, where there was no mark before, was the impress of a red trident.

A man, evidently one of the waiters, who had forced his way into the group, laid his finger on the mark and looked up at the Bishop. There was an unholy exultation in his face as he met the priest's eyes, and said, 'He's marked twice – *curse him*!'

THE MAN WITH THE COUGH

By Mary Louisa Molesworth (1839–1921)

Born in Rotterdam, the daughter of a wealthy British merchant and his wife, Mary Louisa Stewart grew up largely in Manchester, where the family had moved, and married a Major Molesworth, the nephew of an Irish peer, in her early twenties. Her early fiction for adults was published in the 1870s under the pseudonym of Ennis Graham but she became best known for her children's fiction, 'aimed', in the words of the critic Roger Lancelyn Green, 'at girls too old for fairies and princesses but too young for Austen and the Brontës'. Novels such as The Cuckoo Clock, The Children of the Castle *and* The Carved Lion *continue to find occasional readers today, including Jacqueline Wilson, creator of Tracy Beaker, who praised her for her ability to bring her characters to life. Like many women writers of the Victorian era, Molesworth was drawn to the supernatural, and some of the stories in the two collections,* Four Ghost Stories *and* Uncanny Tales, *are as good as any from the period. 'The Man with the Cough' is not a ghost story but an account of its narrator's bizarre and unsettling experiences on a journey from Germany to London, in which he appears to fall into a weird temporal and geographical limbo.*

From Uncanny Tales, *1896*

I am a German by birth and descent. My name is Schmidt. But by education I am quite as much an Englishman as a 'Deutscher', and by affection much more the former. My life has been spent pretty equally between the two countries, and I flatter myself I speak both languages without any foreign accent.

I count England my headquarters now: it is 'home' to me. But a few years ago I was resident in Germany, only going over to London now and then on business. I will not mention the town where I lived. It is unnecessary to do so, and in the peculiar experience I am about to relate I think real names of people and places are just as well, or better, avoided.

I was connected with a large and important firm of engineers. I had been bred up to the profession, and was credited with a certain amount of talent; and I was considered – and, with all modesty, I think I deserved the opinion – steady and reliable, so that I had already attained a fair position in the house, and was looked upon as a 'rising man'. But I was still young, and not quite so wise as I thought myself. I came very near once to making a great mess of a certain affair. It is this story which I am going to tell.

Our house went in largely for patents – rather too largely, some thought. But the head partner's son was a bit of a genius in his way, and his father was growing old, and let Herr Wilhelm – Moritz we will call the family name – do pretty much as he chose. And on the whole Herr Wilhelm did well. He was cautious, and he had the benefit of the still greater caution and larger experience of Herr Gerhardt, the second partner in the firm.

Patents and the laws which regulate them are queer things to have to do with. No one who has not had personal experience of the complications that arise could believe how far these spread and how entangled they become. Great acuteness as well as caution is called for if you would guide your patent bark safely to port – and perhaps more than anything, a power of holding your tongue. I was no chatterbox, nor, when on a mission of importance, did I go about looking as if I were bursting with secrets, which is, in my opinion, almost as dangerous as revealing them. No one, to meet me on the journeys which it often fell to my lot to undertake, would have guessed that I had anything on my mind but an easy-going young fellow's natural interest in his surroundings, though many a time I have stayed awake through a whole night of railway travel if at all doubtful about my fellow-passengers, or not dared to go to sleep in a hotel without a ready-loaded revolver by my pillow.

For now and then – though not through me – our secrets did ooze out. And if, as has happened, they were secrets connected with Government orders or contracts, there was, or but for the exertion of the greatest energy and tact on the part of my superiors, there would have been, to put it plainly, the devil to pay.

One morning – it was nearing the end of November – I was sent for to Herr Wilhelm's private room. There I found him and Herr Gerhardt before a table spread with papers covered with figures and calculations, and sheets of beautifully executed diagrams.

'Lutz,' said Herr Wilhelm. He had known me from childhood, and often called me by the abbreviation of my Christian name, which is Ludwig, or Louis. 'Lutz, we are going to confide to you a matter of extreme importance. You must be prepared to start for London tomorrow.'

'All right, sir,' I said. 'I shall be ready.'

'You will take the express through to Calais – on the whole it is the best route, especially at this season. By travelling all night you will catch the boat there, and arrive in London so as to have a good night's rest, and be clear-headed for work the next morning.'

I bowed agreement, but ventured to make a suggestion.

'If, as I infer, the matter is one of great importance,' I said, 'would it not be well for me to start sooner? I can – yes,' throwing a rapid survey over the work I had before me for the next two days – 'I can be ready tonight.'

Herr Wilhelm looked at Herr Gerhardt. Herr Gerhardt shook his head.

'No,' he replied. 'Tomorrow it must be,' and then he proceeded to explain to me why.

I need not attempt to give all the details of the matter with which I was entrusted. Indeed, to 'lay' readers it would be impossible. Suffice it to say, the whole concerned a patent – that of a very remarkable and wonderful invention, which it was hoped and believed the Governments of both countries would take up. But to secure this being done in a thoroughly satisfactory manner it was necessary that our firm should go about it in concert with an English house of first-rate standing. To this house – the firm of Messrs Bluestone and Fagg, I will call them – I was to be sent with full explanations. And the next half-hour or more passed in my superiors going minutely into the details, so as to satisfy themselves that I understood. The mastering of the whole was not difficult, for I was well grounded technically; and like many of the best things the idea was essentially simple, and the diagrams were perfect. When the explanations were over, and my instructions duly noted, I began to gather together the various sheets, which were all numbered. But, to my surprise, Herr Gerhardt, looking over me, withdrew two of the most important diagrams, without which the others were valueless, because inexplicable.

'Stay,' he said. 'These two, Ludwig, must be kept separate. These we send today, by registered post, direct to Bluestone and Fagg. They will receive them a day before they see you, and with them a letter announcing your arrival.'

I looked up in some disappointment. I had known of precautions of the kind being taken, but usually when the employee sent was less reliable than I believed myself to be. Still, I scarcely dared to demur.

'Do you think that necessary?' I said respectfully. 'I can assure you that from the moment you entrust me with the papers they shall never quit me day or night. And if there were any postal delay – you say time is valuable in this case – or if the papers were stolen in the transit – such things have happened – my whole mission would be worthless.'

'We do not doubt your zeal and discretion, my good Schmidt,' said Herr Gerhardt. 'But in this case we must take even extra precautions. I had not meant to tell you, fearing to add to the certain amount of nervousness and strain unavoidable in such a case, but still, perhaps it is best that you should know that we have reason for some special anxiety. It has been hinted to us that some breath of this' – and he tapped the papers – 'has reached those who are always on the watch for such things. We cannot be too careful.'

'And yet,' I persisted, 'you would trust the post?'

'We do not trust the post,' he replied. 'Even if these diagrams were tampered with, they would be perfectly useless. And tampered with they will not be. But even supposing anything so wild, the rogues in question knowing of your departure (and they are more likely to know of it than of our packet by post), were they in collusion with some traitor in the post-office, are sharp enough to guess the truth – that we have made a Masonic secret of it – the two separate diagrams are valueless without your papers; your papers reveal nothing without Numbers 7 and 13.'

I bowed in submission. But I was, all the same, disappointed, as I said, and a trifle mortified.

Herr Wilhelm saw it, and cheered me up.

'All right, Lutz, my boy,' he said. 'I feel just like you – nothing I should enjoy more than a rush over to London, carrying the whole documents, and prepared for a fight with anyone who tried to get hold of them. But Herr Gerhardt here is cooler-blooded than we are.'

The elder man smiled.

'I don't doubt your readiness to fight, nor Ludwig's either. But it would be by no such honestly brutal means as open robbery that we should be outwitted. Make friends readily with no one while travelling, Lutz, yet avoid the appearance of keeping yourself aloof. You understand?'

'Perfectly,' I said. 'I shall sleep well tonight, so as to be prepared to keep awake throughout the journey.'

The papers were then carefully packed up. Those consigned to my care were to be carried in a certain light, black handbag with a very good lock, which had often before been my travelling companion.

And the following evening I started by the express train agreed upon. So, at least, I have always believed, but I have never been able to bring forward a witness to the fact of my train at the start being the right one, as no one came with me to see me off. For it was thought best that I should depart in as unobtrusive a manner as possible, as, even in a large town such as ours, the members and employees of an old and important house like the Moritzes' were well known.

I took my ticket then, registering no luggage, as I had none but what I easily carried in my hand, as well as the bag. It was already dusk, if not dark, and there was not much bustle in the station, nor apparently many passengers. I took my place in an empty second-class compartment, and sat there quietly till the train should start. A few minutes before it did so, another man got in. I was somewhat annoyed at this, as in my circumstances nothing was more undesirable than travelling alone with one other. Had there been a crowded compartment, or one with three or four passengers, I would have chosen it; but at the moment I got in, the carriages were all either empty or with but one or two occupants. Now, I said to myself, I should have done better to wait till nearer the time of departure, and then chosen my place.

I turned to reconnoitre my companion, but I could not see his face clearly, as he was half leaning out of the window. Was he doing so on purpose? I said to myself, for naturally I was in a suspicious mood. And as the thought struck me, I half started up, determined to choose another compartment. Suddenly a peculiar sound made itself heard. My companion was coughing. He drew his head in, covering his face with his hand, as he coughed again. You never heard such a curious cough. It was more like a hen clucking than anything I can think of. Once, twice, he coughed; then, as if he had been waiting for the slight spasm to pass, he sprang up, looked eagerly out of the window again, and, opening the door, jumped out, with some exclamation, as if he had just caught sight of a friend.

And in another moment or two – he could barely have had time to get in elsewhere – much to my satisfaction, the train moved off.

'Now,' thought I, 'I can make myself comfortable for some hours. We do not stop till M—: it will be nine o'clock by then. If no one gets in there I am safe to go through till tomorrow alone; then there will only be — Junction, and a clear run to Calais.'

I unstrapped my rug and lit a cigar – of course I had chosen a smoking-carriage – and, delighted at having got rid of my clucking companion, the time passed pleasantly till we pulled up at M—. The delay there was not great, and to my enormous satisfaction no one molested my solitude. Evidently the express to Calais was not in very great demand that night. I now felt so secure that, notwithstanding my intention of keeping awake all night, my innermost consciousness had not, I suppose, quite resigned itself to the necessity, for, not more than an hour or so after leaving M—, possibly sooner, I fell fast asleep.

It seemed to me that I had slept heavily, for when I awoke I had great difficulty in remembering where I was. Only by slow degrees did I realise that I was not in my comfortable bed at home, but in a chilly, ill-lighted railway-carriage. Chilly – yes, that it was – very chilly; but as my faculties returned, I remembered my precious bag, and forgot all else in a momentary terror that it had been taken from me. No; there it was – my elbow had been pressed against it as I slept. But how was this? The train was not in motion. We were standing in a station; a dingy deserted-looking place, with no cheerful noise or bustle; only one or two porters slowly moving about, with a sort of sleepy 'night duty', surly air. It could not be the Junction? I looked at my watch. Barely midnight! Of course, not the Junction. We were not due there till four o'clock in the morning or so.

What, then, were we doing here, and what was 'here'? Had there been an accident – some unforeseen necessity for stopping? At that moment a curious sound, from some yards' distance only it seemed to come, caught my ear. It was that croaking, cackling cough! – the cough of my momentary fellow-passenger, towards whom I had felt an instinctive aversion. I looked out of the window – there was a refreshment-room just opposite, dimly lighted, like everything else, and in the doorway, as if just entering, was a figure which I felt pretty sure was that of the man with the cough.

'Bah!' I said to myself. 'I must not be fanciful. I daresay the fellow's all right. He is evidently in the same hole as myself. What in Heaven's name are we waiting here for?'

I sprang out of the carriage, nearly tumbling over a porter slowly passing along.

'How long are we to stay here?' I cried. 'When do we start again for —?' and I named the Junction.

'For —' he repeated in the queerest German I ever heard — was it German? Or did I discover his meaning by some preternatural cleverness of my own? 'There is no train for — for four or five hours, not till—' and he named the time; and leaning forward lazily, he took out my larger bag and my rug, depositing them on the platform. He did not seem the least surprised at finding me there — I might have been there for a week, it seemed to me.

'No train for five hours? Are you mad?' I said.

He shook his head and mumbled something, and it seemed to me that he pointed to the refreshment-room opposite. Gathering my things together I hurried thither, hoping to find some more reliable authority. But there was no one there except a fat man with a white apron, who was clearing the counter — and — yes, in one corner was the figure I had mentally dubbed 'The man with the cough'.

I addressed the cook or waiter — whichever he was. But he only shook his head — denied all knowledge of the trains, but informed me that — in other words — I must turn out; he was going to shut up.

'And where am I to spend the night, then?' I said angrily, though clearly it was not the aproned individual who was responsible for the position in which I found myself.

There was a 'Restauration', he informed me, near at hand, which I should find still open, straight before me on leaving the station, and then a few doors to the right, I would see the lights.

Clearly there was nothing else to be done. I went out, and as I did so the silent figure in the corner rose also and followed me. The station was evidently going to bed. As I passed the porter I repeated the hour he had named, adding, 'That is the first train for — Junction?'

He nodded, again naming the exact time. But I cannot do so, as I have never been able to recollect it.

I trudged along the road – there were lamps, though very feeble ones; but by their light I saw that the man who had been in the refreshment-room was still a few steps behind me. It made me feel slightly nervous, and I looked round furtively once or twice; the last time I did so he was not to be seen, and I hoped he had gone some other way.

The 'Restauration' was scarcely more inviting than the station refreshment-room. It, too, was very dimly lighted, and the one or two attendants seemed half asleep and were strangely silent. There was a fire, of a kind, and I seated myself at a small table near it and asked for some coffee, which would, I thought, serve the double purpose of warming me and keeping me awake.

It was brought me, in silence. I drank it, and felt the better for it. But there was something so gloomy and unsociable, so queer and almost weird about the whole aspect and feeling of the place, that a sort of irritable resignation took possession of me. If these surly folk won't speak, neither will I, I said to myself childishly. And, incredible as it may sound, I did not speak. I think I paid for the coffee, but I am not quite sure. I know I never asked what I had meant to ask – the name of the town – a place of some importance, to judge by the size of the station and the extent of twinkling lights I had observed as I made my way to the 'Restauration'. From that day to this I have never been able to identify it, and I am quite sure I never shall.

What was there peculiar about that coffee? Or was it something peculiar about my own condition that caused it to have the unusual effect I now experienced? That question, too, I cannot answer. All I remember is feeling a sensation of irresistible drowsiness creeping over me – mental, or moral I may say, as well as physical. For when one part of me feebly resisted the first onslaught of sleep, something seemed to reply, 'Oh, nonsense! You have several hours before you. Your papers are all right. No one can touch them without awaking you.'

And dreamily conscious that my belongings were on the floor at my feet – the bag itself actually resting against my ankle – my scruples silenced themselves in an extraordinary way. I remember nothing more, save a vague consciousness through all my slumber of confused and chaotic dreams, which I have never been able to recall.

I awoke at last, and that with a start, almost a jerk. Something had awakened me – a sound – and, as it was repeated to my now aroused ears, I knew that I had heard it before, off and on, during my sleep. It was the extraordinary cough!

I looked up. Yes, there he was! At some two or three yards' distance only, at the other side of the fireplace, which, and this I have forgotten to mention as another peculiar item in that night's peculiar experiences, considering I have every reason to believe I was still in Germany, was not a stove, but an open grate.

And he had not been there when I first fell asleep; to that I was prepared to swear.

'He must have come sneaking in after me,' I thought, and in all probability I should neither have noticed nor recognised him but for that traitorous cackle of his.

Now, my misgivings aroused, my first thought, of course, was for my precious charge. I stooped. There were my rugs, my larger bag, but – no, not the smaller one; and though the other two were there, I knew at once that they were not quite in the same position – not so close to me. Horror seized me. Half wildly I gazed around, when my silent neighbour bent towards me. I could declare there was nothing in his hand when he did so, and I could declare as positively that I had already looked under the small round table beside which I sat, and that the bag was not there. And yet when the man, with a slight cackle, caused, no doubt, by his stooping, raised himself, the thing was in his hand!

Was he a conjurer, a pupil of Maskelyne and Cook? And how was it that, even as he held out my missing property, he managed, and that most cleverly and unobtrusively, to prevent my catching sight of his face? I did not see it then – I never did see it!

Something he murmured, to the effect that he supposed the bag was what I was looking for. In what language he spoke I know not; it was more that by the action accompanying the mumbled sounds I gathered his meaning, than that I heard anything articulate.

I thanked him, of course, mechanically, so to say, though I began to feel as if he were an evil spirit haunting me. I could only hope that the splendid lock to the bag had defied all curiosity, but I felt in a fever to be alone again, and able to satisfy myself that nothing had been tampered with.

The thought recalled my wandering faculties. How long had I been asleep? I drew out my watch. Heavens! It was close upon the hour named for the first train in the morning. I sprang up, collected my things, and dashed out of the 'Restauration'. If I had not paid for my coffee before, I certainly did not pay for it then. Besides my haste, there was another reason for this – there was no one to pay to! Not a creature was to be seen in the room or at the door as I passed out – always excepting the man with the cough.

As I left the place and hurried along the road, a bell began, not to ring, but to toll. It sounded most uncanny. What it meant, of course, I have never known. It may have been a summons to the workpeople of some manufactory, it may have been like all the other experiences of that strange night. But no; this theory I will not at present enter upon.

Dawn was not yet breaking, but there was in one direction a faint suggestion of something of the kind not far off. Otherwise all was dark. I stumbled along as best I could, helped in reality, I suppose, by the ugly yellow glimmer of the woebegone street, or road lamps. And it was not far to the station, though somehow it seemed farther than when I came; and somehow, too, it seemed to have grown steep, though I could not remember having noticed any slope the other way on my arrival. A nightmare-like sensation began to oppress me. I felt as if my luggage was growing momentarily heavier and heavier, as if I should never reach the station; and to this was joined the agonising terror of missing the train.

I made a desperate effort. Cold as it was, the beads of perspiration stood out upon my forehead as I forced myself along. And by degrees the nightmare feeling cleared off. I found myself entering the station at a run just as – yes, a train was actually beginning to move! I dashed, baggage and all, into a compartment; it was empty, and it was a second-class one, precisely similar to the one I had occupied before; it might have been the very same one. The train gradually increased its speed, but for the first few moments, while still in the station and passing through its immediate entourage, another strange thing struck me—the extraordinary silence and lifelessness of all about. Not one human being did I see, no porter watching our departure with the faithful though stolid interest always to be seen on the porter's visage. I might have been alone in the train – it might have had a freight of the dead, and been itself propelled by some supernatural agency, so noiselessly, so gloomily did it proceed.

You will scarcely credit that I actually and for the third time fell asleep. I could not help it. Some occult influence was at work upon me throughout those dark hours, I am positively certain. And with the daylight it was dispelled. For when I again awoke, I felt for the first time since leaving home completely and normally myself, fresh and vigorous, all my faculties at their best.

But, nevertheless, my first sensation was a start of amazement, almost of terror. The compartment was nearly full! There were at least five or six travellers besides myself, very respectable, ordinary-looking folk, with nothing in the least alarming about them. Yet it was with a gasp of extraordinary relief that I found my precious bag in the corner beside me, where I had carefully placed it. It was concealed from view. No one, I felt assured, could have touched it without awaking me.

It was broad and bright daylight. How long had I slept?

'Can you tell me—' I inquired of my opposite neighbour, a cheery-faced compatriot, 'Can you tell me how soon we get to — Junction by this train? I am most anxious to catch the evening mail at Calais, and am quite out in my reckonings, owing to an extraordinary delay at —. I have wasted the night by getting into a stopping train instead of the express.'

He looked at me in astonishment. He must have thought me either mad or just awaking from a fit of intoxication – only I flatter myself I did not look as if the latter were the case.

'How soon we get to — Junction?' he repeated. 'Why, my good sir, you left it about three hours ago! It is now eight o'clock. We all got in at the Junction. You were alone, if I mistake not?' He glanced at one or two of the others, who endorsed his statement. 'And very fast asleep you were, and must have been, not to be disturbed by the bustle at the station. And as for catching the evening boat at Calais—' He burst into a loud guffaw. 'Why, it would be very hard lines to do no better than that! We all hope to cross by the midday one.'

'Then – what train is this?' I exclaimed, utterly perplexed.

'The express, of course. All of us, excepting yourself, joined it at the Junction,' he replied.

'The express?' I repeated. 'The express that leaves—' and I named my own town, 'at six in the evening?'

'Exactly. You have got into the right train after all,' and here came another shout of amusement. 'How did you think we had all got in if you had not yet passed the Junction? You had not the pleasure of our company from M—, I take it? M—, which you passed at nine o'clock last night, if my memory is correct.'

'Then,' I persisted, 'this is the double-fast express, which does not stop between M— and your Junction?'

'Exactly,' he repeated; and then, confirmed most probably in his belief that I was mad, or the other thing, he turned to his newspaper, and left me to my extraordinary cogitations.

Had I been dreaming? Impossible! Every sensation, the very taste of the coffee, seemed still present with me – the curious accent of the officials at the mysterious town, I could perfectly recall. I still shivered at the remembrance of the chilly waking in the 'Restauration'; I heard again the cackling cough.

But I felt I must collect myself, and be ready for the important negotiation entrusted to me.

And to do this I must for the time banish these fruitless efforts at solving the problem.

We had a good run to Calais, found the boat in waiting, and a fair passage brought us prosperously across the Channel. I found myself in London, punctual to the intended hour of my arrival.

At once I drove to the lodgings in a small street off the Strand which I was accustomed to frequent in such circumstances. I felt nervous till I had an opportunity of thoroughly overhauling my documents. The bag had been opened by the Custom House officials, but the words 'private papers' had sufficed to prevent any further examination; and to my unspeakable delight they were intact. A glance satisfied me as to this the moment I got them out, for they were most carefully numbered.

The next morning saw me early on my way to – No. 909, we

will say – Blackfriars Street, where was the office of Messrs Bluestone & Fagg. I had never been there before, but it was easy to find, and had I felt any doubt, their name stared me in the face at the side of the open doorway. 'Second floor,' I thought I read; but when I reached the first landing, I imagined I must have been mistaken. For there, at a door ajar, stood an eminently respectable-looking gentleman, who bowed as he saw me, with a discreet smile.

'Herr Schmidt?' he said. 'Ah, yes; I was on the look-out for you.'

I felt a little surprised, and my glance involuntarily strayed to the doorway. There was no name upon it, and it appeared to have been freshly painted. My new friend saw my glance.

'It is all right,' he said. 'We have the painters here. We are using these lower rooms temporarily. I was watching to prevent your having the trouble of mounting to the second floor.'

And as I followed him in, I caught sight of a painter's ladder – a small one – on the stair above, and the smell was also unmistakable.

The large outer office looked bare and empty, but under the circumstances that was natural. No one was, at the first glance, to be seen; but behind a dulled glass partition screening off one corner I fancied I caught sight of a seated figure. And an inner office, to which my conductor led the way, had a more comfortable and inhabited look. Here stood a younger man. He bowed politely.

'Mr Fagg, my junior,' said the first individual airily. 'And now, Herr Schmidt, to business at once, if you please. Time is everything. You have all the documents ready?'

I answered by opening my bag and spreading out its contents. Both men were very grave, almost taciturn; but as I proceeded to explain things it was easy to see that they thoroughly understood all I said.

'And now,' I went on, when I had reached a certain point, 'if you will give me Numbers 7 and 13, which you have already received by registered post, I can put you in full possession of the whole. Without them, of course, all I have said is, so to say, preliminary only.'

The two looked at each other.

'Of course,' said the elder man, 'I follow what you say. The key of the whole is wanting. But I was momentarily expecting you to bring it out. We have not – Fagg, I am right, am I not? – we have received nothing by post?'

'Nothing whatever,' replied his junior. And the answer seemed simplicity itself. Why did a strange thrill of misgiving go through me? Was it something in the look that had passed between them? Perhaps so. In any case, strange to say, the inconsistency between their having received no papers and yet looking for my arrival at the hour mentioned in the letter accompanying the documents, and accosting me by name, did not strike me till some hours later.

I threw off what I believed to be my ridiculous mistrust, and it was not difficult to do so in my extreme annoyance.

'I cannot understand it,' I said. 'It is really too bad. Everything depends upon 7 and 13. I must telegraph at once for inquiries to be instituted at the post-office.'

'But your people must have duplicates,' said Fagg eagerly. 'These can be forwarded at once.'

'I hope so,' I said, though feeling strangely confused and worried.

'They must send them direct here,' he went on.

I did not at once answer. I was gathering my papers together.

'And in the meantime,' he proceeded, touching my bag, 'you had better leave these here. We will lock them up in the safe at once. It is better than carrying them about London.'

It certainly seemed so. I half laid down the bag on the table, but at that moment from the outer room a most peculiar sound caught my ears – a faint cackling cough! I think I concealed my start. I turned away as if considering Fagg's suggestion, which, to confess the truth, I had been on the very point of agreeing to. For it would have been a great relief to me to know that the papers were in safe custody. But now a flash of lurid light seemed to have transformed everything.

'I thank you,' I replied. 'I should be glad to be free from the responsibility of the charge, but I dare not let these out of my own hands till the agreement is formally signed.'

The younger man's face darkened. He assumed a bullying tone.

'I don't know how it strikes you, Mr Bluestone,' he said, 'but it seems to me that this young gentleman is going rather too far. Do you think your employers will be pleased to hear of your insulting us, sir?'

But the elder man smiled condescendingly, though with a touch of superciliousness. It was very well done. He waved his hand.

'Stay, my dear Mr Fagg; we can well afford to make allowance. You will telegraph at once, no doubt, Herr Schmidt, and – let me see – yes, we shall receive the duplicates of Numbers 7 and 13 by first post on Thursday morning.'

I bowed.

'Exactly,' I replied, as I lifted the now locked bag. 'And you may expect me at the same hour on Thursday morning.'

Then I took my departure, accompanied to the door by the urbane individual who had received me.

The telegram which I at once despatched was not couched precisely as he would have dictated, I allow. And he would have been considerably surprised at my sending off another, later in the day, to Bluestone & Fagg's telegraphic address, in these words:—

'Unavoidably detained till Thursday morning – Schmidt.'

This was after the arrival of a wire from home in answer to mine.

By Thursday morning I had had time to receive a letter from

Herr Wilhelm, and to secure the services of a certain noted detective, accompanied by whom I presented myself at the appointed hour at 909. But my companion's services were not required. The birds had flown, warned by the same traitor in our camp through whom the first hints of the new patent had leaked out. With him it was easy to deal, poor wretch! But the clever rogues who had employed him and personated the members of the honourable firm of Bluestone & Fagg were never traced.

The negotiation was successfully carried out. The experience I had gone through left me a wiser man. It is to be hoped, too, that the owners of 909 Blackfriars Street were more cautious in the future as to whom they let their premises to when temporarily vacant. The repainting of the doorway, etc., at the tenant's own expense had already roused some slight suspicion.

It is needless to add that Numbers 7 and 13 had been duly received on the second floor.

I have never known the true history of that extraordinary night. Was it all a dream, or a prophetic vision of warning? Or was it in any sense true? Had I, in some inexplicable way, left my own town earlier than I intended, and really travelled in a slow train?

Or had the man with a cough, for his own nefarious purposes, mesmerised or hypnotised me, and to some extent succeeded?

I cannot say. Sometimes, even, I ask myself if I am quite sure that there ever was such a person as 'the man with the cough'!

MAN-SIZE IN MARBLE

By Edith Nesbit (1858–1924)

Born in Kennington, the daughter of an agricultural chemist (who died when she was still a child) and his wife, Edith Nesbit had a peripatetic upbringing in England and France, as her mother travelled with her family to find healthier places for Edith's sister who suffered from tuberculosis. As an adult, Edith began her writing career as a poet but moved on to fiction. Starting with The Story of the Treasure Seekers *in 1899, Nesbit wrote many novels for younger readers, several of which (*Five Children and It *from 1902,* The Railway Children *from 1906) are now recognised as classics of children's literature.*

Her personal life was complicated. Already seven months pregnant by him, she married Hubert Bland in 1880, only to discover that he was involved with another woman who had borne him a child. Some years later, Bland engaged in an affair with her friend, Alice Hoatson. Hoatson moved in with the Blands and they adopted the two children Hubert had with her. The Blands were socialists and early members of the Fabian Society. Indeed, some of Nesbit's early novels and short stories were published under the pseudonym 'Fabian Bland' and she named one of her sons Fabian. Outside her writings for children, Nesbit's best work lies in her supernatural stories of which 'Man-Size in Marble' is the most original and unsettling.

Home Chimes December 1887

Although every word of this story is as true as despair, I do not expect people to believe it. Nowadays a 'rational explanation' is required before belief is possible. Let me then, at once, offer the 'rational explanation' which finds most favour among those who have heard the tale of my life's tragedy. It is held that we were 'under a delusion' Laura and I, on that 31st of October; and that this supposition places the whole matter on a satisfactory and believable basis. The reader can judge, when he, too, has heard my story, how far this is an 'explanation', and in what sense it is 'rational'. There were three who took part in this: Laura and I and another man. The other man still lives, and can speak to the truth of the least credible part of my story.

I never in my life knew what it was to have as much money as I required to supply the most ordinary needs – good colours, books, and cab-fares – and when we were married, we knew quite well that we should only be able to live at all by 'strict punctuality and attention to business'. I used to paint in those days, and Laura used to write, and we felt sure we could keep the pot at least simmering. Living in town was out of the question, so we went to look for a cottage in the country, which should be at once sanitary and picturesque. So rarely do these two qualities meet in one cottage that our search was for some time quite fruitless. We tried advertisements, but most of the desirable rural residences which we did look at proved to be lacking in both essentials, and when a cottage chanced to have drains it always had stucco as well and was shaped like a tea-caddy. And if we found a vine- or rose-covered porch, corruption invariably lurked within. Our minds got so befogged by the eloquence of house-agents and the rival disadvantages of the fever-traps and outrages to beauty which we had seen and scorned, that I very much doubt whether either of us, on our wedding morning, knew the difference between a house and a haystack. But when we got away from friends and house-agents, on our honeymoon, our wits grew clear again, and we knew a pretty cottage when at last we saw one. It was at Brenzett – a little village set on a hill over against the southern marshes. We had gone there, from the seaside village where we were staying, to see the church, and two fields from the church we found this cottage. It stood quite by itself, about two miles from the village. It was a long, low building, with rooms sticking out in unexpected places. There was a bit of stone-work – ivy-covered and moss-grown, just two old rooms, all that was left of a big house that had once stood there – and round this stone-work the house had grown up. Stripped of its roses and jasmine it would have been hideous. As it stood it was charming, and after a brief examination we took it. It was absurdly cheap. The rest of our honeymoon we spent in grubbing about in second-hand shops in the county town, picking up bits of old oak and Chippendale chairs for our furnishing. We wound up with a run up to town and a visit to Liberty's, and soon the low oak-beamed lattice-windowed rooms began to be home. There was a jolly old-fashioned garden, with grass paths, and no end of hollyhocks and sunflowers, and big lilies. From the window you could see the marsh-pastures, and beyond them the blue, thin line of the sea. We were as happy as the summer was glorious, and settled down into work sooner than we ourselves expected. I was never tired of sketching the view and the wonderful cloud effects from the open lattice, and Laura would sit at the table and write verses about them, in which I mostly played the part of foreground.

We got a tall old peasant woman to do for us. Her face and figure were good, though her cooking was of the homeliest; but she understood all about gardening, and told us all the old names of the coppices and cornfields, and the stories of the smugglers and highwaymen, and, better still, of the 'things that walked', and of the 'sights' which met one in lonely glens of a starlight night. She was a great comfort to us, because Laura hated housekeeping as much as I loved folklore, and we soon came to leave all the domestic business to Mrs Dorman, and to use her legends in little magazine stories which brought in the jingling guinea.

We had three months of married happiness, and did not have a single quarrel. One October evening I had been down to smoke a pipe with the doctor – our only neighbour – a pleasant young Irishman. Laura had stayed at home to finish a comic sketch of a village episode for the *Monthly Marplot*. I left her laughing over her own jokes, and came in to find her a crumpled heap of pale muslin weeping on the window seat.

'Good Heavens, my darling, what's the matter?' I cried, taking her in my arms. She leaned her little dark head against my shoulder and went on crying. I had never seen her cry before – we had always been so happy, you see – and I felt sure some frightful misfortune had happened.

'What is the matter? Do speak.'

'It's Mrs Dorman,' she sobbed.

'What has she done?' I inquired, immensely relieved.

'She says she must go before the end of the month, and she says her niece is ill; she's gone down to see her now, but I don't believe that's the reason, because her niece is always ill. I believe someone has been setting her against us. Her manner was so queer—'

'Never mind, Pussy,' I said. 'Whatever you do, don't cry, or I shall have to cry too, to keep you in countenance, and then you'll never respect your man again!'

She dried her eyes obediently on my handkerchief, and even smiled faintly.

'But you see,' she went on, 'it is really serious, because these village people are so sheepy, and if one won't do a thing, you may be quite sure none of the others will. And I shall have to cook the dinners, and wash up the hateful greasy plates; and you'll have to carry cans of water about, and clean the boots and knives – and we shall never have any time for work, or earn any money, or anything. We shall have to work all day, and only be able to rest when we are waiting for the kettle to boil!'

I represented to her that even if we had to perform these duties, the day would still present some margin for other toils and recreations. But she refused to see the matter in any but the greyest light. She was very unreasonable, my Laura, but I could not have loved her any more if she had been as reasonable as Whately.

'I'll speak to Mrs Dorman when she comes back, and see if I can't come to terms with her,' I said. 'Perhaps she wants a rise in her screw. It will be all right. Let's walk up to the church.'

The church was a large and lonely one, and we loved to go there, especially upon bright nights. The path skirted a wood, cut through it once, and ran along the crest of the hill through two meadows, and round the churchyard wall, over which the old yews loomed in black masses of shadow. This path, which was partly paved, was called 'the bier-balk', for it had long been the way by which the corpses had been carried to burial. The churchyard was richly treed, and was shaded by great elms which stood just outside and stretched their majestic arms in benediction over the happy dead. A large, low porch let one into the building by a Norman doorway and a heavy oak door studded with iron. Inside, the arches rose into darkness, and between them the reticulated windows, which stood out white in the moonlight. In the chancel, the windows were of rich glass, which showed in faint light their noble colouring, and made the black oak of the choir pews hardly more solid than the shadows. But on each side of the altar lay a grey marble figure of a knight in full plate armour lying upon a low slab, with hands held up in everlasting prayer, and these figures, oddly enough, were always to be seen if there was any glimmer of light in the church. Their names were lost, but the peasants told of them that they had been fierce and wicked men, marauders by land and sea, who had been the scourge of their time, and had been guilty of deeds so foul that the house they had lived in – the big house, by the way, that had stood on the site of our cottage – had been stricken by lightning and the vengeance of Heaven. But for all that, the gold of their heirs had bought them a place in the church. Looking at the bad hard faces reproduced in the marble, this story was easily believed.

The church looked at its best and weirdest on that night, for the shadows of the yew trees fell through the windows upon the floor of the nave and touched the pillars with tattered shade. We sat down together without speaking, and watched the solemn beauty of the old church, with some of that awe which inspired its early builders. We walked to the chancel and looked at the sleeping warriors. Then we rested some time on the stone seat in the porch, looking out over the stretch of quiet moonlit meadows, feeling in every fibre of our being the peace of the night and of our happy love; and came away at last with a sense that even scrubbing and blackleading were but small troubles at their worst.

Mrs Dorman had come back from the village, and I at once invited her to a tête-à-tête.

'Now, Mrs Dorman,' I said, when I had got her into my painting room, 'what's all this about your not staying with us?'

'I should be glad to get away, sir, before the end of the month,' she answered, with her usual placid dignity.

'Have you any fault to find, Mrs Dorman?'

'None at all, sir; you and your lady have always been most kind, I'm sure—'

'Well, what is it? Are your wages not high enough?'

'No, sir, I gets quite enough.'

'Then why not stay?'

'I'd rather not.' – with some hesitation – 'My niece is ill.'

'But your niece has been ill ever since we came.'

No answer. There was a long and awkward silence. I broke it.

'Can't you stay for another month?' I asked.

'No, sir. I'm bound to go by Thursday.'

And this was Monday!

'Well, I must say, I think you might have let us know before. There's no time now to get anyone else, and your mistress is not fit to do heavy housework. Can't you stay till next week?'

'I might be able to come back next week.'

I was now convinced that all she wanted was a brief holiday, which we should have been willing enough to let her have, as soon as we could get a substitute.

'But why must you go this week?' I persisted. 'Come, out with it.'

Mrs Dorman drew the little shawl, which she always wore, tightly across her bosom, as though she were cold. Then she said, with a sort of effort —

'They say, sir, as this was a big house in Catholic times, and there was a many deeds done here.'

The nature of the 'deeds' might be vaguely inferred from the inflection of Mrs Dorman's voice – which was enough to make one's blood run cold. I was glad that Laura was not in the room. She was always nervous, as highly-strung natures are, and I felt that these tales about our house, told by this old peasant woman, with her impressive manner and contagious credulity, might have made our home less dear to my wife.

'Tell me all about it, Mrs Dorman,' I said. 'You needn't mind about telling me. I'm not like the young people who make fun of such things.'

Which was partly true.

'Well, sir,' – she sank her voice – 'you may have seen in the church, beside the altar, two shapes.'

'You mean the effigies of the knights in armour,' I said cheerfully.

'I mean them two bodies, drawed out man-size in marble,' she returned, and I had to admit that her description was a thousand times more graphic than mine, to say nothing of a certain weird force and uncanniness about the phrase 'drawed out man-size in marble'.

'They do say, as on All Saints' Eve them two bodies sits up on their slabs, and gets off of them, and then walks down the aisle, in their marble' – (another good phrase, Mrs Dorman) – 'and as the church clock strikes eleven they walks out of the church door, and over the graves, and along the bier-balk, and if it's a wet night there's the marks of their feet in the morning.'

'And where do they go?' I asked, rather fascinated.

'They comes back here to their home, sir, and if anyone meets them—'

'Well, what then?' I asked.

But no – not another word could I get from her, save that her niece was ill and she must go. After what I had heard I scorned to discuss the niece, and tried to get from Mrs Dorman more details of the legend. I could get nothing but warnings.

'Whatever you do, sir, lock the door early on All Saints' Eve, and make the cross-sign over the doorstep and on the windows.'

'But has anyone ever seen these things?' I persisted.

'That's not for me to say. I know what I know, sir.'

'Well, who was here last year?'

'No one, sir; the lady as owned the house only stayed here in summer, and she always went to London a full month afore the night. And I'm sorry to inconvenience you and your lady, but my niece is ill and I must go on Thursday.'

I could have shaken her for her absurd reiteration of that obvious fiction, after she had told me her real reasons.

She was determined to go, nor could our united entreaties move her in the least.

I did not tell Laura the legend of the shapes that 'walked in their marble', partly because a legend concerning our house might perhaps trouble my wife, and partly, I think, for some more occult reason. This was not quite the same to me as any other story, and I did not want to talk about it till the day was over. I had very soon ceased to think of the legend, however. I was painting a portrait of Laura, against the lattice window, and I could not think of much else. I had got a splendid background of yellow and grey sunset, and Laura was working away with enthusiasm at her lace. On Thursday Mrs Dorman went. She relented, at parting, so far as to say—

'Don't you put yourself about too much, ma'am, and if there's any little thing I can do next week, I'm sure I shan't mind.'

From which I inferred that she wished to come back to us after Hallowe'en. Up to the last she adhered to the fiction of the niece with touching fidelity.

Thursday passed off pretty well. Laura showed marked ability in the matter of steak and potatoes, and I confess that my knives, and the plates, which I insisted upon washing, were better done than I had dared to expect.

Friday came. It is about what happened on that Friday that this is written. I wonder if I should have believed it, if anyone had told it to me. I will write the story of it as quickly and plainly as I can. Everything that happened on that day is burnt into my brain. I shall not forget anything, nor leave anything out.

I got up early, I remember, and lighted the kitchen fire, and had just achieved a smoky success, when my little wife came running down, as sunny and sweet as the clear October morning itself. We prepared breakfast together, and found it very good fun. The housework was soon done, and when brushes and brooms and pails were quiet again, the house was still indeed. It is wonderful what a difference one makes in a house. We really missed Mrs Dorman, quite apart from considerations concerning pots and pans. We spent the day in dusting our books and putting them straight, and dined gaily on cold steak and coffee. Laura was, if possible, brighter and gayer and sweeter than usual, and I began to think that a little domestic toil was really good for her. We had never been so merry since we were married, and the walk we had that afternoon was, I think, the happiest time of all my life. When we had watched the deep scarlet clouds slowly pale into leaden grey against a pale green sky, and saw the white mists curl up along the hedgerows in the distant marsh, we came back to the house, silently, hand in hand.

'You are sad, my darling,' I said, half-jestingly, as we sat down together in our little parlour. I expected a disclaimer, for my own silence had been the silence of complete happiness. To my surprise she said—

'Yes. I think I am sad, or rather I am uneasy. I don't think I'm very well. I have shivered three or four times since we came in, and it is not cold, is it?'

'No,' I said, and hoped it was not a chill caught from the treacherous mists that roll up from the marshes in the dying light. No – she said, she did not think so. Then, after a silence, she spoke suddenly—

'Do you ever have presentiments of evil?'

'No,' I said, smiling, 'and I shouldn't believe in them if I had.'

'I do,' she went on. 'The night my father died I knew it, though he was right away in the north of Scotland.' I did not answer in words.

She sat looking at the fire for some time in silence, gently stroking my hand. At last she sprang up, came behind me, and, drawing my head back, kissed me.

'There, it's over now,' she said. 'What a baby I am! Come, light the candles, and we'll have some of these new Rubinstein duets.'

And we spent a happy hour or two at the piano.

At about half-past ten I began to long for the good-night pipe, but Laura looked so white that I felt it would be brutal of me to fill our sitting-room with the fumes of strong Cavendish.

'I'll take my pipe outside,' I said.

'Let me come, too.'

'No, sweetheart, not tonight; you're much too tired. I shan't be long. Get to bed, or I shall have an invalid to nurse tomorrow as well as the boots to clean.'

I kissed her and was turning to go, when she flung her arms round my neck, and held me as if she would never let me go again. I stroked her hair.

'Come, Pussy, you're over-tired. The housework has been too much for you.'

She loosened her clasp a little and drew a deep breath.

'No. We've been very happy today, Jack, haven't we? Don't stay out too long.'

'I won't, my dearie.'

I strolled out of the front door, leaving it unlatched. What a night it was! The jagged masses of heavy dark cloud were rolling at intervals from horizon to horizon, and thin white wreaths covered the stars. Through all the rush of the cloud river, the moon swam, breasting the waves and disappearing again in the darkness. When now and again her light reached the woodlands they seemed to be slowly and noiselessly waving in time to the swing of the clouds above them. There was a strange grey light over all the earth; the fields had that shadowy bloom over them which only comes from the marriage of dew and moonshine, or frost and starlight.

I walked up and down, drinking in the beauty of the quiet earth and the changing sky. The night was absolutely silent. Nothing seemed to be abroad. There was no scurrying of rabbits, or twitter of the half-asleep birds. And though the clouds went sailing across the sky, the wind that drove them never came low enough to rustle the dead leaves in the woodland paths. Across the meadows I could see the church tower standing out black and grey against the sky. I walked there thinking over our three months of happiness – and of my wife, her dear eyes, her loving ways. Oh, my little girl, my own little girl, what a vision came then of a long, glad life for you and me together!

I heard a bell-beat from the church. Eleven already! I turned to go in, but the night held me. I could not go back into our little warm rooms yet. I would go up to the church. I felt vaguely that it would be good to carry my love and thankfulness to the sanctuary whither so many loads of sorrow and gladness had been borne by the men and women of the dead years.

I looked in at the low window as I went by. Laura was half lying on her chair in front of the fire. I could not see her face, only her little head showed dark against the pale blue wall. She was quite still. Asleep, no doubt. My heart reached out to her, as I went on. There must be a God, I thought, and a God who was good. How otherwise could anything so sweet and dear as she have ever been imagined?

I walked slowly along the edge of the wood. A sound broke the stillness of the night, it was a rustling in the wood. I stopped and listened. The sound stopped too. I went on, and now distinctly heard another step than mine answer mine like an echo. It was a poacher or a wood-stealer, most likely, for these were not unknown in our Arcadian neighbourhood. But whoever it was, he was a fool not to step more lightly. I turned into the wood, and now the footstep seemed to come from the path I had just left. It must be an echo, I thought. The wood looked perfect in the moonlight. The large dying ferns and the brushwood showed where through thinning foliage the pale light came down. The tree trunks stood up like Gothic columns all around me. They reminded me of the church, and I turned into the bier-balk, and passed through the corpse-gate between the graves to the low porch. I paused for a moment on the stone seat where Laura and I had watched the fading landscape. Then I noticed that the door of the church was open, and I blamed myself for having left it unlatched the other night. We were the only people who ever cared to come to the church except on Sundays, and I was vexed to think that through our carelessness the damp autumn airs had had a chance of getting in and injuring the old fabric. I went in. It will seem strange, perhaps, that I should have gone half-way up the aisle before I remembered – with a sudden chill, followed by as sudden a rush of self-contempt – that this was the very day and hour when, according to tradition, the 'shapes drawed out man-size in marble' began to walk.

Having thus remembered the legend, and remembered it with a shiver, of which I was ashamed, I could not do otherwise than walk up towards the altar, just to look at the figures – as I said to myself; really what I wanted was to assure myself, first, that I did not believe the legend, and, secondly, that it was not true. I was rather glad that I had come. I thought now I could tell Mrs Dorman how vain her fancies were, and how peacefully the marble figures slept on through the ghastly hour. With my hands in my pockets I passed up the aisle. In the grey dim light the eastern end of the church looked larger than usual, and the arches above the two tombs looked larger too. The moon came out and showed me the reason. I stopped short, my heart gave a leap that nearly choked me, and then sank sickeningly.

The 'bodies drawed out man-size' were gone, and their marble slabs lay wide and bare in the vague moonlight that slanted through the east window.

Were they really gone? Or was I mad? Clenching my nerves, I stooped and passed my hand over the smooth slabs, and felt their flat unbroken surface. Had someone taken the things away? Was it some vile practical joke? I would make sure, anyway. In an instant I had made a torch of a newspaper, which happened to be in my pocket and, lighting it, held it high above my head. Its yellow glare illumined the dark arches and those slabs. The figures were gone. And I was alone in the church; or was I alone?

And then a horror seized me, a horror indefinable and indescribable — an overwhelming certainty of supreme and accomplished calamity. I flung down the torch and tore along the aisle and out through the porch, biting my lips as I ran to keep myself from shrieking aloud. Oh, was I mad — or what was this that possessed me? I leaped the churchyard wall and took the straight cut across the fields, led by the light from our windows. Just as I got over the first stile, a dark figure seemed to spring out of the ground. Mad still with that certainty of misfortune, I made for the thing that stood in my path, shouting, 'Get out of the way, can't you!'

But my push met with a more vigorous resistance than I had expected. My arms were caught just above the elbow and held as in a vice, and the raw-boned Irish doctor actually shook me.

'Would ye?' he cried, in his own unmistakable accent — 'Would ye, then?'

'Let me go, you fool,' I gasped. 'The marble figures have gone from the church; I tell you they've gone.'

He broke into a ringing laugh. 'I'll have to give ye a draught tomorrow, I see. Ye've bin smoking too much and listening to old wives' tales.'

'I tell you, I've seen the bare slabs.'

'Well, come back with me. I'm going up to old Palmer's – his daughter's ill; we'll look in at the church and let me see the bare slabs.'

'You go, if you like,' I said, a little less frantic for his laughter. 'I'm going home to my wife.'

'Rubbish, man,' said he. 'D'ye think I'll permit of that? Are ye to go saying all yer life that ye've seen solid marble endowed with vitality, and me to go all me life saying ye were a coward? No, sir – ye shan't do ut.'

The night air – a human voice – and I think also the physical contact with this six feet of solid common sense, brought me back a little to my ordinary self, and the word 'coward' was a mental shower-bath.

'Come on, then,' I said sullenly. 'Perhaps you're right.'

He still held my arm tightly. We got over the stile and back to the church. All was still as death. The place smelt very damp and earthy. We walked up the aisle. I am not ashamed to confess that I shut my eyes: I knew the figures would not be there. I heard Kelly strike a match.

'Here they are, ye see, right enough; ye've been dreaming or drinking, asking yer pardon for the imputation.'

I opened my eyes. By Kelly's expiring vesta I saw two shapes lying 'in their marble' on their slabs. I drew a deep breath, and caught his hand.

'I'm awfully indebted to you,' I said. 'It must have been some trick of light, or I have been working rather hard, perhaps that's it. Do you know, I was quite convinced they were gone.'

'I'm aware of that,' he answered rather grimly. 'Ye'll have to be careful of that brain of yours, my friend, I assure ye.'

He was leaning over and looking at the right-hand figure, whose stony face was the most villainous and deadly in expression.

'By Jove,' he said. 'Something has been afoot here – this hand is broken.'

And so it was. I was certain that it had been perfect the last time Laura and I had been there.

'Perhaps someone has tried to remove them,' said the young doctor.

'That won't account for my impression,' I objected.

'Too much painting and tobacco will account for that, well enough.'

'Come along,' I said, 'or my wife will be getting anxious. You'll come in and have a drop of whisky and drink confusion to ghosts and better sense to me.'

'I ought to go up to Palmer's, but it's so late now I'd best leave it till the morning,' he replied. 'I was kept late at the Union, and I've had to see a lot of people since. All right, I'll come back with ye.'

I think he fancied I needed him more than did Palmer's girl, so, discussing how such an illusion could have been possible, and deducing from this experience large generalities concerning ghostly apparitions, we walked up to our cottage. We saw, as we walked up the garden path, that bright light streamed out of the front door, and presently saw that the parlour door was open too. Had she gone out?

'Come in,' I said, and Dr Kelly followed me into the parlour. It was all ablaze with candles, not only the wax ones, but at least a dozen guttering, glaring tallow dips, stuck in vases and ornaments in unlikely places. Light, I knew, was Laura's remedy for nervousness. Poor child! Why had I left her? Brute that I was.

We glanced round the room, and at first we did not see her. The window was open, and the draught set all the candles flaring one way. Her chair was empty and her handkerchief and book lay on the floor. I turned to the window. There, in the recess of the window, I saw her. Oh, my child, my love, had she gone to that window to watch for me? And what had come into the room behind her? To what had she turned with that look of frantic fear and horror? Oh, my little one, had she thought that it was I whose step she heard, and turned to meet – what?

She had fallen back across a table in the window, and her body lay half on it and half on the window seat, and her head hung down over the table, the brown hair loosened and fallen to the carpet. Her lips were drawn back, and her eyes wide, wide open. They saw nothing now. What had they seen last?

The doctor moved towards her, but I pushed him aside and sprang to her; caught her in my arms and cried—

'It's all right, Laura! I've got you safe, wifie.'

She fell into my arms in a heap. I clasped her and kissed her, and called her by all her pet names, but I think I knew all the time that she was dead. Her hands were tightly clenched. In one of them she held something fast. When I was quite sure that she was dead, and that nothing mattered at all any more, I let him open her hand to see what she held.

It was a grey marble finger.

SANDY THE TINKER

By Charlotte Riddell (1832–1906)

Born in County Antrim in what is now Northern Ireland, Charlotte Riddell published her first novel in her twenties and went on to produce dozens of others in the last four decades of the nineteenth century. Unusually for a woman writer, many of them, with titles like City and Suburb *and* The Head of the Firm, *dealt with the worlds of business and finance. Her best known book in her own lifetime was* George Geith of Fen Court, *the story of a cleric who abandons family and religious life for a career in the City. Regularly reprinted, it was adapted as a play which was a success on the London stage. Today she is remembered not for any of her novels but for her ghost stories, a genre in which she proved herself a highly skilful practitioner. Stories such as 'Forewarned, Forearmed', 'Nut Bush Farm' and 'The Old House in Vauxhall Walk' still regularly appear in anthologies. Her collection* Weird Stories *was published in 1882. Despite the title, most of the tales which appear in it are more accurately described as ghost stories but 'Sandy the Tinker', about a Scottish minister's encounter with the 'Evil One', is most definitely a 'weird story'.*

From the collection, Weird Stories, *1882*

'Before commencing my story, I wish to state it is perfectly true in every particular.'

'We quite understand that,' said the sceptic of our party, who was wont, in the security of friendly intercourse, to characterise all such prefaces as mere introductions to some tremendously exaggerated tale.

On the occasion in question, however, we had donned our best behaviour, a garment which did not sit ungracefully on some of us; and our host, who was about to draw out from the stores of memory one narrative for our entertainment, was scarcely the person before whom even Jack Hill, the sceptic, would have cared to express his cynical and unbelieving views.

We were seated, an incongruous company of ten persons, in the best room of an old manse among the Scottish hills. Accident had thrown us together, and accident had driven us under the minister's hospitable roof. Cold, wet and hungry, drenched with rain, sorely beaten by the wind, we had crowded through the door opened by a friendly hand, and now, wet no longer, the pangs of hunger assuaged with smoking rashers of ham, poached eggs, and steaming potatoes, we sat around a blazing fire, drinking toddy out of tumblers, whilst the two ladies who graced the assemblage partook of a modicum of the same beverage from wine glasses.

Everything was eminently comfortable, but conducted upon the most correct principles. Jack could no more have taken it upon himself to shock the minister's ear with some of the opinions he aired in Fleet Street than he could have asked for more whisky with his water.

'Yes, it is perfectly true,' continued the minister, looking thoughtfully at the fire. 'I can't explain it, I cannot even try to explain it. I will tell you the story exactly as it occurred, however, and leave you to draw your own deductions from it.'

None of us answered. We fell into listening attitudes instantly, and eighteen eyes fixed themselves by one accord upon our host.

He was an old man, but hale. The weight of eighty winters had whitened his head, but not bowed it. He seemed young as any of us – younger than Jack Hill, who was a reviewer and a newspaper hack, and whose way through life had not been altogether on easy lines.

'Thirty years ago, upon a certain Friday morning in August,' began the minister, 'I was sitting at breakfast in the room on the other side of the passage, where you ate your supper, when the servant girl came in with a letter. She said a laddie, all out of breath, had brought it over from Dendeldy Manse. "He was bidden to rin a' the way," she went on, "and he's fairly beaten."

'I told her to make the messenger sit down, and put food before him; and then, when she went to do my bidding, proceeded, I must confess with some curiosity, to break the seal of a missive forwarded in such hot haste.

'It was from the minister at Dendeldy, who had been newly chosen to occupy the pulpit his deceased father had occupied for a quarter of a century and more.

'The call from the congregation originated rather out of respect to the father's memory than any extraordinary liking for the son. He had been reared for the most part in England, and was somewhat distant and formal in his manners; and, though full of Greek and Latin and Hebrew, wanted the true Scotch accent, that goes straight to the heart of those accustomed to the broad, honest, tender Scottish tongue.

'His people were proud of him, but they did not like some of his ways. They could remember him as a lad running about the whole countryside, and they could not understand, and did not approve of his holding them at arm's length, and shutting himself up among his books and refusing their hospitality, and sending out word he was busy when maybe some very decent man wanted speech with him. I had taken it upon myself to point out that I thought he was wrong, and that he would alienate his flock from him. Perhaps it was for this very reason, because I was blunt and plain, he took to me kindly, and never got on his high horse, no matter what I said to him.

'Well, to return to the letter. It was written in the wildest haste, and entreated me not to lose a moment in coming to him, as he was in the very *greatest distress* and *anxiety*.

'"Let *nothing* delay you," he proceeded. "If I cannot speak to you soon I believe I shall go out of my senses."

'What could be the matter? I thought. What in all the wide earth could have happened?

'I had seen him but a few days before and he was in good health and spirits, getting on better with his people, feeling hopeful of so altering his style of preaching as to touch their hearts more sensibly.

'What could have happened, however, puzzled me sorely. As I made my hurried preparations for setting out, I fairly perplexed myself with speculation. I went into the kitchen, where his messenger was eating some breakfast, and asked if Mr Crawley was ill.

'"I dinna ken," he answered. "He mad' no complaint, but he luiked awful bad, just awful."

'"In what way?" I inquired.

'"As if he had seen a ghaist," was the reply.

'This made me very uneasy, and I jumped to the conclusion the trouble was connected with money matters. Young men will be young men.'

Here the minister looked significantly at the callow bird of our company, a youth who had never owed a sixpence in his life or given away a cent; while Jack Hill – no chicken, by the way – was over head and ears in debt, and could not keep a sovereign in his pocket, though spending or bestowing it involved going dinnerless the next day.

'Young men will be young men,' repeated the minister, in his best pulpit manner ('Just as though anyone expected them to be young women!' grumbled Jack to me afterwards), 'and I feared that now he was settled and comfortably off some old creditor he had been paying as best he could, might have become pressing. I knew nothing of his liabilities, or, beyond the amount of the stipend paid him, the state of his pecuniary affairs; but, having once in my own life made myself responsible for a debt, I was aware of all the trouble putting your arm out further than you can draw it back involves. And I considered that most probably money, which is the root of all evil' ('and all good' Jack's eyes suggested to me), 'was the cause of my young friend's agony of mind. Blessed with a large family – every one of whom is now alive and doing well, I thank God, out in the world – you may imagine I had not much opportunity for laying by. Still, I had put aside a little for a rainy day, and that little I placed in my pocket-book, hoping even a small sum might prove of use in case of emergency.'

'By the road,' proceeded our host, 'Dendeldy is distant from here ten long miles, but by a short cut across the hills it can be reached in something under six. For me it was nothing of a walk, and accordingly I arrived at the manse ere noon.'

He paused and, though thirty years had elapsed, drew a handkerchief across his forehead before he continued his narrative.

'I had to climb a steep brae to reach the front door, but before I could breast it my friend met me.

'"Thank God you are come," he said, pressing my hand in his. "Oh, I am grateful."

'He was trembling with excitement. His face was a ghastly pallor.

'His voice was that of a person suffering from some terrible shock, labouring under some awful fear.

'"What *has* happened, Edward?" I asked. I had known him since he was a little boy. "I am distressed to see you in such a state. Rouse yourself; be a man; whatever may have gone wrong can possibly be righted. I have come over to do all that lies in my power for you. If it is a matter of money—"

'"No, no; it is not money," he interrupted. "Would that it were!" and he began to tremble again so violently that really he communicated some part of his nervousness to me, and put me into a state of perfect terror.

'"Whatever it is, Crawley, out with it," I said. "Have you murdered anybody?"

'"No, it is worse than that," he answered.

'"But that's just nonsense," I declared. "Are you in your right mind, do you think?"

'"I wish I were not," he returned. "I'd like to know I was stark staring mad; it would be happier for me – far, far happier."

'"If you don't tell me this minute what is the matter, I shall turn on my heel and tramp my way home again," I said, half in anger at what I thought was his folly.

'"Come into the house," he entreated, "and try to have patience with me; for indeed, Mr Morison, I am sorely troubled. I have been through my deep waters, and they have gone clean over my head."

'We went into his little study and sat down. For a while he remained silent, his head resting upon his hand, struggling with some strong emotion; but after about five minutes he asked in a low subdued voice, "Do you believe in dreams?"

'"What has my belief to do with the matter in hand?" I inquired.

'"It is a dream, an awful dream, that is troubling me."

'I rose from my chair.

"'Do you mean to say," I asked, "you have brought me from my business and my parish to tell me you have had a bad dream?"

"'That is just what I do mean to say," he answered. "At least it was not a dream – it was a vision; no, I don't mean a vision – I can't tell you what it was; but nothing I ever went through in actual life was half so real, and I have bound myself to go through it all again. There is no hope for me, Mr Morison. I sit before you a lost creature, the most miserable man on the face of the whole earth."

"'What did you dream?" I inquired.

'A dreadful fit of trembling again seized him; but at last he managed to say: "I have been like this ever since, and I shall be like this for evermore, till – till – the end comes."

"'When did you have your bad dream?" I asked.

"'Last night, or rather this morning," he answered. "I'll tell you all about it. I was as well when I went to bed about eleven o'clock as ever I was in my life. I had been considering my sermon and felt satisfied I should be able to deliver a good one next Sunday morning. I had taken nothing after my tea and I lay down in my bed feeling at peace with all mankind, and satisfied with my lot. How long I slept, or what I dreamt about at first, if I dreamt at all, I don't know; but after a time the mists seemed to clear from before my eyes, to roll away like clouds from a mountain summit, and I found myself walking on a beautiful summer's evening beside the River Deldy."

'He paused for a moment, and an irrepressible shudder shook his frame.

"'Go on," I said, for I felt afraid of his breaking down again.

'He looked at me pitifully, with a hungry entreaty in his weary eyes, and continued.

"'It was a lovely evening and I never thought the earth had looked so beautiful before. I walked on and on, till I came to that point where, as you may perhaps remember, the path, growing very narrow, winds round the base of a great crag, and leads the wayfarer suddenly into a little green amphitheatre, bounded on one side by the river, and on the other by rocks, that rise in places sheer to a height of a hundred feet or more."

"'I remember it,' I said. 'A little farther on three streams meet and fall with a tremendous roar into the Witches' Cauldron. A fine sight in the winter time, only there is scarce any reaching it from below, as the path you mention and the little green oasis are mostly covered with water.'

"'I had not been there before since I was a child,' he went on mournfully, 'but I recollected it as one of the most solitary spots possible; and my astonishment was great, to see a man standing in the pathway, with a drawn sword in his hand. He did not stir as I drew near, so I stepped aside on the grass. Instantly he barred my way.

"''You can't pass here,' he said.

"''Why not?' I asked.

"''Because I say so,' he answered.

"''And who are you that say so?' I inquired, looking full at him.

"'He was like a god. Majesty and power were written on every feature, were expressed in every gesture. But, oh, the awful scorn of his smile, the contempt with which he regarded me! The beams of the setting sun fell full upon him, and seemed to bring out, as in letters of fire, the wickedness and terrible beauty of his face.

"'I felt afraid; but I managed to say, 'Stand out of my way, the river bank is as free to me as to you.'

"''Not this part of it,' he answered. 'This place belongs to me.'

"''Very well,' I agreed, for I did not want to stand there bandying words with him, and a sudden darkness seemed to be falling around. 'It is getting late, and so I'll turn round.'

"'He gave a laugh, the like of which never fell on human ear before, and made reply: 'You can't turn back – of your own free will you have come on my ground and from it there is no return.'

"'I did not speak; I only just turned round and made as fast as I could for the path at the foot of the crag. He did not pass me, yet before I could reach the point I desired he stood barring my progress, with the scornful smile still on his lips, and his gigantic form assuming tremendous proportions in the narrow way.

"'"Let me pass," I entreated, 'and I will never come here again, never trespass more on your ground.'

"'"No, you shall not pass.'

"'"Who are you that takes such power on yourself?' I asked.

"'"Come closer, and I will tell you,' he said.

"'I drew a step nearer, and he spoke one word. I never heard it before, but, by some extraordinary intuition, I knew what it meant. He was the Evil One. The name seemed to be taken up by the echoes, and repeated from rock to rock and crag to crag. The whole air seemed full of that one word – and then a great horror of darkness came about us, only the place where we stood remained light. We occupied a small circle walled round with the thick blackness of night.

"'"You must come with me,' he said.

"'I refused and then he threatened me. I implored and entreated and wept, but at last I agreed to do what he wanted if he would promise to let me return. Again he laughed, and said, Yes, I should return – and the rocks and trees and mountains, ay, and the very rivers, seemed to take up the answer and bear it in sobbing whispers away into the darkness."

'He stopped, and lay back in his chair, shivering like one in an ague fit.

'"Go on," I repeated again, "It was only a dream, you know."

"'Was it?" he murmured, mournfully. "Ah, you have not heard the end of it yet."

"'Let me hear it then," I said. "What happened afterwards?"

"'The darkness seemed in part to clear away and we walked side by side across the grass in the twilight, straight up to the bare, black wall of rock. With the hilt of his sword he struck a heavy blow, and the solid rock opened as though it were a door. We passed through and it closed behind us with a tremendous clang – yes, it closed behind us"; and at that point he fairly broke down, crying and sobbing as I had never seen a man even in the most frightful grief cry and sob before.'

The minister paused in his narrative. At that moment there came a tremendous blast of wind which shook the windows of the manse, and burst open the hall door, and caused the candles to flicker and the fire to go roaring up the chimney. It is not too much to say that, what with the uncanny story and the howling storm, we all felt that creeping sort of uneasiness which so often seems like the touch of something from another world – a hand stretched across the boundary-line of time and eternity, the coldness and mystery of which make the stoutest heart tremble.

'I am telling you this tale,' said Mr Morison, resuming his seat after a brief absence to see that the fastenings of the house were properly attended to, 'exactly as I heard it. You must draw your own deductions from the facts I put before you. Part of that great and terrible region in which he found himself, my friend went on to tell me, he penetrated, compelled by a power he could not resist, to see the most awful sights and the most frightful sufferings. There was no form of vice that had not there its representative. As they moved along, his companion told him the special sin for which such horrible punishment was being inflicted. Shuddering, and in mortal agony, he was unable to withdraw his eyes from the dreadful spectacle. The atmosphere grew more unendurable, the sights more and more terrible, the cries, groans, blasphemies more awful and heartrending.

'"I can bear no more," he gasped at last. "Let me go!"

'With a mocking laugh, the Presence beside him answered the appeal; a laugh which was taken up, even by the lost and anguished spirits around.

'"There is no return," said the pitiless voice.

'"But you promised," he cried. "You promised me faithfully."

'"What are promises here?" and the words were the sound of doom.

'Still he prayed and entreated; he fell on his knees and in his agony spoke words that seemed to cause the purpose of the Evil One to falter.

'"You shall go," he said, "on one condition: that you agree to return to me on Wednesday next – or send a substitute."

'"I could not do that," said my friend. "I could not send any fellow-creature here. Better stop myself than do that."

'"Then stop," said Satan, with the bitterest contempt; and he was turning away when the poor distracted soul asked for a minute more before he made his choice.

'He was in an awful strait: on the one hand, how could he remain himself? On the other, how could he doom another to such fearful torments? Who could he send? Who would come? And then suddenly there flashed into his mind the thought of an old man to whom it could not signify much whether he took up his place in this abode a few days sooner or a few days later. He was travelling to it as fast as he knew how. He was the reprobate of the parish; the sinner without hope that successive ministers had striven in vain to reclaim from the error of his ways; a man marked and doomed – Sandy the Tinker. Sandy, who was mostly drunk and always godless.

'Sandy, who, it was said, believed in nothing, and gloried in his infidelity. Sandy, whose soul really did not signify much. He would send him. Lifting his eyes, he saw those of his tormentor surveying him scornfully.

'"Well, have you made your choice?" he asked.

'"Yes, I think I can send a substitute," was the hesitating answer.

'"See you do then," was the reply, "for if you do not, and fail to return yourself, *I shall come for you*. Wednesday, remember, before midnight." And with these words ringing in his ears he was flung violently through the rock, and found himself in the middle of his bedroom floor, as if he had just been kicked there.'

'This is not the end of the story, is it?' asked one of our party, as the minister came to a full stop, and looked earnestly at the fire.

'No,' he answered, 'it is not the end; but before proceeding I must ask you to bear carefully in mind the circumstances already recounted. Especially remember the date mentioned – *Wednesday next, before midnight.*

'Whatever I thought, and you may think, about my friend's dream, it made the most remarkable impression upon *his* mind. He could not shake off its influence; he passed from one state of nervousness to another. It was in vain I entreated him to exert his common sense, and call all his strength of mind to his assistance. I might as well have spoken to the wind. He implored me not to leave him, and I agreed to remain. Indeed, to leave him in his then frame of mind would have been an act of the greatest cruelty. He wanted me also to preach in his place on the Sunday following; but this I flatly refused.

'"If you do not make an effort now," I said, "you will never make it. Rouse yourself; get on with your sermon, and if you buckle down to work you will soon forget all about that foolish dream."

'Well, to cut a long story short, the sermon was somehow

composed and Sunday came, and my friend, a little better and getting over his fret, walked up into the pulpit to preach. He looked dreadfully ill; but I thought the worst was over now and that he would go on mending.

'Vain hope! He gave out the text and then looked over the congregation – and the first person on whom his eyes lighted was Sandy the Tinker. Sandy, who had never before been known to enter a place of worship of any sort; Sandy, whom he had mentally chosen as his substitute, and who was *due on the following Wednesday* – sitting just below him, quite sober, and comparatively clean, waiting with a great show of attention for the opening words of the sermon.

'With a terrible cry my friend caught the front of the pulpit, then swayed back and fell down in a fainting fit. He was carried home and a doctor sent for. I said a few words, addressed apparently to the congregation, but really to Sandy, for my heart somehow came into my mouth at the sight of him. And then, after I had dismissed the people, I paced slowly back to the manse, almost afraid of what might meet me.

'Mr Crawley was not dead; but he was in the most dreadful state of physical exhaustion and mental agitation. It was dreadful to hear him. How could he go himself? How could he send Sandy? – Poor old Sandy whose soul, in the sight of God, was just as precious as his own.

'His whole cry was for us to deliver him from the Evil One; to save him from committing a sin which would render him a wretched man for life. He counted the hours and the minutes before he must return to that horrible place.

'"I can't send Sandy," he would moan. "I cannot. Oh, I cannot save myself at such a price!"

'And then he would cover his face with the bedclothes, only to start up and wildly entreat me not to leave him; to stand between the enemy and himself, to save him, or, if that were impossible, to give him the courage to do what was right.

"'If this continues," said the doctor, "Wednesday will find him either dead or a raving lunatic."

'We talked the matter over, the doctor and I, as we walked to and fro in the meadow behind the manse; and we decided, having to make our choice of two evils, to risk giving him such an opiate as should carry him over the dreaded interval. We knew it was a perilous thing to do even with one in his condition, but, as I said before, we could only take the lesser of two evils.

'What we dreaded most was his awaking before the time expired, so I kept watch beside him.

He lay like one dead through the whole of Tuesday night and Wednesday and Wednesday evening. Eight, nine, ten, eleven o'clock came and passed – then twelve.

"'God be thanked!" I said, as I stooped over him and heard he was breathing quietly.

"'He will do now, I hope," said the doctor, who had come in just before midnight. "You will stay with him till he wakes?"

'I promised that I would and in the beautiful dawn of a summer's morning he opened his eyes and smiled. He had no recollection then of what had occurred; he was as weak as an infant and, when I bade him try to go to sleep again, turned on his pillow and sank to rest once more.

'Worn out with watching, I stepped softly from the room and passed into the fresh, sweet air. I strolled down to the garden gate, and stood looking at the great mountains and the fair country, and the Deldy wandering like a silver thread through the green fields below.

'All at once my attention was attracted by a group of people coming slowly along the road leading from the hills. I could not at first see that in their midst something was being borne on men's shoulders; but when at last I made this out, I hurried to meet them and learn what was the matter.

"'Has there been an accident?' I asked, as I drew near.

'They stopped and one man came towards me.

"'Ay," he said, "the warst accident that could befa' him, puir fella. He's deid."

"'Who is it?' I asked, pressing forward; and lifting the cloth they had flung over his face, I saw *Sandy the Tinker*!

"'He had been coming home, I tak' it,'" remarked one who stood by, "'puir Sandy, and gaed over the cliff afore he could save himself. We found him just on this side of the Witches' Cauldron, where there's a bonny strip of green turf, and his cuddy was feeding on the hill-top with the bit cart behind her.'"

There was silence for a minute – then one of the ladies said softly, 'Poor Sandy.'

'And what became of Mr Crawley?' asked the other.

'He gave up his parish and went abroad as a missionary. He is still living.'

'What a most extraordinary story!' I remarked.

'Yes, I think so,' said the minister. 'If you like to go round by Deldy tomorrow, my son, who now occupies the manse, would show you the scene of the occurrence.'

The next day we all stood looking at the frowning cliff and at the Deldy, swollen by recent rains, rushing on its way.

The youngest of the party went up to the rock and knocked upon it loudly with his cane.

'Oh, don't do that, pray!' cried both the ladies nervously – the spirit of the weird story still brooded over us.

'What do you think of the coincidence, Jack?' I inquired of my friend, as we talked apart from the others.

'Ask me when we get back to Fleet Street,' he answered.

THE MAN-EATING TREE

By Phil Robinson (1847–1902)

Born in India, the son of an army chaplain, Philip Stewart Robinson was educated in England at Marlborough College and then returned to his native land to work as a journalist and teacher. In his thirties he left India again to join the Daily Telegraph *in London and, for the next twenty years, he was a foreign correspondent for that paper and others throughout the world, reporting from Afghanistan, Zululand, Egypt during the Anglo-Egyptian War of 1882 and Cuba during the Spanish-American War of 1898. His career was a turbulent one and involved a scandalous divorce, bankruptcy, and a brief period of imprisonment. In his lifetime, Robinson was admired for his tales set in India and was compared to Rudyard Kipling. Today, when he is remembered at all, it is for his speculative fiction. 'The Hunting of the Soko', which has appeared in many anthologies, is a short story about a hunter in Africa coming across an enigmatic creature as much human as ape. 'The Man-Eating Tree' was first published in a collection of articles, sketches and stories entitled* Under the Punkah. *Both his younger brothers, Edward and Harry, were also writers and* Tales by Three Brothers *(1902) gathers together nearly a dozen previously published stories, including 'The Man-Eating Tree', a number of which can be described as 'weird'.*

from Under the Punkah, *1881*

Peregrine Oriel, my maternal uncle, was a great traveller, as his prophetical sponsors at the font seemed to have guessed he would be. Indeed he had rummaged in the garrets and cellars of the earth with something more than ordinary diligence. But in the narrative of his travels he did not, unfortunately, preserve the judicious caution of Xenophon between the thing seen and the thing heard, and thus it came about that the town-councillors of Brunsbüttel (to whom he had shown a duck-billed platypus, caught alive by him in Australia, and who had him posted for an importer of artificial vermin) were not alone in their scepticism of some of the old man's tales.

Thus, for instance, who could hear and believe the tale of the man-sucking tree from which he had barely escaped with life? He called it himself more terrible than the Upas.

'This awful plant, that rears its splendid death-shade in the central solitude of a Nubian fern forest, sickens by its unwholesome humours all vegetation from its immediate vicinity, and feeds upon the wild beasts that, in the terror of the chase, or the heat of noon, seek the thick shelter of its boughs; upon the birds that, flitting across the open space, come within the charmed circle of its power, or innocently refresh themselves from the cups of its great waxen flowers; upon even man himself when, an infrequent prey, the savage seeks its asylum in the storm, or turns from the harsh foot-wounding sword-grass of the glade, to pluck the wondrous fruit that hang plumb down among the wondrous foliage.' And such fruit! – 'Glorious golden ovals, great honey drops, swelling by their own weight into pear-shaped translucencies. The foliage glistens with a strange dew, that all day long drips on to the ground below, nurturing a rank growth of grasses, which shoot up in places so high that their spikes of fierce blood-fed green show far up among the deep-tinted foliage of the terrible tree, and, like a jealous body-guard, keep concealed the fearful secret of the charnel-house within, and draw round the black roots of the murderous plant a decent screen of living green.'

Such was his description of the plant; and the other day, looking it up in a botanical dictionary, I find that there is really known to naturalists a family of carnivorous plants; but I see that they are most of them very small, and prey upon little insects only. My maternal uncle, however, knew nothing of this, for he died before the days of the discovery of the sun, dew, and pitcher plants; and grounding his knowledge of the man-sucking tree simply on his own terrible experience of it, explained its existence by theories of his own. Denying the fixity of all the laws of nature except one, that the stronger shall endeavour to consume the weaker, and holding even this fixity to be itself only a means to a greater general changefulness, he argued that – since any partial distribution of the faculty of self-defence would presume an unworthy partiality in the Creator, and since the sensual instincts of beast and vegetable are manifestly analogous – the world must be as percipient as sentient throughout. Carrying on his theory (for it was something more than hypothesis with him) a stage or two further, he arrived at the belief that, given the necessity of any imminent danger or urgent self-interest, every animal or vegetable could eventually revolutionise its nature, the wolf feeding on grass or nesting in trees, and the violet arming herself with thorns or entrapping insects.

'How,' he would ask, 'can we claim for man the consequence of perceptions to sensations, and yet deny to beasts that hear, see, feel, smell, and taste, a percipient principle co-existent with their senses? And if in the whole range of the animate world there is this gift of self-defence against extirpation, and offence against weakness, why is the inanimate world, holding as fierce a struggle for existence as the other, to be left defenceless and unarmed? And I deny that it is. The Brazilian epiphyte strangles the tree and sucks out its juices. The tree, again, to starve off its vampire parasite, withdraws its juices into its roots, and piercing the ground in some new place, turns the current of its sap into other growths. The epiphyte then drops off the dead boughs on to the fresh green sprouts springing from the ground beneath it – and so the fight goes on. Again, look at the Indian peepul tree; in what does the fierce yearning of its roots towards the distant well differ from the sad struggling of the camel to the oasis, or of Sennacherib's army to the saving Nile.

'Is the sensitive plant unconscious? I have walked for miles through plains of it, and watched, till the watching almost made me afraid lest the plant should pluck up courage and turn upon me, the green carpet paling into silver grey before my feet, and fainting away all round me as I walked. So strangely did I feel the influence of this universal aversion that I would have argued with the plant; but what was the use? If only I stretched out my hands, the mere shadow of the limb terrified the vegetable to sickness; shrubs crumbled up at every commencement of my speech; and at my periods great sturdy-looking bushes, to whose robustness I had foolishly appealed, sank in pallid supplication. Not a leaf would keep me company. A breath went forth from me that sickened life. My mere presence paralysed life, and I was glad at last to come out among a less timid vegetation, and to feel the resentful spear-grass retaliating on the heedlessness that would have crushed it. The vegetable world, however, has its revenges. You may keep the guinea-pig in a hutch, but how will you pet the basilisk? The little sensitive plant in your garden amuses your children (who will find pleasure also in seeing cockchafers spin round on a pin), but how could you transplant a vegetable that seizes the running deer, strikes down the passing bird, and once taking hold of him, sucks the carcass of man himself, till his matter becomes as vague as his mind, and all his animate capabilities cannot snatch him from the terrible embrace of – God help him! – an inanimate tree?

'Many years ago,' said my uncle, 'I turned my restless steps towards Central Africa, and made the journey from where the Senegal empties itself into the Atlantic to the Nile, skirting the Great Desert, and reaching Nubia on my way to the eastern coast. I had with me then three native attendants – two of them brothers, the third, Otona, a young savage from the Gaboon uplands, a mere lad in his teens; and one day, leaving my mule with the two men, who were pitching my tent for the night, I went on with my gun, the boy accompanying me, towards a fern forest, which I saw in the near distance. As I approached it I found the forest was cut into two by a wide glade; and seeing a small herd of the common antelope, an excellent beast in the pot, browsing their way along the shaded side, I crept after them. Though ignorant of their real danger the herd was suspicious, and, slowly trotting along before me, enticed me for a mile or more along the verge of the fern growths. Turning a corner I suddenly became aware of a solitary tree growing in the middle of the glade – one tree alone. It struck me at once that I had never seen a tree exactly like it before; but, being intent upon venison for my supper, I looked at it only long enough to satisfy my first surprise at seeing a single plant of such rich growth flourishing luxuriantly in a spot where only the harsh fern-canes seemed to thrive.

'The deer meanwhile were midway between me and the tree, and looking at them I saw they were going to cross the glade. Exactly opposite them was an opening in the forest, in which I should certainly have lost my supper; so I fired into the middle of the family as they were filing before me. I hit a young fawn, and the rest of the herd, wheeling round in their sudden terror, made off in the direction of the tree, leaving the fawn struggling on the ground.

Otona, the boy, ran forward at my order to secure it, but the little creature seeing him coming, attempted to follow its comrades, and at a fair pace held on their course. The herd had meanwhile reached the tree, but suddenly, instead of passing under it, swerved in their career, and swept round it at some yards' distance.

'*Was I mad, or did the plant really try to catch the deer?* On a sudden I saw, or thought I saw, the tree violently agitated, and while the ferns all round were standing motionless in the dead evening air, its boughs were swayed by some sudden gust towards the herd, and swept, in the force of their impulse, almost to the ground. I drew my hand across my eyes, closed them for a moment, and looked again. The tree was as motionless as myself!

'Towards it, and now close to it, the boy was running in excited pursuit of the fawn. He stretched out his hands to catch it. It bounded from his eager grasp. Again he reached forward, and again it escaped him. There was another rush forward, and the next instant boy and deer were beneath the tree.

'And now there was no mistaking what I saw.

'The tree was convulsed with motion, leant forward, swept its thick foliaged boughs to the ground, and enveloped from my sight the pursuer and the pursued; I was within a hundred yards, and the cry of Otona from the midst of the tree came to me in all the clearness of its agony There was then one stifled, strangling scream, and except for the agitation of the leaves where they had closed upon the boy, there was not a sign of life!

'I called out, "Otona!" No answer came. I tried to call out again, but my utterance was like that of some wild beast smitten at once with sudden terror and its death wound. I stood there, changed from all semblance of a human being. Not all the terrors of earth together could have made me take my eye from the awful plant, or my foot off the ground. I must have stood thus for at least an hour, for the shadows had crept out from the forest half across the glade before that hideous paroxysm of fear left me. My first impulse then was to creep stealthily away lest the tree should perceive me, but my returning reason bade me approach it. The boy might have fallen into the lair of some beast of prey, or perhaps the terrible life in the tree was that of some great serpent among its branches. Preparing to defend myself, I approached the silent tree – the harsh grass crisping beneath my feet with a strange loudness, the cicadas in the forest shrilling till the air seemed throbbing round me with waves of sound. The terrible truth was soon before me in all its awful novelty.

'The vegetable first discovered my presence at about fifty yards' distance. I then became aware of a stealthy motion among the thick-lipped leaves, reminding me of some wild beast slowly gathering itself up from long sleep, a vast coil of snakes in restless motion. Have you ever seen bees hanging from a bough – a great cluster of bodies, bee clinging to bee – and by striking the bough, or agitating the air, caused that massed life to begin sulkily to disintegrate, each insect asserting its individual right to move? And do you remember how without one bee leaving the pensile cluster, the whole became gradually instinct with sullen life and horrid with a multitudinous motion?

'I came within twenty yards of it. The tree was quivering through every branch, muttering for blood, and, helpless with rooted feet, yearning with every branch towards me. It was that terror of the deep sea which the men of the northern fiords dread, and which, anchored upon some sunken rock, stretches into vain space its longing arms, pellucid as the sea itself, and as relentless – maimed Polypheme groping for his victims.

'Each separate leaf was agitated and hungry. Like hands they fumbled together, their fleshy palms curling upon themselves and again unfolding, closing on each other and falling apart again – thick, helpless, fingerless hands (rather lips or tongues than hands) dimpled closely with little cup-like hollows. I approached nearer and nearer, step by step, till I saw that these soft horrors were all of them in motion, opening and closing incessantly.

'I was now within ten yards of the farthest reaching bough. Every part of it was hysterical with excitement. The agitation of its members was awful – sickening yet fascinating. In an ecstasy of eagerness for the food so near them, the leaves turned upon each other. Two meeting would suck together face to face, with a force that compressed their joint thickness to a half, thinning the two leaves into one, now grappling in a volute like a double shell, writhing like some green worm, and at last, faint with the violence of the paroxysm, would slowly separate, falling apart as leeches gorged drop off the limbs. A sticky dew glistened in the dimples, welled over, and trickled down the leaf. The sound of it dripping from leaf to leaf made it seem as if the tree was muttering to itself. The beautiful golden fruit as they swung here and there were clutched now by one leaf and now by another, held for a moment close enfolded from the sight, and then as suddenly released. Here a large leaf, vampire-like, had sucked out the juices of a smaller one. It hung limp and bloodless, like a carcass of which the weasel has tired.

'I watched the terrible struggle till my starting eyes, strained by intense attention, refused their office, and I can hardly say what I saw. But the tree before me seemed to have become a live beast. Above me I felt conscious was a great limb, and each of its thousand clammy hands reached downwards towards me, fumbling. It strained, shivered, rocked, and heaved. It flung itself about in despair. The boughs, tantalised to madness with the presence of flesh, were tossed to this side and to that, in the agony of a frantic desire. The leaves were wrung together as the hands of one driven to madness by sudden misery. I felt the vile dew spurting from the tense veins fall upon me. My clothes began to give out a strange odour. The ground I stood on glistened with animal juices.

'Was I bewildered by terror? Had my senses abandoned me in my need? I know not – but the tree seemed to me to be alive. Leaning over towards me, it seemed to be pulling up its roots from the softened ground, and to be moving towards me. A mountainous monster, with myriad lips, mumbling together for my life, was upon me!

'Like one who desperately defends himself from imminent death, I made an effort for life, and fired my gun at the approaching horror. To my dizzied senses the sound seemed far off, but the shock of the recoil partially recalled me to myself and, starting back, I reloaded. The shot had torn their way into the soft body of the great thing. The trunk as it received the wound shuddered, and the whole tree was struck with a sudden quiver. A fruit fell down – slipping from the leaves, now rigid with swollen veins, as from carven foliage. Then I saw a large arm slowly droop, and without a sound it was severed from the juice-fattened bole, and sank down softly, noiselessly, through the glistening leaves. I fired again, and another vile fragment was powerless – dead. At each discharge the terrible vegetable yielded a life. Piecemeal I attacked it, killing here a leaf and there a branch. My fury increased with the slaughter till, when my ammunition was exhausted, the splendid giant was left a wreck – as if some hurricane had torn through it. On the ground lay heaped together the fragments, struggling, rising and falling, gasping. Over them drooped in dying languor a few stricken boughs, while upright in the midst stood, dripping at every joint, the glistening trunk.

'My continued firing had brought up one of my men on my mule. He dared not, so he told me, come near me, thinking me mad. I had now drawn my hunting-knife, and with this was fighting – with the leaves. Yes – but each leaf was instinct with a horrid life; and more than once I felt my hand entangled for a moment and seized as if by sharp lips. Ignorant of the presence of my companion, I made a rush forward over the fallen foliage, and with a last paroxysm of frenzy drove my knife up to the handle into the soft bole and, slipping on the fast-congealing sap, fell exhausted and unconscious, among the still-panting leaves.

'My companions carried me back to the camp, and after vainly searching for Otona awaited my return to consciousness. Two or three hours elapsed before I could speak, and several days before I could approach the terrible thing. My men would not go near it. It was quite dead; for as we came up a great-billed bird with gaudy plumage that had been securely feasting on the decaying fruit, flew up from the wreck. We removed the rotting foliage, and there among the dead leaves still limp with juices, and piled round the roots, we found the ghastly relics of many former meals, and – its last nourishment – the corpse of little Otona. To have removed the leaves would have taken too long, so we buried the body as it was with a hundred vampire leaves still clinging to it.'

Such, as nearly as I remember it, was my uncle's story of the man-eating tree.

THE GREEN PHIAL

By T W Speight (1830–1915)

Thomas Wilkinson Speight was born in Liverpool and worked for forty years for the Midland Railway Company. He began to write non-fiction articles for an assortment of magazines while in his twenties, often on subjects relating to the railways, and later graduated to fiction, both novels and short stories. Speight wrote works which fall into a variety of genres. Some of his earliest novels might best be described as 'sensation fiction' and owe an obvious debt to Wilkie Collins. Later books are more original and include straightforward mysteries, thrillers and historical romances. The Strange Experiences of Mr Verschoyle, *published towards the end of his career, is a fantasy in which a young man is granted the power to leave his own body and adopt the identity of another person, using this strange gift to take his revenge on the family that he believes ruined his life. Throughout his writing life, Speight published short stories in magazines such as Dickens's* Household Words *and* All the Year Round, *and* Belgravia. *Some of these had supernatural elements and 'The Green Phial', with its plot that focuses on a dream shared by two individuals, is probably the most memorable of them.*

From Belgravia, *February 1884*

I

It was at the house of the Rev. Percival Milburne, where I had gone to read, that I made the acquaintance of Victor Langholme, who was my senior by about three years. His parents were dead, and although he was rich he had no home. Mr Milburne having been one of his father's oldest friends, Victor had taken up his quarters at the rectory for a time, pending the settlement of certain claims connected with his inheritance. Despite the difference in our ages and the dissimilarity of our dispositions, Langholme and I, being thrown much together, soon struck up one of those youthful friendships which are so pleasant while they last, but are scarcely calculated to stand the wear and tear of life in afteryears.

I had been brought up in a country house where hunting, shooting, boating, and cricketing were looked upon as the legitimate amusements of English gentlemen, and were pursued with a degree of energy conducive alike to health of body and mind. But here was a young man, rich and of good family, who cared for none of these things; a young man addicted through choice to vegetable diet, who made one suit of clothes last him a year, who kept himself aloof from polite society, who had never been on horseback in his life, and who held the cultivation of his intellect and the acquisition of knowledge as the only ends worth living for. The contrast puzzled me at first, and ended by attracting me, the result being the friendship of which mention has been already made.

In person Langholme was tall, thin, and fragile-looking, with a slight stoop of the shoulders probably induced by poring so many hours over his books. He was an intellectual egotist, living the introspective, self-contained life of an Eastern mystic, and regarding with indifference or ill-concealed contempt all those minor accidents and circumstances of everyday life by which the majority of people are so powerfully swayed. He was of Scotch extraction, and he possessed to some extent the gift of second sight. Young though he was, he was already an adept in the use of opium, and he would sometimes relate to me with as much earnestness as though they were based on fact some of the singular visions induced by the imbibition of that dangerous drug. He devoured books, rather than read them, of any and every kind, and was the only reading man I ever knew who had no favourite authors.

When my twelve months came to an end I bade adieu to my good friends at the rectory and set out for Cambridge. Langholme announced his intention of shortly proceeding to Paris, there to study anatomy and walk the hospitals in furtherance of a certain crotchet which of late had found lodgment in his brain, but would probably die there of inanition before many months were over.

So each of us set out on his own road in life, and after some half-dozen epistles had passed between us we lost sight of each other for several years. Letter-writing was always my detestation, and Langholme was too deeply immersed in his own mental experiences to care greatly about keeping up a correspondence with one who, as he probably thought, had passed out of the circle of his observation for ever.

II

Several years passed away, and the image of Victor Langholme had all but faded from my memory, when one autumn evening, while rambling through the streets of Heidelberg, I suddenly encountered him as he was emerging from a second-hand book store. We recognised each other in a moment, and after a hearty greeting I walked back with him to his hotel, where we dined together and had a pleasant gossip about old times.

Langholme looked even taller and leaner than of yore, and was as eccentric in manners and dress as I always remembered him to have been. He had come abroad for the benefit of his health, which had been injured by over-study, and he was now wandering from one town to another in a desultory aimless sort of way, not caring greatly where he found himself so long as his craving for variety and continual change of scene was gratified. We were both of us so well pleased with the renewal of our broken friendship that we agreed to join company and wander about together till my holidays should be at an end.

A few days later found us at Kaiserbad, at which place we decided to make some little stay, neither of us having visited it before.

Kaiserbad was, at the period of which I write, and probably is now, one of the most enjoyable of places to those who visit it for the first time. The town in itself is charming, and is surrounded by some of the loveliest scenery in Germany, in addition to which there were at that time certain phases of society to be seen there the like of which could be encountered at few places elsewhere.

Neither Victor nor I gambled. It is true that we now and then ventured a little loose change on the red or black, but when the croupier's rake had swept it away we shrugged our shoulders and contented ourselves with being lookers-on for the rest of the evening.

We were strolling through the Kursaal as usual one evening watching the company, when Langholme stopped suddenly in front of one of the tables and plucked me by the sleeve.

'Observe that man,' he said, indicating one of the players on the opposite side. 'Notice him particularly; I shall have something to tell you concerning him when we get back to the hotel. Strange that I should encounter him here!'

We drew nearer the table, and placed ourselves directly opposite the spot where the stranger indicated by Langholme was seated.

The face of the man in question was certainly an uncommon one—one which, once seen, would not readily be forgotten. His features were bold, well formed, and regular; his eyes were large, black, and piercing; black also were his thick moustache and imperial and his close-cropped hair. The singularity of his appearance lay in the fact that both sides of his face were artistically tattooed, after the fashion of various savage tribes, with an elaborate pattern picked out in dark blue. He was lame, one of his legs having recently been broken by the kick of a horse, as we learned later on, and he was now seated in an invalid chair, behind which stood a servant in livery ready to wheel him away whenever he should grow tired of the game. He was dressed in the extreme Parisian fashion of the period, and wore a cluster of brilliants on one finger which had cut through his tightly fitting primrose-coloured glove. He was nervously anxious about the play, although he strove hard to assume a mask of impassibility, and his keen black eyes lighted up with gleams of avaricious joy, or shot forth lurid, angry flashes from under his thick brows, in accordance with the varying chances of the game, while a slight trembling of the hands whenever a fresh rouleau was handed to him by his servant indicated still further how futile was his assumption of indifference.

But he only gambled indirectly and by deputy.

Immediately in front of him, but so as to allow him a clear view of the table, sat a lady, young, fascinating, and richly dressed, who did all the work of winning and losing. She was very handsome after a certain sinister style of beauty – a style which has for some men such an attraction that they yield themselves body and soul to its influence, while others there are whom it repels, who, warned by some instinct of harm, shrink from it as from something baleful and malign. Small regular features; a complexion which by that light looked as pure and delicate as the tints of the wild rose; large grey eyes shaded by dark eyelashes; a magnificent profusion of yellow silky hair – not auburn or golden, but genuine pale yellow – plaited and coiled round her head after some strange snaky fashion which looked thoroughly original; a figure lithe and slender, but not too tall. There she sat, drawing to herself the eyes of everyone in the room.

'Unhappy the mortal round whom yonder siren weaves her spells,' muttered Langholme in my ear. 'Not until she has compassed his utter ruin will she rend the magic web that binds him to her. Had she lived three centuries ago, she would have stood a chance of being burnt as a witch. For you may rely upon it, if we could only drag out of the past and see enacted over again a few of those trials for witchcraft which, especially when the victim was young and beautiful, seem to us so strange and barbarous, we should find that the popular conscience which gave utterance to the verdict was in many cases justified to some extent by seeing, or believing that it saw, in its victim such half-hidden but veritable signs of the fiend's own marking that its rough, sharp justice and summary method of purgation are hardly to be wondered at.'

'The stranger calls himself Monsieur De Montillac,' I heard someone behind me remark, with a sneering emphasis on the 'De'. 'He is reported to be immensely rich, and the lady is his wife, or passes for such.'

'Adventurers both,' muttered Langholme contemptuously.

Madame was certainly an accomplished player as far as preserving her coolness went. Not the quiver of a nerve, not the trembling of an eyelid, betrayed her whether she won or lost, and yet there was an avidity about her style of play which seemed to indicate that she was a thorough gambler.

We wandered about the rooms and the alleys outside for an hour or more, and then we retraced our way to the table, where we found De Montillac and his wife still busy. They had won largely, and there was quite a crowd round the table watching their run of luck. De Montillac could not hide his exultation, but Madame sat as cold and impassive as some marble goddess behind her rapidly increasing pile of gold. And still the croupier's everlasting croak went on.

No sooner, however, did the finger of the clock point to ten than De Montillac touched Madame lightly on the shoulder and whispered a word in her ear. She rose at once, and while her husband swept the heap of winnings into a velvet sachet, she pulled off the gloves in which she had been playing, dropped them under the table, and proceeded to draw on another pair. A minute later they were ready to go. The servant behind turned the chair and proceeded to wheel it slowly down the saloon, followed by Madame with downcast eyes, still patiently drawing on her gloves.

'I told you that I had seen De Montillac before,' said Langholme as soon as we were alone in his room at the hotel, 'but I did not tell you when and where. I saw him six months ago in a dream.'

'And you pretend to recognise him again! You must be dreaming still, *mon ami.*'

'So be it,' answered Langholme quietly. 'But pretermit your further observations till you have read something I am about to show you.'

Without a word more he unlocked his writing-desk and drew from it a thin morocco-bound book – his diary, in fact – in which he quickly found the passage he wanted. He then laid the book open before me and bade me read. The passage pointed out by him bore the date of 13 March of the current year, and ran as follows:

'Last night I had a singular and very vivid dream, the particulars of which seem to me worthy of finding a record here.

'All at once, as it seemed to me, and with that strange absence of any known foregone cause capable of leading up to such a result so common in dreams, I found myself among the ruins of some moyen-age castle or baronial residence, the features of which were utterly strange to me. I was digging a hole with spade and pick in one corner of the courtyard. The scene was dimly lighted by an old-fashioned horn lantern, whose function would shortly cease, for a dull, grey, ghostly light was beginning to broaden in the east and night was nearly over. It had been revealed to me by some occult means that below the spot where I was digging lay buried an ancient treasure of immense value, the finding of which would make me rich beyond the dreams of avarice. But underlying the feeling of exultation induced by the hope of finding the treasure was a secret dread of discovery – for, in such a case, discovery meant death. Still, I kept on digging while the dawn slowly broadened, bringing into sharp relief against the clear sky every fantastic feature of the grass-grown ruins. At length my pick struck against something hard. I carefully removed the surrounding earth and laid bare a small iron box. There was no need to open it; it was what I had been told to search for. I knew that its contents consisted of diamonds and rubies of incalculable value unsunned since the reign of Charlemagne. I wrapped the box in my cravat and hid it away within the folds of my vest, buttoning my coat over it for further protection.

'Leaving my implements behind me I emerged from the twilight corner where I had been digging, crossed the courtyard and the castle fosse, and came out on a steep grassy mound which sloped down to some level meadows, beyond which lay a little town, whether French or German I could not tell. I paused for a moment to consider the path I ought to follow. That pause was fatal to me. Suddenly, as if it had dropped from the clouds, a thick cloth was flung over my head and shoulders. The next moment I was seized tightly round the body, my feet slipped from under me on the damp grass, and with a loud cry I fell heavily to the ground.

'Scarcely had I touched the earth when the cloth that enveloped my head was withdrawn and someone was seated astride my chest – a man whom I had never seen before, who glared down at me with black eyes that were at once mocking and malignant. Judging from his dress, he was a gentleman; his hands, too, were white and delicate and laden with rings; but his face was a remarkable one, not from any peculiarity of features, but from the fact of both his cheeks being tattooed, stamped with a network or reticulation of thin blue lines arranged in some fantastic pattern, after the fashion of a New Zealander or Malayan chief. I struggled desperately but unavailingly to throw him off. He waited without speaking till I sank back breathless and exhausted, then, drawing a small green phial from his pocket, he held it up to the light for a moment. The golden stopper flew open and the mocking light in his eyes deepened as he proceeded to press the phial to my nostrils. A delicious odour seemed to fill my brain and to steal away my senses not unpleasantly. I felt myself sinking softly into a sleep against which I had neither the power nor the wish to struggle. Softly and slowly I seemed to be sinking down through delicious dreamy spaces into a sleep within a sleep – when I was recalled suddenly and rudely from the land of shadows by an importunate knocking at my bedroom door, and on the instant all my cobweb fancies vanished into thinnest air.

'My dream was gone, but the impression left behind it was a particularly vivid one, owing, doubtless, to the fact of my having been so suddenly awakened while its pictures were still painted freshly on my brain.

'Mem. – One would like to know whether the curious-looking stranger with the green phial has a real existence, or whether he was merely a figment of my own distempered fancy. Further, if there be such a person, whether he in his turn dreamt that he played the part which I in my dream saw him enact.'

'Then you wish me to believe,' said I with a smile, as I gave the diary back to Langholme, 'that the man you saw in your dream and De Montillac are one and the same?'

'As to that I have no doubt whatever. It must, however, be borne in mind that, had not the man in the first instance been strikingly different in some one point from the ordinary run of people, I should probably not have recognised him again. It was the fact of his being tattooed that first drew my attention to him in the Kursaal and then brought back to my recollection, one by one, the more minute traits of his appearance – the colour and expression of his eyes, his sharp aquiline nose with the mark of an old scar, a peculiar twitching of the under lip, and the same large ring set with brilliants which I saw in my dream.'

'Granting for a moment,' said I, 'that De Montillac and the man you saw in your dream are the same, you do not, I suppose, imagine, as the remark in your diary would lead me to infer, that the man himself had a similar dream, that is to say, one in which he enacted the part of your assailant, at the same time that you had yours?'

'I am certainly inclined to believe that he had such a dream,' answered Langholme, 'although, even if we could question him on the point, it might be difficult to prove it; for he might have such a dream and yet on waking retain such a vague and confused impression of it that in the course of a few hours it would fade entirely from his memory, or, which I think quite as likely, he might have such a dream with all its seeming vivid reality and yet remember nothing whatever of it when he awoke.'

'You are becoming charmingly obscure, my dear Langholme,' I remarked. 'Take care that you don't lose yourself among the clouds.'

'The subject of dreams,' resumed Langholme, without noticing my interruption, 'is one that for me has always had a peculiar fascination, and one on which at times I have pondered deeply. I believe that dreams may, as a rule, be divided into two classes, which, for the purpose of illustration, we may term normal and abnormal ones. The latter are generally the result of extraneous circumstances, or may follow as the further unwinding of some thread of thought on which the brain has been busy during the day and now proceeds to take up again in a sort of wild tangle during sleep. Perhaps, indeed, it would be safe to put down all such dreams as the sequence of unhealthy action or over-excitement of the brain or stomach, producible by a hundred different causes, known and unknown. Of the other class of dreams, those I have termed normal ones, few in number as regards our recollection of them in comparison with those of the first-named class, I believe that we seldom retain any waking impression; with rare exceptions they pass away in the fumes of sleep and are forgotten. For I believe this, and it is the groundwork of my airy edifice – that we seldom sleep without dreaming. At the close of day, when brain and body are alike wearied, we retire to bed gratefully, to sleep and to gather up new vigour for the morrow; but while our earthly husk reposes, slumbers, is dead but for the mechanical action of certain pulses, the brain – or rather, the busy unresting Ariel which tenants that strange domicile – is far away, gathering from fresh woods and pastures new, from the cloudy, illimitable realms of dreamland, stores of strength and elasticity to meet the dull earthly requirements of the morrow. We awake, and we know not that we have been visitants of a strange mysterious land, that we have been enacting a part in some fantastic drama wilder often than the day-dreams of the maddest poet. In change, not in inaction, lie the elements of strength. Whenever, in a morning, I feel my mind to be more than usually clear and buoyant, I say to myself, "Last night I had happy dreams." Further, I hold with the old poetic dictum that "All which seems is." And this brings us back to the starting-point. According to my theory, in all cases of normal, healthy dreams, the actors in the visionary drama, however numerous they may be, all dream that they are filling the parts which the others in their dreams see them filling; thus De Montillac should have dreamt at the same time that I dreamt that he enacted the part of my assailant in our imaginary encounter. But, as I said before, to prove that such was the case would be next to impossible.'

'What foundation,' said I, 'is there for supposing, or what proof have you to offer, that the theory you put forward is anything more than a wild flight of imagination on your part?'

'Alas, my friend,' answered Langholme, 'this is precisely one of those things which cannot be proved – at least, not by any rules of mental arithmetic at present known to us. My wild-goose theory has for its foundation nothing more substantial than certain remarkable coincidences which have come under my notice at different times, a few apparently authentic dream narratives which I have picked up in the course of much desultory reading, and some half-dozen dream stories told me by sundry friends and acquaintances on whose veracity I can rely. Beyond that it is indeed nothing more than a flight of imagination.'

De Montillac and his wife were making their game as usual the following evening, and for three nights after that, winning largely on each occasion, but always leaving the table punctually as the clock struck ten.

On the morning of the fifth day of our sojourn, Victor and I left Kaiserbad for an excursion into the surrounding country. We were away nearly a week, and after a late dinner on the evening of our return we mechanically bent our steps towards the Kursaal. As before, we found the Frenchman, his wife, his valet, and his chair in front of one of the tables, only this evening, contrary to precedent, there was no little heap of winnings at the elbow of Madame, while De Montillac's hands trembled more than ever, and his former cynical smile was replaced by a thunderous frown as one rouleau after another was drawn from the velvet sachet.

Except the croupier, the only person at the table who seemed to be winning was a tall, thin, melancholy-looking young Italian of decidedly shabby appearance, who sat directly opposite Madame. As usual, there was quite a crowd round the table, and it was amusing to hear the comments of some of the veteran gamblers upon the singular change of fortune which had befallen the Frenchman and his wife since the advent of the young Italian. They were now as unlucky as they had been fortunate before. On two points these ancient rooks were all agreed – that the melancholy-looking stranger was the *bête noire* who had brought ill-luck to the Frenchman, and that if the latter were wise, he would quit Kaiserbad at once before the tide of ruin had set in too strongly.

For six consecutive evenings the Frenchman's run of ill-luck continued. The Italian always occupied the seat opposite Madame, silently constituting himself, as it were, her special antagonist; and every evening a hundred greedy eyes gazed enviously at the heap of gold, sometimes light, sometimes heavy, which he carried away at the end of his play. One evening he was later than usual in taking his seat at the table, and till he came fortune smiled brightly on De Montillac, only to desert him the moment his opponent began to play. On the sixth evening the agony of the Frenchman seemed to be culminating. Great drops of sweat stood on his brow as, in accordance with the exigencies of the game, he handed one rouleau after another to Madame and watched the croupier rake them one by one away; and when the clock pointed to ten, he struck his clenched fist on the table and said with an oath, in French, 'Another week of this work and I shall be a ruined man!'

'Fi donc, Henri!' said Madame reprovingly in low liquid tones. 'Do not make a scene, I pray of you,' and as she rose she flashed down on the Italian a swift venomous shaft of hatred that would have struck him dead on the spot had her power been equal to her will.

Early next morning Langholme and I set out for a drive, getting back just in time for the *table d'hôte*. The first news that greeted us was that the young Italian had been found dead in bed that morning under very mysterious circumstances, some people opining that he had committed suicide, while others averred that he had been robbed and murdered. But the doctors and the authorities had the case under investigation, and we should doubtless know more about it on the morrow.

III

I was so tired and good-for-nothing on the evening of our return from our excursion that I decided to stay indoors. So Langholme sallied out by himself when dinner was over, promising me that on his return he would furnish me with whatever particulars he might be able to pick up concerning the affair of the young Italian. It was late when he got back and I had gone off to bed, but he came to my room, and, finding I was not asleep, he sat down and proceeded to give me an account of what he had heard.

'Sure enough,' said he, 'the young Italian is dead – dead, too, under very singular circumstances. He arrived at Kaiserbad about nine days ago, and was, it seems, in the habit of depositing his winnings with the landlord of his hotel every night for safety. Last night, however, the landlord, being ill, had gone to bed before the

Italian got back from the Kursaal. So the young fellow took the bag containing the money into his bedroom, saying with a laugh in the hearing of several people that he would make a pillow of his winnings, and so ensure golden dreams. He then went and smoked a cigar on the terrace, drank half a bottle of wine, asked for his candlestick, bade one or two casual acquaintances good night, and retired to his room; and that was the last that was seen of him alive. On his arrival at Kaiserbad he complained to his landlord of an affection of the lungs, and got assigned to himself a bedroom on the ground floor, so as to avoid the labour of going upstairs. This bedroom, originally intended for a sitting-room, opened by means of two French windows on to a balcony on which were ranged a number of shrubs and evergreens. Both these windows were securely bolted by one of the servants just before the Italian retired for the night. When the servants knocked at the door this morning there was no reply, and after the scene usual on such occasions, the door was broken open, and the young man was found lying in bed, apparently in a pleasant sleep, but in reality stone dead. Near the bed was found a small empty phial, which gave rise to the rumour that he had poisoned himself, but all his winnings of last night had disappeared. A more minute examination showed that a square piece of glass had been cut out of one of the windows by means of a diamond, in such a position that anyone from the outside by putting his hand through the aperture could at once draw back the bolt by which the window was secured. There seems to be no doubt that such was the method adopted for effecting an entrance, but whoever did it was cool enough to rebolt the window on leaving the room.

'There being no external marks of violence to account for death, the doctors have decided upon making a post-mortem examination of the body.

'For these and other particulars I am indebted to our obliging friend Herr Volckmann, who, as you are probably aware, is a Government functionary of high position.

'There are one or two points connected with the case respecting which I have not spoken to anyone. Firstly, I discovered that the suite of apartments occupied by De Montillac and his wife are situated directly over the bedroom of the Italian. Secondly, the empty phial found near the dead man's bed is made of thick green cut glass and has a gold stopper – the very phial, in fact, seen by me in that dream with which our French friend was so signally mixed up, of which you read an account a few days ago in my diary. The phial, though empty, still retained a peculiar, faint, aromatic odour, very refreshing and delightful, the inhalation of which brought vividly to my mind every little half-forgotten incident connected with that visionary struggle among the ruins.'

Next morning Langholme and I went to the hotel where the body of the Italian lay. The influence of Herr Volckmann procured me a sight of the phial, which was now in the hands of the police. It tallied exactly with the description given in my friend's diary.

'It has just been whispered to me,' said Langholme on our way back, 'that strong suspicions attach to the Frenchman and his wife, and that their rooms and effects are about to undergo a strict examination by the police.'

'Do you intend to say anything to Volckmann respecting the phial in connection with your dream?' I asked.

Victor shook his head. 'What I could tell would not be accepted as evidence by anyone but a dreamer and visionary like myself. Volckmann would scout the idea of acting on such a suggestion. Besides, De Montillac is already under surveillance, and should the perquisition of the police bring to light nothing inculpatory, I don't think that I should be justified in endeavouring, on the mere strength of what you and I know, to build up an accusation against a man who may possibly be innocent, however much I myself may feel inclined to believe the contrary.'

Next morning Langholme and I set out for Munich, and were away ten days. We had scarcely alighted at the hotel on our return to Kaiserbad before we encountered Volckmann. 'What about the affair of the young Italian?' was Langholme's first question.

'Ah, bah! That bagatelle is hushed up and all but forgotten in our gay little pandemonium here,' answered the lively Herr, with a lift of the shoulders that was quite as expressive as Lord Burleigh's historical nod could ever have been. 'The result confirmed the opinion whispered by you at the first. There is no doubt that he died from the results of some strange poison, but by whom administered there was no evidence to show. That it was not his own act there can be no moral doubt; besides which, his winnings had disappeared. However, as the police could make nothing of the case, and as the doctors were puzzled and could not agree among themselves, and as on examination of the dead man's papers it was found that he was a nobody – merely the son of a Customs official at some petty Italian port – it was not thought advisable to make too much bother about a trifle, so the affair was allowed to lapse quietly into oblivion. For, as you are doubtless aware, it is the policy of a paternal Government as regards this favoured spot to imbue its visitors with the conviction that dining, flirtation, roulette, and rouge-et-noir are the sole ends worth living for.'

'And De Montillac and his wife?'

'They left here several days ago,' answered the German. 'It did not suit them to have their effects examined, although nothing was discovered bearing on the case in hand, and the day after they were released from surveillance away they went to try their luck elsewhere. As for the Frenchman, it was proved by medical evidence that he was incapable of walking six yards except on crutches; and as regards Madame, in the first place it was not a likely deed for a woman to do, and, secondly, she was seen by two or three of the servants to retire to her room shortly after eleven o'clock. Now, in order to effect an entrance into the Italian's room by way of the window she would have had to pass along a much-frequented corridor, down the principal staircase of the house, and out at the front door, round which there is generally a knot of young men smoking till a late hour, and after that the door is secured and left in charge of the night porter and could not possibly be opened by a stranger without attracting attention. But even supposing she reached the room without discovery, she would have to come the same way back. No, I don't see how it would be possible for her to do it and escape detection.'

'Nevertheless,' whispered Victor to me as we passed on into the hotel, 'I for one believe that the secret of the young Italian's death rests between De Montillac and his wife, and nothing short of proof positive would convince me to the contrary.'

'And that you are never likely to have in this world,' said I.

A fortnight later my holiday came to an end, and after bidding Langholme a cordial farewell I set off for London and hard work, leaving my friend to pursue his tour alone.

IV

Extract from a Letter by Victor Langholme, Esq.
Washington, US: December 1862

… I have already apprised you that I lately fell in with the ci-devant De Montillac while wandering in the neighbourhood of one of the many fields of slaughter which signalised McClellan's disastrous retreat from the Chickahominy to the Potomac, and I now proceed to give you some further particulars of our meeting. An announcement of my profession (you are aware that I hold a French diploma) procured me admission into places where as a mere stranger I should have been denied.

The moment I set eyes on him I knew him again. He was lying on a rude pallet in a corner of a large barn, which for lack of a better place had been converted into a temporary hospital. You remember his appearance at Kaiserbad – his tattooed face, his jewellery, his invalid chair, his servant in livery, and his siren of a wife. Now, in a bundle by the side of his pallet, was tied up the uniform, torn and dirty, of a private in the Federal Army. He had been struck some days before by a splinter of a shell, and the doctors had given him up. His period of intense pain was over when I saw him; he suffered little now; it was a fatal sign, and he knew it. Firmly clutched in one hand he held a common horn box containing a little snuff, of which he inhaled a pinch occasionally with an air of thorough miserly enjoyment, his last earthly care evidently being to make his snuff last out till he should be past needing another pinch. I sat down on a rude plank by his side.

'Good-day, Monsieur De Montillac. How do you find yourself?' I said in French.

'How! Monsieur knew me during my *beaux jours*, and he recognises me again – and here!' he exclaimed, turning on me with a momentary vivacity. 'But Monsieur is English,' he added, peering up curiously into my face, 'and he must pardon me when I say that I do not remember ever having had the pleasure of meeting him in society.' He gave a ghastly smirk, tapped his box, and peered into it as though debating with himself whether he could afford to offer me a pinch. Finally he decided that he could not.

'I encountered you at Kaiserbad some few summers ago,' I said. 'You and Madame De Montillac were there and had a great run of luck, if I remember rightly. May I venture to hope that Madame is well and happy?'

An evil light leaped into his eyes, and his lips tightened over his teeth as he muttered a string of execrations under his breath.

'And the young Italian,' I said in a low voice, 'the poor young man who died so mysteriously one night, after winning heavily at the tables?'

'What of him?' he asked. 'Why do you speak to me about him?'

'Because you know the secret of his death,' I whispered.

His lips turned livid, and a sudden terror looked at me out of his eyes. For a little while he lay without speaking.

'Well – yes – I do know the secret of his death,' he answered after a time, 'and if you are at all curious about it, I will tell you the story; though how you happen to know that I was in any way mixed up with the affair is more than I can imagine. However, that matters nothing now. A minute ago, when you spoke of the Italian, a sudden chill came over me. I forgot for the moment that I was past all earthly hopes and fears, that if I were the veriest murderer on earth, Justice could not touch me now, that if all the riches in the world were mine, they would be as so much dust in my hands – to such a bitter strait have I come at last.'

He lay still for a little while with shut eyes and a troubled look on his face. His thoughts were travelling back into the past; his memories were steeped in gall.

What follows was told me in a fragmentary way, in the course of the half-dozen visits I paid De Montillac before he died, and with many breaks and abrupt changes of subject between. I jotted down a few notes from time to time in the course of the recital, and now give you the narrative as nearly as possible in the man's own words.

'I am the son of one of the most eminent professors of the art of legerdemain which France has ever had the honour of producing. As a youth I wandered up and down the Continent with my father, assisting him in his performances and being gradually initiated into the mysteries of the profession. But I never took kindly to it. That, however, did not greatly matter, for my father's gains were large, I was his only son, and he indulged me in every way as though I were a young aristocrat.

'But when I was about twenty-two years old my father and I had a terrible quarrel. There was a *jupon* in the case, you may be sure. Neither of us would give way to the other, and it ended by my father turning me out of doors. I borrowed a thousand francs from a friend and set out for England, a country which I had long wished to visit.

'But a thousand francs will not last for ever, and before long I saw starvation staring me in the face. Accordingly, I at once proceeded to furbish up my half-forgotten acquirements, designing, monsieur, to astonish your phlegmatic nation with a display of legerdemain such as they had never been privileged to witness before. Suddenly I saw the announcement of an exhibition by one of your great English wizards. I went to assist at it, and discovered to my dismay that the Englishman knew far more than I did, and that without long years of practice I could not hope to enter into competition with him.

'I will not weary you, monsieur, by dwelling on this part of my career. It is enough to say that I sank lower and lower, till at length I was glad to accept the offer of an eminent caravan proprietor to fill the post of New Zealand chief in his establishment, his last chief having lately died. The only condition was that I should allow myself to be tattooed. I was reckless and desperate, and acceded to the proposal. The operation was skilfully performed by an ex-sailor who had lived for years among a tribe of aborigines; and I then made my appearance before the public in the paint, feathers, and paraphernalia of a genuine Maori chief. It was a life that suited me well enough for a time; I had always a sufficiency of spare cash for absinthe and cigarettes.

'After a few years I was recalled to France by the death of my father. He had forgiven me at the last moment and had left me all his property. After airing my fortune in Paris for six months I set out on an extended tour. But I did not go alone.

'How or where I first met Élise Duvrier, it matters not to say. I knew nothing of her antecedents – know nothing of them to this day – and nothing I cared. I knew only that I loved her. Élise was wise; she loved no one but herself. I bought her a diamond bracelet, gave her ample proof that my fortune was a substantial reality, and she agreed to follow my fortunes.

'For two years we travelled from place to place as the caprices of Élise dictated. She was not without her little extravagances, and my fortune was slowly melting away; but I was powerless to help myself. After a time we grew tired of sightseeing, and then Élise took to gambling; at first merely *pour passer le temps*, but after a time the passion grew upon her and became the one absorbing occupation of her life. As a rule she was wonderfully lucky, and for a time her winnings served to prop my tottering fortunes.

'After a time we came to Kaiserbad, and fortune befriended us as usual till the young Italian of whom you lately spoke appeared on the scene. But with his arrival everything changed, and before long I half began to believe in the theory of Élise that he had brought some diabolical influence to bear upon us. Élise, who was terribly superstitious, had indeed urged me to go away after the first night, but for once I decided contrary to her wishes and determined to remain. At the end of a week I found a frightful hole in my fast-decreasing resources, but Élise only laughed when I spoke of it, and said that I ought to have taken her warning in time.

'One night about eleven o'clock she came into my dressing-room and seated herself on a low stool at my feet. "Henri," she said, looking up and speaking very slowly and distinctly, "Justine tells me that she heard our Italian friend say downstairs just now that he intended to make a pillow of his rouleaux tonight and so have golden dreams."

'"What has that to do with us?"

'"Nothing – nothing at all. You like to hear the gossip of the place, so I thought I would tell you. But it is almost time for you to take your draught."

'Shortly afterwards I went to bed. Élise brought me my customary potion, after which I at once fell asleep, and did not awake again till aroused by the noise of someone effecting an entrance into my room by way of the window. Next moment I recognised the intruder as Élise. She was in male attire, having dressed herself for the occasion in a masquerade suit which formed a portion of her wardrobe, while a small black bag was slung by a strap from her shoulder. Having drawn up the rope-ladder by means of which she had both left and entered the room, she took off her slouched hat, wig, and mask, turned up the night-lamp, and came and sat down beside me.

'"Where have you been?" I asked, although I had already guessed the truth.

'"I have been paying our Italian friend a visit, and he has kindly made me a present of his last evening's winnings," and she pointed carelessly to the bag.

'"You have robbed him!" I exclaimed. "You are—"

'She laid her hand over my mouth. "You forget, my Henri, that you are addressing yourself to a lady."

'I stared at her, astounded by the audacity of the exploit.

'"You would like some particulars," she said. "Good; you shall have them. I put on my masquerade dress of Monsieur Smeeth the Englishman. I took the rope-ladder which you, in your foolish dread of fire, always keep by you wherever you go; I fixed the hooks in the window-frame, let down the ladder outside, and then descended with my empty bag as nimbly as a squirrel. After listening for a minute, I took my ring and cut neatly and deftly a little square out of one of the lower panes of the window. To unbolt the window, open it, and glide behind the curtains was the work of a few moments – then forward, into the room, step by step, till I stood by the bedside and bent silently over the sleeper. A night-lamp was burning on the chimney-piece.

'"Naturally, I may say unconsciously, my fingers strayed to his pillow. Yes – underneath it was certainly some hard substance – a bag of gold! But something disturbed him; he turned over, flung up one arm, muttered a few words, and seemed as if he were about to awake. What a predicament for your poor Élise! But thanks to you, my Henri, I had not come unprepared for such an emergency."

'"Thanks to me! I do not understand you, Élise."

'"I had the green phial concealed in the breast pocket of my coat."

'I looked at her in astonishment. "And, pray, who revealed to you the secret of the green phial?"

'"You yourself, dear friend; no one else."

'"I had forgotten."

'"Being, then, prepared, no sooner did my sleeper begin to grow restless than I applied the phial to his nostrils for a few seconds. It quieted him almost immediately. I then gently raised his head and drew the bag from under his pillow, together with a small box of very excellent bonbons which I found there. Unfortunately as I was crossing the room the phial slipped from my fingers and rolled under the bed, but nobody will know it for yours when it is found. I refastened the window, climbed the ladder, and here I am. Signor l'Italiano will be rather astonished when he wakes in the morning and finds that his gold has taken to itself wings, and vanished for ever. Really these bonbons are very nice."

'Next morning, when the news spread through the hotel that the young Italian had been found dead in bed, even Élise paled for a time, and a deadly fear caused her to tremble in every limb. But she soon recovered her *sang-froid*. "I never intended that it should end thus – never!" she asseverated, and I believed her.

'Probably, monsieur, you know as well as I how the affair ended. The police made a perquisition into our effects, but found nothing inculpatory – Élise was too wary for that – and as soon as we were free to do so, we left Kaiserbad for ever.

'From the night of the young Italian's death a cloud seemed to grow up between Élise and myself – an intangible something, easily felt, but difficult to describe. I loved her, and yet I feared her. I knew that if I should ever stand in the way of her interests she would sacrifice me with as little compunction as she had sacrificed the Italian, and yet I could not bear to part from her. It seemed to me, when I thought of such a thing, as if all the light and gladness of my life would be shut out for ever were she to leave me.

'After a time we found ourselves at Nice, where I fell ill of a fever. Élise was disconsolate. As soon as my wits began to wander she ordered me to be taken to the hospital; then she paid the hotel bill, packed up her trinkets, and fled away. And from that day to this I have never seen her again.

'How I gradually sunk in the world till I came to be what you see me now were a weary story for me to tell, and twice as weary for you, monsieur, to listen to. Enough that I am here, but not for long now—not for long!'

When De Montillac had ceased speaking, I said to him: 'You made mention just now of a certain green phial, and seemed to attribute the death of the Italian to the inhalation of its contents. As a medical man I am interested in such matters. Can you give me any further particulars concerning the phial in question?'

'It was originally the property of my father,' answered De Montillac, 'and descended to me, together with many other curious objects, at his decease. My father dabbled a good deal in toxicology, and professed, with what degree of truth I know not, to have discovered the secret of some of those subtle poisons of which such terrible use was made by the Borgias and other great Italian families during the Middle Ages. The green phial was supposed to be nothing more harmful than a tiny flask of perfume, but its properties were peculiar. It emitted a faint but delightful odour different from any other perfume with which I am acquainted. Inhale this odour for a quarter of a minute with the phial close to your nostrils, and the effect upon the system was refreshing and exhilarating in the highest degree, stimulating the brain, brightening the eyes, and causing the blood to course more generously through the veins – an effect delicious but transitory. Inhale the perfume of the phial for half a minute, and you would fall without warning into a profound lethargy lasting for several hours. Let someone hold the phial to your nostrils for sixty seconds, and you would never wake more on earth.

'I had kept this singular drug by me as a curiosity, never making further use of it – as, indeed, why should I? – than at rare intervals to take an exhilarating sniff, thinking sometimes that, should my troubles ever become greater than I could bear, I knew of an easy and pleasant mode of ending them for ever.

'When Élise made mention of the phial on the night of the Italian's death, there came into my mind the picture of a half-forgotten dream, in which, after overpowering a man – a stranger whom I had never seen before – I rendered him insensible by means of the phial and then robbed him of a box of precious stones which he had just dug out of the ruins of some old castle. I told the story laughingly to Élise over breakfast next morning, never thinking that she would ever call it to mind again or turn to such strange use in real life an incident based on nothing but a dream.'

I had learnt from De Montillac all I wanted to know.

He lay back in a state of exhaustion after he had finished his narrative, of which the latter part had been told in low, broken accents which showed how weak he was becoming. I administered a restorative and then rose to leave him, telling him that I would visit him again towards evening.

'You won't forget to come, Doctor?' he said, his eyes gazing into mine with strange yearning wistfulness.

'I will not forget.'

At five o'clock I went back to the hospital. De Montillac was lying with his face turned to the wall, his empty snuff-box firmly grasped in one hand. I thought he was asleep. I touched him.

He was dead.

About the Author

NICK RENNISON is a writer, editor and bookseller with a particular interest in the Victorian era and in crime fiction. He is the editor of six anthologies of short stories for No Exit Press, plus *A Short History of Polar Exploration*, *Peter Mark Roget: A Biography*, *Freud and Psychoanalysis*, *Robin Hood: Myth, History & Culture* and *Bohemian London*, published by Oldcastle Books. He is also the author of *The Bloomsbury Good Reading Guide to Crime Fiction*, *100 Must-Read Crime Novels* and *Sherlock Holmes: An Unauthorised Biography*. His crime novels, *Carver's Quest* and *Carver's Truth*, both set in nineteenth-century London, are published by Corvus. He is a regular reviewer for both the *Sunday Times* and the *Daily Mail*.

NO EXIT PRESS
More than just the usual suspects

— CWA DAGGER —
AWARDED BEST CRIME & MYSTERY PUBLISHER

'A very smart, independent publisher delivering the finest literary crime fiction' **Big Issue**

MEET NO EXIT PRESS, an award-winning crime imprint bringing you the best in crime and suspense fiction. From classic detective novels, to page-turning spy thrillers and literary writing that grabs the attention. Our books are carefully crafted by some of the world's finest writers and delivered to you by a small, but passionate, team.

In over 30 years of business, we have published award-winning fiction and non-fiction including the work of a Pulitzer Prize winner, the British Crime Book of the Year, numerous CWA Dagger Awards, a British million-copy bestselling author, the winner of the Canadian Governor General's Award for Fiction and the Scotiabank Giller Prize, to name but a few. We are the home of many crime and noir legends from the USA whose work includes iconic film adaptations and TV sensations. We pride ourselves in uncovering the most exciting new or undiscovered talents. New and not so new – you know who you are!

We are a proactive team committed to delivering the very best, both for our authors and our readers.

Want to join the conversation and find out more about what we do?

Catch us on social media or sign up to our newsletter for all the latest news from No Exit Press.

f fb.me/noexitpress   **X** @noexitpress

noexit.co.uk